Dear Reader,

I am so incredibly pleased and proud to share Mariko Tamaki's *Anne of Greenville* with you! For the debut from my new studio, I wanted to take a beloved classic—*Anne of Green Gables*—and update it for the modern reader. Anne Shirley has always been one of my favorite heroines of all time—spunky, eccentric, warm, kind, and over-the-top—and Mariko's adaptation brings us an Anne completely of the moment but with the same lovable, garrulous, outsize personality that has endeared her to our hearts forever.

Anne has two moms, a best friend named Berry, and an irrepressible urge to shake things up in this smallest of small towns that she finds herself in. Her story made me laugh out loud and shed a happy tear or two as Anne battles closed-mindedness and finds true love.

This joyous, diverse, feel-good story inspired by a beloved classic is the epitome of what Melissa de la Cruz Studio hopes to bring to the publishing and entertainment worlds.

I hope *Anne of Greenville* roller-skates into your heart with a crash as it did mine.

Melissa de la Cruz

MELISSA de la CRUZ STUDIO

ANNE OF GREENVILLE

MARIKO TAMAKI

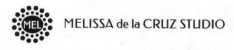

MELISSA de la CRUZ STUDIO

HYPERION   Los Angeles   New York

First Edition, October 2022
10 9 8 7 6 5 4 3 2 1
FAC-004510-22231
Printed in the United States of America

This book is set in Adobe Garamond Pro/Adobe.
Designed by Marci Senders
Illustrations copyright © 2022 by Shutterstock

Library of Congress Cataloging-in-Publication Data
Names: Tamaki, Mariko, author. • Montgomery, L. M. (Lucy Maud), 1874–1942.
Anne of Green Gables.
Title: Anne of Greenville / by Mariko Tamaki.
Description: First edition. • Los Angeles ; New York : MDLC Studio, 2022.
• Audience: Ages 14–18. • Audience: Grades 10–12. • Summary: In this contemporary
retelling of Anne of Green Gables, Anne Shirley, a queer, half-Japanese disco
superfan, moves to a town that seems too small for her big personality and where
she becomes embroiled in a series of dramatic and unfortunate events.
Identifiers: LCCN 2021050338 • ISBN 9781368078405 (hardcover)
• ISBN 9781368083379 (ebook)
Subjects: CYAC: Bullying—Fiction. • Lesbians—Fiction. • Racially mixed people—Fiction.
• Adoption—Fiction. • City and town life—Fiction. • High schools—Fiction.
• Schools—Fiction. • LCGFT: Novels.
Classification: LCC PZ7.T1587 An 2022 • DDC [Fic]—dc23
LC record available at https://lccn.loc.gov/2021050338

Reinforced binding
Visit www.hyperionteens.com

SUSTAINABLE FORESTRY INITIATIVE
Certified Sourcing
www.sfiprogram.org
SFI-01681

Logo Applies to Text Stock Only

For all the kindred spirits out there

NOTE FROM THE PUBLISHER

This story explores experiences relating to racism and homophobia and includes some offensive language that may be triggering for readers. If these topics are sensitive for you, please read with care.

ONE

Technically a story starts wherever you want it to start.

When you start writing it down, that could be the start of the story. Or maybe the story started *before* you started writing it down, but then the story was *so good* you thought . . .

This is really good; I should write this down.

It's possible the answer to where and when a story starts has something to do with the space-time continuum, and if it does, I would *not* be the person to talk about that. I am not a space-time continuum kind of person. I'm more of an arts-and-crafts kind of person, which can be just as serious as space-time, especially if you spill purple glitter (or any other color of glitter) on the carpet.

Pretty serious.

I don't recommend you do this because then glitter will be in that space between the fibers of your carpet for the time period of *forever*.

Of course, sometimes you're working on a particularly cool objet d'art in your living room because you just moved into a new house and your craft area hasn't been set up yet and these things can't be helped.

And now we're into the story.

It's already started!

If we're being picky about it, all this already happened and I'm going *back* in time to tell you the story of how I became Anne of Greenville (formerly Anne of a Few Cities Other Than Greenville). It's also the story of how I found my true true, and how I needed to maybe come to Greenville, of all places, to make that happen.

Speaking of Greenville, I should probably set the scene a little. Because if you don't know Greenville, and arguably, if you don't live here, you've probably never heard of Greenville (I hadn't), you might need a little wiki info to get you started.

Greenville is a very small town in a state that is about six states to the east of any state I have ever lived in. It's what Millie, my mom, who was born in a small town called Pepperdown, North Carolina (so cute, right?), calls The Ultimate Small Town. Greenville's total pop. when we arrived was 5,004 (5,007 once my family moved in—so that sign will need to be changed).

My first impression of Greenville was that it was very, very hard to see anything, because it was night. And night in Greenville is, like, really *really* dark. I arrived with my two moms in a U-Haul full of mostly books and cooking supplies, as well as our ginger cat, Bjorn, and our golden retriever, Monty. Greenville dark is not like city dark, where every street is lit up by a streetlight, as if you had a house and every room had a lamp on. Greenville felt like a house with *no* lamp on. Admittedly, when I first looked out the moving-van window at our new town, awakened from an in-van nap by a "we're almost there," my heart kind of sank. I felt like I was looking out into the void, and it was looking back at me. And not in a pleasant way.

As we pulled into our driveway, Monty looked out the window and whined. I opened the van door and the only thing in the wind was the soft rustle of leaves and crickets.

That's it.

"Hear that quiet?" Millie said, stretching her arms from the drive. "That's country quiet."

"This isn't the *country*," Lucy, my other mom, corrected, digging our new house key out of her purse.

"Oh, it's country all right." Millie grinned, striding to the front door. "Just you wait."

A few more things about Greenville I noticed once I actually saw it in the daylight:

1. Greenville is the kind of place where everyone keeps a wreath on their door. Even if it isn't a winter holiday. Most of these wreaths are decorated with plastic flowers.
2. Greenville is the kind of place where everyone has two cars because everything is so far apart you have to drive everywhere (unless you roller-skate, which I think is preferable).
3. Most of Greenville doesn't have sidewalks, maybe because everyone drives (see #2).
4. All the trees in Greenville are puffy and green, like someone drew them with a crayon.
5. Greenville is a place that feels both very very big and very very small. Like maybe because there's no tall buildings, there's so much more room for the ground and the sky to stretch out, which feels big. But also there's so little to look at *besides* the green ground and the blue sky, it feels . . . small.

Mostly I couldn't decide if any of the things I noticed about Greenville were good or bad. Maybe because I couldn't decide what they meant. And where in them would fit the puzzle that was me. Or vice versa.

I tried not to think about it those first few days. I unpacked (sort of), lost Bjorn (three times), found Bjorn (three times), and made papier-mâché disco globes (because I had all the materials).

And then, on the day of the beginning of my story, which, yes, we're now getting to, it was sunny, I had to start thinking about it.

Greenville and me.

It was August, so, it was hot. Not like your-sequins-are-going-to-melt-off-you hot (which is too hot). But *hot*.

I loaded my newly (sort of) dry disco globes into the back of Millie's car because she was going to drop me off in the town center while she went off to do house stuff like go buy forks because we still couldn't find any forks, which was weird because we *could* find spoons and we definitely *packed* forks! (What, were the forks and spoons fighting or something? Did the spoons win?) During the drive, Millie eyeballed my disco balls. "Those aren't going to get glitter all over my car, are they?"

"Probably, yes."

I'd lived in small cities before Greenville, just FYI, but most of them had at least three grocery stores and a corporate retail chain or two. Greenville had: A grocery store, A drugstore, and A post office, plus An ice cream parlor, A place to get wings, and A place to buy running shoes. OH. And A pizza place.

It was Saturday and pretty much everyone seemed to be out and about; everywhere you could see the citizens of Greenville walking around with ice cream cones and shopping bags in groups of three or four, in what I would call Greenville's Times Square, the intersection of the streets of Main, Center, and Division. One thing I will say, as far as town squares went, Greenville's was at least *very* clean. No garbage anywhere. Everyone seemed to have their natural hair color, and everyone except me was wearing sandals and nice shirts. And shorts/pants obviously.

Imagine moving to a town where no one wears pants.

After assessing what space was available, I picked a spot by a big brass statue of an old white man and started hanging up my globes on the signposts, at which point an old guy with white hair under a white baseball cap started surveilling me with what I hoped was a mix of curiosity and anticipation.

I taped my last papier-mâché disco ball to the last post and placed my speaker at the edge of what I determined to be my "performance space." I strapped on my favorite pair of roller skates, which are orange leather with green sparkly wheels and yellow laces, which not coincidentally matched the orange and green of my amazing polyester sequined jumpsuit with extra-wide bell-bottom cuffs (custom, obv). Putting on my skates is very often, if not the best part of my day, like, pretty high up there on the list. I personally, not that anyone has asked, think everyone should own a pair of roller skates. It's like putting wings on your feet, like that god Hermes, but with way less family baggage.

I took a breath.

"Here we go," I whispered to myself.

I pressed play and set the wheels in motion (literally) for my introduction to Greenville, by way of a hastily assembled roller disco performance to the best song in the world: "Funkytown."

Extended mix.

"Funkytown," by Lipps Inc, is a track from their debut album,

Mouth to Mouth. It was written by musician, composer, and record producer Steven Greenberg and sung by Cynthia Johnson, who later became a member of the gospel group Sounds of Blackness. I'll say the album, on the whole, is not a full-on collection of hits. "All Night Dancing" is a little slow, and you've probably never heard of "Rock It" and "Power." But "Funkytown," the hit single, has survived many decades as an amazing and relevant dance track for a reason: It is *so so so so* good. "Funkytown" is a song I often use as the base or first act of my various performances.

My moms say I have a tendency to get "lost" in things: Millie says I am a daydreamer, Lucy will say I am sometimes easily distracted. Both are definitely true when I am making art or performing. I don't know what a person is supposed to be *thinking* when they're making art, or dancing, or singing. I mean it's not like my brain stops working when I'm doing any of these things. But it definitely works different. Like when I'm just normal me, I can see the things that are in front of me, like a tree, or a fountain, or a lamp. When I'm making art, it's like everything gets . . . intense? Or like, lighter but deeper?

Like, I can see the things, but I can also see all these things that *could* be. Like all the symbolism jumps out, and the fountain is suddenly "flow" and "rejuvenation" and all that junk. And I can see me in those things, in these evolving worlds, I guess? And in those evolving worlds, anything is possible.

Anything is possible feels like a fresh slice of lemon in your brain.

I could feel the smile spreading out over my lips as my skates glided over the pavement.

"Boop boop boop boop boop boop boop boop boop boop."

As my wheels rolled over the concrete, everything went rainbow gooey. The sequins on my outfit flashed in the sun and sent little prism rainbows around the square, which was what I'd hoped would happen. About two minutes into the song, after a series of slow swoops around the fountain, just to let people know what I was about, I did a back walkover into a spin and down into the splits.

That kind of move is what is called a "crowd pleaser" in that way most circus/gymnastics–type stuff is crowd pleasing (or Cirque du Soleil wouldn't exist). This move is normally where I pause, if only for a moment, and take in what Lucy calls "the temperature of the room."

Or the square in this case.

I looked up from my splits, my palms pressed onto the baking pavement of the square, to the equally heated glares of the residents of Greenville, some with ice creams, some without.

Not the best reception.

Which was not entirely unpredictable.

TWO

Okay. For most of the time I have known myself, I have always been a person who is . . . different.

Mostly when other people talk about me being different they want to talk about the fact that I have two moms, which is not *super* different depending on where you are, but it's a little different than a lot of the kids I've gone to school with.

I'm adopted; both my moms are white and I'm half-Japanese. I am the biological child of my mom Millie's cousin Susan and was adopted after Susan and my bio dad, Dean, died in a car accident. I was three when this happened, so I mostly only have vague glowy memories of my biological parents. I know my grandma Hana looks like an old female version of Dean. (I have a sum total of four grandmothers, two moms, one grandfather, and one step-grandfather as a result of this family setup, which is either a lot or enough depending on what I need at any given time).

Really, I think the thing that sets me apart from my moms, like if you look at us from a distance, is the fact that when I was ten, I started dying my hair orange because it's my favorite color and my parents said so long as I didn't get it all over the bathtub it was okay.

(I totally get it in the bathtub, though.)

Once, when I was twelve, an old lady stopped me in the elevator and told me I shouldn't dye it. To which I replied, "Maybe YOU should mind your own business." Lucy said this would have been an acceptable response to the lady's very rude comment if I hadn't yelled it super loud into her face.

No one in my household is okay with yelling. Which means you can pretty much say whatever you want if you say it in an even tone. Nothing you say in anything resembling a shout is going to be okay.

Ahem.

Of course, you could *also* say that everyone's upbringing and hair is unique and not really worth calling out as "different." Both of my moms hate the word *normal*, like as in what is a "normal" family? Like who defines that, right? The patriarchy? Probably.

Unfortunately, a complete discussion of the origins of the so-called normal and why normal is a construct would get us *way* off course storywise, so let's say the previously mentioned things are part of who I am and things that have been called out as being different. But really there are just so many other more interesting ways a person can be . . . unusual.

And I am all of them. I think.

Like, I'm pretty sure I don't think like other people. Aside from the things I see when I'm making art, I bet I spend *way* more time than most people thinking about things that *could* exist versus all the things that *do* exist. Like once I spent a week dreaming about all the different ways an elephant could look. Like what if their ears were softer and covered in fur and stuck up in the air?

When I was six, I had an imaginary friend named Danny, a purple unicorn who was also a lawyer and a model. And I would spend all this time talking to Danny about fashion and my dreams, and my moms would have to remind me that he was imaginary so I would calm down about getting him to his auditions and court appearances on time.

"If Danny's not there, who else is going to stand up for the little creatures of the magic forest?" I wailed, on a particularly vexing day. "Who will grace the cover of *Unicorn Fair*?"

"Oh, sweetie," Lucy cooed, "why do you insist on using your imagination to worry yourself into more problems?"

I had a friend once who was obsessed with knowing which of my moms I was "actually related to." Which to me was and is just absurd (and I would never tell her, which is why we stopped being friends). Like, honestly, who cares? One, we're a family; two, they both have to look after me—it's not like biology changes that; and three, I am so clearly the result of both of their influences and obsessions. Like how Lucy likes to learn as many new things as possible. For example, the whole reason

I learned how to roller-skate was because she saw a movie about roller-skating and then she wanted to learn how *and* teach me how.

The gift that keeps on giving.

And Millie is the artist who likes to try to look at things from as many different angles as possible. Like how she takes pictures of people from a camera mounted over their heads or at their feet, which is the series she started working on before we moved to Greenville.

As moms, sometimes I think Lucy has more patience for my stuff because she's a teacher. But I think Millie gets me more because she's an artist. Like, I think Millie gets why I need to make a thing because it's in my head and I want to see it in the world. Even if the trip from my head to the world can be . . . rocky.

(Side note: Millie and Lucy are both kind of athletic and wear what I would describe as sensible shoes. I can almost immediately tell whether someone else is queer by whether they think Millie and Lucy are sisters or partners. Like *sisters*? Are you for real? Look at their matching sensible shoulder bags!)

Actually one of my first performances was a tribute to mothers, created for Lucy's grandmother's ninetieth birthday when I was seven. (Originally it was supposed to be a ninety-minute performance, but I was told I had six minutes, max—a time allowance I know Lucy fought for.)

It was a dance, not to "Funkytown," but a song Grandma Shirley liked, "Sing Sing Sing (with a Swing)" originally written by Louis Prima and covered by Benny Goodman. I made tap shoes and decorated my leotard so I would look like what in my mind was an old-timey dancer.

Halfway through the dance, Lucy's cousin Herbert ran up and pulled me off the stage because he said I was up there "shaking my hips in my underwear" and it was disgusting.

The first abrupt end to one of my performances.

But not the last.

Not everyone gets it. Or almost no one gets it.

I know that.

And sometimes, the *not getting it* can be louder than disco.

Oh. Also, I go off on what Millie calls "epic tangents." Which are (almost) always relevant. And eventually connect back to the story.

THREE

S ee?

   Okay, so there I was. In Greenville. The last strains of "Funkytown" fading into the sunny day. Either my audience was not loving what was happening *or* they were the quietest audience in the history of audiences. Or both.

   I was getting up from my epic splits, brushing the bits of gravel off my palms, thinking.

   I had two choices: One, keep going. Like, the show must go on (a theater saying that people used to say way back in the 1900s and also a song by the epic band Queen). Two, act like the three-part disco roller performance was actually a *one* part, take my bow, and roll off into the sunset.

If you're caught up, it's not going to surprise you to hear that I took option one.

Heck yeah, I did! Gloria Gaynor's "I Will Survive" came on (recorded in 1978 and originally released as a B-side if you can believe it). That's like the most powerful gay song (not sung by a gay person) in the world!

I blew a kiss to the crowd, did a jump turn, pumped twice, and flew into a sit spin. I came out of that, waved to the crowd, and went right back into a series of hurricane kicks that I then transitioned into a heel toe spin, because I love spinning; the world flew into a stream of light and dark when suddenly . . .

The music cut out.

So fast it was like someone pulled the rug out from under me, like, literally. Before I could catch myself, my left skate skidded out from beneath me, then my right, and I landed *hard* on my butt.

The butt, the softest but hardest landing of them all.

I don't know if you've ever landed on your butt on roller skates. It is discombobulating. First, I was dizzy, with this weird whooshing sound that took over all the space inside my brain, then the whooshing was replaced by another sound . . . laughter.

Not happy fun laughter, the laughter of joy and joining, the laughter of beach balls and lollipops. No. *Unhappy* laughter, which only comes at someone else's expense. As my butt throbbed, I looked up and spotted the source of the chortles.

It was a group of kids, but I saw the boy first, tall with spiky brown hair. He was wearing a green soccer jersey and shorts. A girl with bright, but I think natural, red hair tied into pigtails, dressed entirely in baby pink, was balanced on his shoulders.

I blinked.

They were ripping my disco balls off the lampposts!

"HEY!" I scrambled to my feet, or tried to, but it is hard to scramble to your feet in roller skates, which is the only uncool thing about them.

A wave of heat rose up through my jumpsuit and turned my neck into a ring of fire. "HEY!"

The boy with spiky brown hair grinned a big toothy grin, as the girl on his shoulders wrenched the disco ball free and held it over her head, triumphant.

"HEY!" she screeched back, waving the ball like a broken flag, "YOU GOT A PERMIT FOR THIS TRASH?"

"HA-HA-HA-HA-HA!" The boy's face was turning red.

But the laughter wasn't just coming from him.

I swiveled as best I could and spotted the other pair, at another lamppost closer to the fountain. This pair had one shorter boy with curly hair, also in a soccer jersey, who was almost eclipsed by the girl on *his* shoulders, who was long like spaghetti with equally long blond hair. She had ripped two of my disco balls free and was holding them in her hands like deflated cheerleader pom-poms.

"CUT IT OUT!" I finally got to my feet. "THOSE ARE MINE!"

"HO-HO!" the curly-haired boy laughed as he bent forward and the girl vaulted off.

As I (finally) got my skates under me, all four kids were off like a shot. Laughing and waving my disco balls in the air as they ran.

"STOP!" I screamed, catching the eye of the girl with long blond hair.

She slowed down, just a little, like there was suddenly something in my voice worth paying attention to. Maybe because my voice had reached the pitch of a fire engine.

"THOSE! ARE! MINE!" I howled.

The girl's eyes went wide. She glanced down at the now unrecognizable lumps of disco art in her hands.

"TOSS IT!" the boy with spiky hair hollered back. "GILLY! TOSS THEM!"

The redheaded girl with the pigtails cupped her hands over her mouth. "COME ON, GILLY!"

The tall blond looked at me again with watery blue eyes, and then she heaved my disco balls into the fountain and sprinted off.

"YOU ASSHOLES!" I hollered.

And then suddenly everyone in the square stopped and looked at me. Possibly because I screamed *assholes*. My face had its own pulse as I slunk down, slamming my butt on the fountain's edge, producing a flash of pain that ripped through my lower half as I unstrung my laces.

"Hey."

This is the moment when I first met Berry. Or right before.

"WHAT?" I roared.

Like yeah, I kind of instantly reacted with yelling, because I was trying not to break my lace with my rage fingers and listening to the gurgling of the fountain.

But then I looked up.

The first thing I noticed, which calmed me in a way that I cannot explain, was that the person who was standing in front of me, who was probably my age, had hair that was all different colors of green. Like moss and fluorescent and forest and pine green. They had more hair than most people I had ever met. It was curly, like spiral-curls curly, its mass only barely tamed by a white headband that matched their white coveralls.

They were holding a skateboard in one hand, looking down at their paint-splattered work boots; their cheeks were blushing hard, maybe because I had just yelled at them. Also because they were super pale, and pale people, in my experience, blush like nobody else. I think it's cool, but I get that some of the pale do not think it's cool.

I dropped my skate. "UGH. Sorry." I looked back into the fountain. "I just— It just— I thought you were— Sorry."

"I saw what happened." The person I didn't know yet as Berry looked up with hazel eyes. "I'm sorry. But, uh, I did manage to save this one."

In their hand was the only disco ball that hadn't been shredded or destroyed, my one glittering paper child that had survived Greenville's apparent disco hatred. They placed the ball in my hands like a fragile egg. "Sorry about, you know, them."

"RIGHT? What was THAT?! Who does that?" I fumed, suddenly re-enraged. I gestured at the water fountain. "Do they even know what glitter does to a water fountain?"

"They probably don't care."

"Well, THAT sucks," I seethed, carefully placing my last disco ball next to my skates and rolling up my pant legs.

As the crowd watched, I slipped one leg at a time into the fountain to dig out the pulpy messes of my other balls. "It could, like, seriously screw with the water systems, *hello*," I groused, raking my fingers through the disturbingly warm water. "Who were they, anyway?"

"The big one's Tanner." The person I still didn't know was Berry reached into the fountain to pull out a scrap of purple paper. "The other boy is John. The girls are Sarah and Gilly."

"Well, they're ALL JERKS," I fumed, my hands full of disco pulp.

"Like, pretty much always. Anyway. I think you got all the stuff out of here. So that's good."

It didn't feel especially good, which was also probably because everyone was staring at me like I was stealing wishes from the bottom of the fountain or something.

Instead of saving them! Hello!

I heaved my rolled-up but still magically soaked to the core pant legs out of the fountain. Did Greenville even have a dry cleaner who could handle sequins?

"I thought it was cool," the person who would soon become my one Greenville friend said. "Your thing. With the tricks and stuff? Gloria Gaynor. Great track."

A shard of light pierced my dark mood. I raised an eyebrow. "You know Gloria Gaynor?"

Not just Gloria Gaynor music but her *name*. Huge points.

It was just nice for a moment of feeling like I wasn't the only one talking disco that day.

"Sure." They grinned, showing a giant gap between two front teeth.

Also, I noticed, this person had more freckles than I had ever seen on one face. Maybe it came with the hair. "My dad is kind of a vinyl fiend."

"Well." I held up my one surviving disco ball, my wet fingers sticking to the paper and glue. "Thanks. For grabbing this."

"Anytime." The person I still hadn't introduced myself to, who hadn't really introduced themselves to me, hence still *person*, shrugged. "Welcome to Greenville, I guess?"

"Thanks."

"No problem." With a sort of awkward salute, they spun artfully, flopped their skateboard on the ground, and with a light step, rolled away, the gravel crunching under their wheels. "See you at school on Monday!"

"Oh!" I said, because I had actually forgotten about school, because that's how my mind works. "Yeah."

And yes, it's true, I had that *whole* exchange with my first nice person in Greenville, and I hadn't even managed to get a name, or say mine.

I frowned, shoving my feet in my running shoes and tying up my skates.

"ANNE!" Millie strode toward me, lugging a big bag of what looked like Christmas lights. "Gimme a hand?"

"Sure," I said as I shook as much water out of my pant leg as I could.

Millie looked at my hands. "What happened to your other . . . globes?"

"They are, were, disco balls and . . . they were the casualty of the day."

"Oh." Millie looked around, catching some of the locals with ice creams who were clearly straining to hear our conversation. "So. How was the performance?"

"Mixed reviews." I took the bag from her hand.

"Right." Millie, who has also received her fair share of mixed reviews over the years, including a man who called her a pestilence on the photography community, nodded, waited for me to say more, and when I didn't, started walking toward the car.

For the drive home, Millie mostly let me percolate, which is what she calls a thinking silence.

A productive silence.

I don't know if it was all that productive. Mostly I was letting the rolling green slide by the window and thinking about what it would be like to have an audience appreciate your three-act disco opera.

"Some of the best reviews are mixed," Millie said finally as we closed in on our street. "Like mixed nuts. Right?"

"If you like Brazil nuts."

"Wait. You don't like Brazil nuts? Have I raised you right?" Millie gave me an exaggerated look of horror.

"Brazil nuts are disgusting," I said, "and yes, you did."

Millie snuck a quick glance in my direction. "Do you know what you can do to make it better next time? Your performance?"

"No," I said. "Maybe."

"Well, work on that," Millie said, spinning the wheel as we rounded the corner. "And don't forget to wish Lucy good luck," she added as we pulled into the driveway. "It's her big day tomorrow."

Millie calls Lucy the traveling educator, because Lucy has taught pretty much everything you can imagine a person teaching in pretty much everywhere a person could teach in the United States. A lot of us moving around has been my mom trying to get different experiences teaching in different places for different schools. She was a substitute teacher for years. Then she worked for this company that trains teachers in what my mom calls "community skills." Then she taught English and geography in Petaluma, California. Then she applied to be a vice principal.

And now we're here. Greenville, where Lucy will be the new vice principal at Greenville High.

In almost every movie where a character is a vice principal, that person is the least cool person in the movie. The vice principal is usually the person who hates their job and takes it out on others.

Lucy is the opposite of that, by the way. And yet, being a vice principal is Lucy's dream job. Lucy really really likes teaching and teachers and school. She wants to be a vice principal so she can help people have a better time at their school. Like, if Lucy was in charge, and she sometimes is, all our vacations would be learning experiences.

So this whole Greenville thing was a really big deal.

Which is why the night before the first day of school Lucy was holed up in her office. I brought her a plate of leftover fried rice and tofu lumps. Inside, the room that was going to be her office was a traffic jam of boxes. Surrounded by stacks of paper, Lucy had three elastics in her hair—I think because she kept forgetting she'd put her hair up already. When she's not working, Lucy wears school sweatshirts from the schools that she's taught in. She has *a lot* of sweatshirts with badly drawn school mascots on them. The one she was wearing that night was supposed to be a hawk, but it looked like an angry owl. I think it was from a school in Ohio.

"Oh," Lucy said. She glanced up from a pile, looking a little owly herself. "Hey! How was your show?"

Lucy calls them *shows*.

"My *performance* . . . was fine," I said, moving a stack of papers to put the plate on.

"OH!" Lucy lurched forward, reaching for the papers I was holding. "Those are— Sorry, sweetie. I need those. Give them here. Thanks."

I handed her the stack. "Sorry."

"Just trying to get everything together." Lucy surveyed the many *other* stacks that I imagined *also* couldn't be moved. "*So* much paperwork! I just—" She shoved a few piles over and pointed at a pile of books. "Just put the plate here is fine, sweetie. Thank you."

I rested the plate of reheated food I was pretty sure she was going to forget to eat on a folder of educational standards she probably was going to read, and leaned against the doorway. "So, are you ready? Do you have your outfit? For school?"

"Oh." Lucy pulled a hair elastic off her wrist. "Oh yes, that's right. Ha-ha. Clothes. Yes I'll find something. Do you? Have your outfit?"

"Obviously," I said. "I have a few options. I'll review them tonight. Consider all the angles. Debate possible body modifications. Piercings. You know? To pull the whole thing together."

"Good good." Lucy's eyes darted back to her laptop, which was pinging like an alarm clock. "That's great."

She wasn't listening, of course. Lucy is very anti-piercing for reasons I don't completely understand.

"You'll be great." I sighed. "Tomorrow, I mean. And this year, you'll be great at this."

Like I said, Lucy is the person who has given me pretty much everything that means anything in my life, including disco (also her fave) and roller skating. I once asked Lucy to show me how to sew, and she learned so she could teach me. I wasn't going to give her something else to worry about. Like the fact that my first meet-and-greet with Greenville had gone . . . poorly. I mentally slipped it under the tall stack of things we could talk about later.

" 'Night!"

" 'Night, Anne! Oh! Can you take Monty for her walk?"

Easier said than done. Apparently Monty wasn't all that fond of the sound of the "country," including the crickets. (What did she think they were? I wondered). As soon as I opened the door and the first cricket cricketed she plastered herself to the ground and started whining.

"Okay, so walking is out?"

A low squeal escaped from Monty's snout.

"Fine."

I wrapped my arms around her middle and pulled our now angry golden area rug out the door so I could walk her onto the front porch, where she pinned herself against my side.

"This is exposure therapy, Monty," I said, looking around, noting that she wasn't going to the bathroom, which couldn't be a good thing.

I put my hand on her head, and she pinned her big brown eyes on me.

I do not want to be here, those eyes said.

"I hear you," I said. "I mean, obviously we can't do anything about being in Greenville, but it's nice just for a moment to not have to pretend to be happy about it."

In what I took as agreement, Monty shoved her wet nose under my thigh, which probably smelled like Greenville fountain water, the perfume of copper and disapproval.

"At least tomorrow's another day," I offered.

I mean, come on, I hadn't even gotten to school yet.

FOUR

t's possible to make a day good, or at least better, by starting it off with a small dance party in which you get dressed in some of your favorite clothing items.

Or that's my theory.

That's why I chose to prepare for my first day at Greenville High with "Le Freak" by the band Chic (from the album *C'est Chic*, released 1978) blasting while I dug through a bunch of boxes I was supposed to unpack but didn't, because I was making the pieces of my, let's say "failed" or "ill-received," disco moment.

All my clothing is vintage, or most of it, partly because my moms don't like buying anything new that we can buy used. For most of my life I've made kind of a game of finding clothing that's the perfect match for my aesthetic. It's like searching out magic gemstones, only those gemstones often smell like mothballs. And need to be hemmed.

For my first day of school, I rummaged for one of my favorite finds, a pair of legit seventies suede shorts in orange, yellow, and blue, pairing it with peach sparkly leggings, and a lavender-and-neon-orange sweatshirt with massive bell sleeves I think someone made and then hid in a Value Buys in Arizona just for me to find. The tag on the sweatshirt says DAZZLING DUDS, which is like a secret piece of awesome just for me or whoever is doing the laundry.

What's the best kind of dud? A *dazzling* dud!

Of course now you're asking, what kind of *shoes* go with that ensemble? The answer is, obviously, neon-green kicks that someone was generous enough to add a three-inch platform to before they donated them to *Good Willing* in Eureka, where I found them.

Really what you want as the finale to that sort of dressing routine is a slide down a banister, but our new house didn't have one, so I settled for dancing down the stairs like the Beatles in their "Your Mother Should Know" from the *Magical Mystery Tour* movie. (You can view this sequence online without having to see the whole, not great movie. It's not disco, but it's very cool.)

Millie was in the kitchen, which was momentous because Millie is an artist who once told me that the whole point of being an artist is you don't have to wake up early in the morning.

But it was the first day of school, so Millie was there with a pot of fresh coffee and a few inspiring words of encouragement.

"Finally! I'm getting you guys out of my hair." She sighed with exaggerated contentment.

But Lucy didn't catch said exaggerated contentment, as she was clearly *very* nervous.

"What time is it?" she asked, searching the counter for the phone that was right in front of her.

"You've got lots of time," Millie said, filling up a travel mug and setting it next to Lucy's phone. "I'll take the kid to school. You go on ahead."

I searched the fridge for the leftover fried rice, which is the best breakfast, especially when served with coffee.

"Does this look okay?" Lucy stood back and pressed her hands down the front of her green jacket and matching pencil skirt.

I thought she looked a little military-ish, but I was clearly in no position to criticize, as I was wearing what could easily be interpreted as the uniform of a psychedelic cheerleader from Jupiter.

Also there's a time and place for thoughts about a person's outfit. I think these things are always better noted in retrospect. Or internally.

Plus Lucy clearly needed a boost, so I gave her a *whomp* on the back and said, "HEY! YOU LOOK SUPER PROFESH!"

I also (mentally) noted she'd set her hair in a strange bob helmet that looked protective and maybe older? Also she was wearing eyeliner, which she normally didn't.

"You look very . . . in charge," Millie said, dropping an apple into Lucy's lunch bag. "You're going to knock them dead."

"Principal Lynde already left six messages," Lucy fretted, pocketing her phone. "She must have expected me to be there at the stroke of six."

Millie looked at me with a silent *Yikes* Lucy didn't see because she was already searching for the phone she had just slid into her pocket.

"You're going to be amazing at this," Millie said, taking Lucy's face in her hands and giving her a peck. "Your phone is in your pocket."

I paused scarfing my rice to point at my outfit. "How do *I* look?"

Millie squinted. "A little like me when I was your age, which is disturbing, but only to me."

"Double bonus," I cheered.

"You look lovely," Lucy said, grabbing her keys and doing a cool backward walk out the door. "Love you."

"LOVE YOU!" I scooped the last of the rice out of the container. "See you at school, sort of."

"Have a good day, sweetie!" Lucy called back as she blasted out of the house like a military hurricane.

A few seconds after the door slammed shut and Monty barked her the-door-is-shut bark, Millie stretched. "All right. How do you feel about grabbing a doughnut chaser for your leftovers?"

"Good, obviously."

Millie fished her keys out of her robe pocket and took Monty's leash off the wall hook. "Let's go."

"In your robe?" I asked, in what I hoped wasn't a judgmental tone.

"Says the girl dressed like she's hosting an aerobic marathon on Mars," Millie noted, standing in the doorway. "Are those shorts suede?"

"Yeah." I pointed at my legs. "Suede and polyester *and* nylon in one outfit!"

Millie shrugged. "What you will soon learn, my dear sweet child, is that while small-town folks might *not* dig your perfectly reasonable cacophony of fabrics, wearing your pajamas out of the house is going to be totally acceptable."

And with that, Millie swung open the door, twirling her keys around her finger. "Come on, MONTY!"

By the time we got to the school, full of doughnuts (*no* one blinked at Millie's pj's at the doughnut place, by the way), the road was jammed with people dropping off some kids while other kids zipped past on boards and bikes, and other kids in groups charged the door and shoved one another. As Millie idled and finished her jelly doughnut, I took a moment of respite to breathe in Monty's doggy smell and give her doggy kisses.

"Wish me luck Monty o' Mine," I whispered into her fur.

Monty snuffled and licked a spot on my face very close to my eyeball.

"Right." Lifting my head, pulling my knapsack up on my shoulder, I shifted into happy voice. "High school! Hooray!"

I hopped out of the car, full of forced vigor.

"GOOD LUCK!" Millie called out as she skidded out of the parking lot, Monty's head hanging out the window like a party favor. I watched as Millie drove off with the rest of the doughnuts and my stomach.

That morning, before I even got up, I had three texts from my actual real best friend, Danny, who I've known since I was ten.

Danny and I share the following things in common: We are both half-Japanese, we have both read all the books people give you to read when you are, we both prefer brightly colored hair, and we both love clothes other people deem to be tacky. Danny is "aggressively gay" and I am "deliriously queer." We haven't lived in the same city for like many many years. So. Lots of texts.

I had already messaged Danny about my disco debacle. He was unsurprised and helpfully enraged.

DANNY
Never stop throwing your balls in their faces.

ANNE
I don't think that's helpful but I appreciate the sentiment

I paused in front of the school to take a photo.

From the outside, Greenville High was a redbrick building with the grid of windows you expect to see in high schools. In every pane, there were little green paw prints taped to the glass, which made it look like someone's green cat had walked over the front of the building and no one had bothered to clean up afterward. Clearly the most important thing about the front of the school was the massive marquee sign that towered over it. Squatting on top of the sign was a giant green plaster creature with the body of a tiger and the neck of a giraffe (maybe?), with a pointed spiky head. I'm guessing this was probably the creature responsible for the paw prints in the windows. Its muzzle was pointed, like a hunting dog, away from the school. Its eyes were made of what looked like yellow lightbulbs. Were they lit up at night?

From the ground, I could see the little white teeth, bared. It looked like someone probably cleaned those teeth, and the sign, on the regular.

The text on the sign read: GO, DRAGONS, GO! DON'T COME FOR US!

"'Don't come for us'?"

As Lucy's sweatshirts can attest, every school has a mascot. They're all kind of weird.

I wondered what this mascot was standing on watch for.

I mean, I had a guess. But I wasn't letting my brain follow up on those thoughts. Instead, I forced my feet to walk the twenty steps between the parking lot and the front entrance.

"Okay, Anne, let's do this."

Inside, Greenville High smelled like every other high school in the world: a mix of floor polish and sweat. The music of kids yelling bounced aggressively off the walls of green and gray lockers as students crisscrossed the green tile floor and did what kids do, which at Greenville High seemed to be punch one another on the shoulder and say stuff like "WHAT UP, DICK?"

Three people smashed past me as I dug into my pockets and pulled out the piece of paper I'd printed with my locker number and schedule. As if on cue, the final kid slammed past me so hard he knocked my bag onto the floor, spilling its contents everywhere.

So I was on all fours trying to get my stuff together when I heard a familiar voice.

"Welcome to Greenville High!"

I smiled as I recognized the paint-spattered work boots.

"Hey!" I looked up.

It was still-unknown person from the day before, who was wearing pretty much the same thing, only with a bright blue sweater on over their coveralls. They held out their hand, which was also covered in freckles (and a little blue paint?) and yanked me off the floor.

"Nice outfit."

"Thanks," I said, flooded with relief. "I didn't ask your name yesterday, or anything else really," I apologized, wiping the dust and pain from my knees. "Sorry, it was kind of a weird—"

"It's Berry." Berry smiled and adjusted their ponytail/pile of hair. "I mean, I'm Berry. Uh. She/her. If that's also what you're asking."

"Oh, it wasn't but that is cool?!" I said, dazzled. "Is it, uh, with an 'e'? Your name?"

"Yeah like Blueberry, or whatever." Berry scratched her chin. "I didn't ask your name because . . . I mean it's Anne, right?"

I blinked. "What?"

"Oh, uh, yeah." Berry held up her hands, "Sorry. Welcome to small-town high school life, where like everyone knows everyone. Like, I mean NBD, but I kind of already know everything about you. Not to freak you out."

I pointed at my chest. "Freaked out."

"I mean." Berry shrugged. "Just maybe close your curtains when you get home."

My eyes popped open. "What?"

"Joke." Berry smiled. "Small-town humor. Not very funny. More menacing, really. I have no idea if you have curtains."

"I mean . . ." I looked around, suddenly realizing how aware of me everyone else seemed to be. "We don't, but *now* I'm *gonna* put some up."

"Maybe not a bad idea." Berry pulled me to the left so I would avoid being slammed to the floor for the second time in the all of ten minutes I'd been at Greenville High. "So. Okay. Here's what I know. . . ."

Berry held up a hand and ticked off the facts about my existence on her fingers, which really were dotted in paint. "I know that your moms are gay. That one of your moms is a big-time photographer who takes pictures of naked people."

"Uh," I said as I mentally scanned Millie's gallery of works, "she takes *portraits*. Sometimes. They're not ALL naked. Not that nudes are, like, bad."

"I mean around here that's porn," Berry said. "Just so you know. People will say your mom makes porn."

"Cool." I sighed. "I'll let her know."

"You moved here from California; some people say LA." Berry raised an eyebrow as if to check on this one.

I shook my head.

Berry looked disappointed for a flash, but then she looked at her watch. "Okay, and also we have to start walking to get to homeroom."

"It was Petaluma," I said, walking next to Berry, "which is *not* LA. Petaluma is actually kind of small, but apparently not Greenville small because no one there knew my bio from the moment I arrived."

"Well." Berry sped up a little. "People are going to say you're from

LA. Because that's what they've decided is true, and basically California around here is just west."

"Riiiiiight." I silently prayed Berry was taking me somewhere I needed to go. "What else?"

Berry rounded a corner. "Your *other* not-porn-making mom is a left-wing socialist militant who will be our first female vice principal in fifty years."

"Yikes again," I said. "Militant? Is that all-encompassing like *west* or what?"

The eyes on me suddenly seemed all that much more potent. Wasp stingers. If wasps were insects that categorized people without actually knowing the person they were talking about.

"Don't worry," Berry said, gesturing for me to catch up. "I'm in your homeroom. And I'm, like, maybe the only person in this town who *was* excited you were from LA. And that your moms are cool and gay and artists."

"Well, good." I mean, heck yeah, my parents are awesome.

"Whatever you need to know about Greenville, I'll, you know, try to tell you all the stuff," Berry assured me in a tone that was actually assuring.

"Thank God."

Berry grinned, gap showing. "Don't you mean 'thank goddess'?"

"Is that a feminist militant reference, because we do worship Gaia," I joked. "I mean not ALL the time but on the harvest moon, you know, we strip, dance in circles around a fire, that whole thing."

"I mean that's what people are saying."

"I'm kidding."

"Yeah, okay," Berry said. Which made me think that that *was* what people were saying.

As if my moms didn't actually spend their weekends bingeing TV and cleaning the kitchen like everyone else. My moms went to sleep at like nine. Not exactly a full-moon house. Although Millie did walk around naked sometimes when she felt like it.

Curtains, I reminded myself. Must get curtains.

We rounded another corner (I was NOT keeping track of where we were going) and ended up in a small classroom where Berry navigated us through a sea of seats to the far side. In each seat sat a kid in muted earth tones who looked at me like I was an alien. Either because two of the fabrics I was wearing were sparkly or because they thought I came from a cult of angry lesbians.

Which, think about it, most cults are heterosexual. Just saying.

The bell finally rang, at which point our homeroom teacher, a tall woman with a blond bob and pearls, walked into the classroom, followed by a set of familiar faces: Tanner, the boy who had basically brought my opening number to a close in Greenville Square a day earlier, and what was clearly his crew. The four of them took their seats at the back of the class, which looked like they had almost been reserved for them.

The homeroom teacher clapped her hands. "Okay, class! Take your seats. It's good to see you all back. Many familiar faces. And it looks like we have a new student with us, uh, Anne? Anne, can you stand up?"

Twenty sets of eyes trained on me as I slowly rose from my seat.

"Hi, I'm Anne," I said, waving as I stood. "Uh. She/her. Not from LA."

I had prepared more casual introductory material, including a brief summary of my three last schools, my three favorite albums, and an inspirational quote.

Apparently none of these were needed or desired.

I had just cracked my mouth open to talk when my new homeroom teacher made a clam-slamming-shut motion with her hand, followed by a "sit down" motion with her other hand.

I sat.

"Anne. My name is Mrs. Sherman," she said, with the crispness of a snapped cracker, "and I will be your homeroom teacher. If you need any assistance, I'm sure there will be no shortage of students prepared to help the adopted daughter of our new school vice principal."

It was like being pricked by an unexpected thorn. Why did she say I was adopted? Like, accurate but also kind of *rude*. Adopted daughter instead of just, you know, daughter? Kid?

I caught Berry's glance like a butterfly net, her eyes wide with "Yes, Anne, this is going to happen. I am very sorry."

I opened my mouth to say something, but then the bell rang.

And there ended the final (ish?) introduction of me to Greenville.

Of course, *my* introduction to Greenville was just getting started.

Berry continued her primer in Gym a few periods later, while we ran in circles like planets orbiting our gym teacher, Mrs. Harras, who took a moment to eye me and give me a curt handshake of introduction when I walked onto the field.

"Harras," she said, holding out her hand. "*Coach* Harras. Physical education. I also coach girls soccer and tennis."

"Anne," I said, shaking with a firm grip that was not as firm as Harras's. "I will be your student, but probably not on any teams. No offense."

"Annie?" Harras looked momentarily interested.

"No, *Anne*. With an *e*."

"Really?"

"Anne with an *e*?" I repeated. "It's . . . my name?"

Harras sniffed. "I thought it was Annie."

She was very clearly disappointed.

In addition to somehow having a preference for Annie over Anne, Harras also seemed to like blowing her whistle a lot for no reason. Like three tweets for every lap? Why? I tried to zone out and focus in on my lesson and jog, something I hadn't done since my last gym class a few months earlier, because who jogs?

According to Berry, Greenville is made up of two groups of people.

"Okay, so." Berry looked around. "Possibly this is weird to talk about, like, categorizing people and stuff. I mean, I think it's weird."

"Acknowledging before you begin that many categories of people are subjective," I noted. "And imposed. And likely oppressive. Yes."

"Right! Yeah, okay, so there's people who have been here since what *they* would say is *the beginning*. They're, like, the *locals*." Berry rounded the turn, her hands balled into fists as she ran, in the boots I thought she would have changed out of. "I mean," she added, "obviously, like, everyone in the United States *came* here from another country unless you are Indigenous or Native American."

I pointed at Berry, pleased because American history and the history of what actually happened in America is sometimes a thing I think only my moms and I talk about. "Yes. That is TRUE."

"And then there are the *newcomers*," Berry said, "which is everyone else in Greenville, even if your family has been here for fifty years."

"And the locals are the people who determine the newcomers," I assumed.

"Oh. Yeah." Berry took a gulp of air. Her cheeks were apple red. "But, you know, sometimes it's the newcomers who call themselves newcomers, too."

"So, I am *definitely* a newcomer," I said.

"I mean, oh yeah, you definitely are, but, like, I am, too," Berry pointed at herself. "I mean, everyone here is always like, *Your family is Polish. Right?* Even though we've been here for like two generations. In Greenville years that's like five minutes."

"Yikes," I said, because it seemed the most appropriate response. Or the shortest. But also, wow. Like super prejudicial and problematic?

"Super yikes." Berry nodded, stopping to tie her laces, which were thick with paint. "But that's how it is here."

I looked around at all the kids all bundled in groups. "What about Tanner?" I asked. "I'm assuming he's local."

Berry looked over her shoulder. "Tanner and crew? They call themselves the *Forevers*."

Tanner and the boys from his crew weren't around (since gym in Greenville adhered to the archaic definitions of the gender binary) but the two girls from his crew were standing with a few other blonds in the center of the track, stretching.

"The Forevers are the kids whose families have been here since, you know, *they* would say, *forever*. Again, super erasing and problematic. It's like the whole Founding Fathers–type thing. Also, they all have like tons of money. Tanner Spencer, the tall guy who always wears his soccer stuff, his family is all mayors and councilmen. The kid with the black hair and the freckles from yesterday was John Maxwell; his family owns the grocery store and the car dealership. And Gilly Henderson, the girl with the long hair, her dad is on the city council and her grandfather manages the bank. Her mom died a few years ago. The girl with the pigtails is Sarah Pye. They're just rich . . . I don't know how. Her mom is PTA."

"That's too bad about her mom." I looked over at Gilly, who was in the center of the track, bending to touch her toes. "So, like the Forevers, they *founded* the city?"

"Oh, I mean, no, probably not. Maybe?" Berry shrugged as Coach Harras tweeted us back into our laps with—I thought—an excessive number of blasts. "I mean, they sort of . . . own it?"

The best way to run a place is to *act* like you run it.

And somewhere now Lucy, the "militant lesbian," had been given a position of power.

I was pretty sure that wouldn't be good.

Fortunately, for me at least, Berry and I had almost the same schedule except for Band, which Berry had (tuba!) but I didn't, so I could pretty much follow her around all day soaking up as much information as she was willing to dish out. And clinging to Berry like a life jacket.

Berry showed me the two water fountains that worked, how to open my locker, which stuck, and how to navigate the Greenville High building, which was basically a doughnut. Also where the bathrooms with the working stalls were.

"So what do people do around here," I asked as we walked from Chemistry to Spanish, "for fun?"

"For fun?" Berry tapped her chin. "*Some* kids stay home and play video games and watch makeup youvids. Mostly, though, around *here*, everything is sports. Like Greenville is ninety percent soccer season and ten percent academics. Soccer is the big thing at Greenville."

"Hence the dragon perched on top of the sign outside."

"Yeah, you don't mess with the Dragons. Like parents here are super intense about that stuff."

"Yeah?"

"Like"—Berry surreptitiously pointed to the arm of a kid walking next to us—"if you want to get a dragon tattoo around here, you can do that from the age of like six."

"Do you have one?" I asked.

"Uh, no way." Berry frowned. "When I get a tattoo, it's not going to be a Greenville tattoo!"

"So there's a lot of patchy dragon tattoos around Greenville is what you're saying."

"Mmm-hmm."

My next class was English, which is normally my favorite class. Because what is better than a class that asks you to read a thing and then give your opinion about it? Even if you don't like the thing you're reading, at least you get to give your thoughts on it later, and, if you're a super nerd, teachers usually give in and let you give an opinion on whatever else you happen to be reading.

Which is why I've given at least three book reports over the years on books about disco.

This teacher was a tall and reedy man with a smooth face and a thumb-size ponytail of curly hair at the back of his head. He smiled and nodded as I walked into the classroom, which was the first hint of any kind of warm welcome I'd gotten from any teacher. I nodded back and mentally told him that I 100 percent approved of his deliciously russet-orange vest with the wide shirt collar winged over top. Even if it was paired with a curious light blue denim.

A choice. A bold choice, really.

I could have sworn I got a little vibe back on my ensemble, but it was late in the day and I was kind of desperate for some acknowledgment, so I could have been projecting.

We were starting the semester with poetry, which was clear from the cursive message on the board.

Mr. Davidson. English.
Take out your poetry intro books.
Now.

"Hello, hello," Mr. Davidson trilled, fanning his hand out over the class. "Sit, sit, sit."

He picked up a list from his desk, his lips moving slightly as he ran down what I assumed was an attendance sheet. Mr. Davidson preferred the arena style of desk arrangement. I sat at the top side of the O, which unfortunately meant I was across from Tanner and crew.

"You must be Anne." Davidson looked up from the list with a smile. "Welcome. We're of course very happy to have your mother as our new vice principal, and we look forward to your contribution to our school."

"Thanks!"

"Maybe you could start by telling us what you read this summer," Mr. Davidson said. "So we can get a little sense of your literary tastes?"

"Um. I read a biography of the singer Sylvester and a bunch of graphic novels."

Mr. Davidson nodded. "Excellent. Well, we'll look forward to hearing your thoughts on our reading list, Anne."

"Cool." I grinned.

"Cool," someone on my left mimicked.

Someone else stifled a giggle.

Mr. Davidson straightened. "All right. Let's get out your textbooks."

I looked up to see Sarah Pye staring back at me, her little cherry-red ponytails sticking out either side of her head, each tied with a green bow. "Coooool," she mouthed exaggeratedly.

As Davidson wiped off the board at the front of the class, Tanner, his head tilted, faux-whispered to Sarah. His voice was only barely audible under the flutter of papers shifting, books coming out of bags and slapping onto the desktops. But I heard it. "Yeah, I mean I heard she's a DYKE."

I froze, my poetry textbook gripped in my hand.

Next to me, Berry shifted in her seat.

"Guess the city would rather give a job to a dyke than someone who can actually do it for real," Tanner's voice crept up in volume, as the sound of books flopping open, throats clearing, shoes on the floor, got louder.

Gilly, the girl with long hair, dropped her head into her hand, staring at her desk.

"I heard they're *all* dykes," Sarah loud whispered back.

My stomach flopped in my belly.

Suddenly there was a loud *bang* at the front of the classroom. Everyone looked up to see Mr. Davidson, his hands still hovering in the air over the book he'd dropped. He picked the book up. "We're in *class* now. And in *class* we *listen* until spoken *to*."

Across the room, Tanner gave a big stretch and yawned.

"Mr. Spencer." Mr. Davidson stepped into the open circle of desks, walked over to Tanner and put his finger on the desk in front of him. "SIT. UP."

Tanner slowly unfolded his body until he was sitting up straight.

I could feel Berry looking at me.

She mouthed, "Sorry."

I could see a sheen of sweat beaded on her forehead.

"It's okay," I whispered back.

I opened my poetry book and flipped through it, my lips numb.

Mr. Davidson strode through the classroom back to his desk.

"Why don't we start with . . . Gilly? Read our first poem on page six."

Gilly raised her head slowly. "What?"

"Reading," Davidson repeated. "Which we all enjoy. Please open your book, Gilly."

I flipped through the contents while Gilly opened her book and started reading the first poem, by Robert Frost. The textbook was about 70 percent white guys, but it had a poem by Mary Oliver in it, "Wild Geese." Which is Lucy's favorite poem.

Ideally seeing Mary Oliver's words would have carried me past this very stressful situation. Because she is a very very amazing writer. But all I could feel was a buzzing in my head during the rest of English. When the bell rang, I followed Berry to the cafeteria like there was cement in my sneakers, selecting a boat of fries to go with my apple juice. Outside, there was a paved area filled with tables. We sat at one near the edge.

"Yeah so," Berry said, dropping down onto her seat and biting into her apple.

"Yeah."

"I'm not going to ask if you're okay, by the way. I mean, it's cool if you're not okay is what I'm saying. It's not okay . . . what Tanner said. I mean he's going to say it again, but I feel like, yeah, it's worth always saying that it's not okay."

"He say it to you, ever?" I asked.

Berry pulled up the edge of her overalls with her thumb and fore-finger. "Obv."

"Right. Okay. That sucks." I took a deep breath.

"I should have mentioned the element of small-town homophobia on top of the racism," Berry said as we walked our trays to an empty table.

"Yeah," I said. "I mean, it's not like I haven't heard it before. It's not just small towns, BTW."

"Wait, really?" Berry raised her eyebrows, highlighting a spatter of neon-orange paint on her eyebrow.

"Yeah," I said.

Berry looked at the apple in her hand. "People are homophobic in *California?*"

I shrugged. "Yeah, I'm pretty sure there are people who are horrible in every city. I mean in some bigger cities I think it's just not, like, as accepted. Or obvious? But it does happen."

Berry blinked, shook.

"But I'm not, like, an expert or anything," I added.

People having an issue with LGBTQIA people, or BIPOC people, wasn't new. It just sucked. Consistently. I'd spent a lot of time as a kid with my moms advocating for their existence to teachers who sent me home with "draw your family tree" exercises that were tricky for me as someone who was both adopted and had two moms.

"Tell them we're not a tree. We're a garden," Millie said.

Actually one of the reasons Lucy went into education was stuff like that. Like curriculum and how it normalizes stuff. Lucy came up with this whole exercise she taught to teachers in schools all over the place. So we could *all* be gardens.

But maybe not in Greenville. On this particular day.

Berry artfully changed the subject to what movies I had and hadn't seen, and we were knee-deep in a debate about whether or not animation is better than live action (it's not) when I heard Tanner's voice rise up into the air like a flock of angry seagulls.

"Hey, NEW GIRL!!!"

I put my drink down on the table.

"NEW GIRL! DYKE!"

"Anne," Berry said quietly.

I was already up and walking before I realized it.

Tanner and his crew of Forevers were sitting at a picnic table a few feet away. It was clearly the good table. Half shaded by tree, half in the sun, the full buffet of teen snacks spread out for those in attendance to enjoy. Tanner was spinning his soccer ball on the table, which to me seemed doubly rude, not that his friends seemed to care.

As I stepped up to the table, Tanner smiled at me, his big teeth whiter than I thought they should be.

"Excuse me." Sarah leaned forward, her fingers spread out displaying a pale pink mani that matched her lip gloss and shirt. "I don't think you're *invited* to be near this table. And, um, maybe in whatever fucked-up place you came from being *rude* is okay, but it's not here."

Tanner grinned up at me.

"So maybe you can dyke off." Sarah smiled acid.

Gilly covered her mouth with her hand, her eyes wide.

They were all eating pizza, big droopy cafeteria slices with brick-like red pepperonis, all laid out on paper plates on beat-up cafeteria trays on the table. It was the special of the day, which I didn't get because it didn't *smell* like pizza and that's a major component of food for me.

"Here for some lunch meat, new girl?" The boy I was pretty sure was John Maxwell sneered, dropping his hands under the table.

"Nah, New Girl's here 'cause I got a message for her mom." Tanner leaned back, pulling his foot up on the bench.

"I don't take messages for my mother," I said, trying to keep my heart from jumping out of my chest. "I'm here to tell you not to use the word *dyke*. It's not yours. It's *mine*."

I turned and started walking away.

"HEY!" Tanner called after me. "Hey, I'm not finished! DYKE! You gotta give your ma a message? OKAY?"

I could hear Sarah laughing.

I was three feet away when Tanner added, "Tell your SLUT of a mother to go back to California so we can get a real vice principal who knows what he's doing."

I spun around.

"What did you say?"

You talk about my mom . . .

"I said your mom's a SLUT." Tanner grinned. His teeth were as big as boats. "You wanna know how I know that?"

I didn't let him answer. In a blur of pure rage, I charged at him like a freight train.

Suddenly my body wasn't a body. It was a volcano, connected to the darkest, fiercest, hottest matter on the face of the earth.

Tanner's pretty lucky I only hit him with a piece of pizza.

I had other options.

FIVE

Okay, so it's probably worth taking a moment to say that my life is not all rainbows and glitter. How could it be? A person can't live on glitter alone. Not that anyone's ever put in the effort and tried.

For example, that performance I did at my grandmother's ninetieth birthday, where my uncle pulled me off the stage because he thought I was in my underwear? (To be *very very* clear, I wasn't in my underwear. Also why do girls always get accused of being "in their underwear" and boys never do? How are shorts so different from boxers?) Okay, so, what I didn't tell you is what happened *after* he got me off the stage.

First of all the whole thing was a scene out of a family sitcom. Millie, who was running music and lights for my performance (like a desk lamp that I brought from home because the hotel didn't have an actual lighting setup), jumped off the stage, ripping her phone free from the audio cord that was plugged into the sound system in the process, cutting off the music. In a flash she'd also yanked me out of my uncle's grip.

Lucy, who was at the back of the room filming, bolted to the front of the room. I remember hearing the *clip-clop* of her heels on the floor as she raced toward us.

I, it was said later, was howling like a cat in the shower (not my description) this whole time.

Before Lucy got to the stage, Millie got into it with my uncle because Millie is not a fan of my uncle because he does stuff like this.

Millie got her face very close to my uncle's face and growled. "Herbert! You TOUCH my kid one more time and they'll be wheeling you out of here on a STRETCHER."

Herbert doubled down, shoving me out of the way. "Maybe your kid shouldn't be parading around my grandmom's birthday party in her undies."

Undies?

"Herbert." Millie got even closer. "You SHOVE MY KID or say *undies* around my kid one more time, you won't remember the experience of being rolled out of here on a stretcher because I'm going to beat you unconscious."

At that point, Lucy arrived.

"Okay." She stepped in between Millie and Herbert. "I need everyone to take a deep breath. Herbert. You owe Anne an apology."

"WHAT? This is Grandmom's BIRTHDAY, Lucy! You think you can come in here with your—"

Lucy cut him off. "*Herbert.* I'm going to have to insist that you bring your voice down."

As Lucy attempted to de-escalate and Millie, I believe, considered the possible legal consequences of decking my uncle, I, still in my outfit and taps, released from my uncle's grip, was walking through the crowd, toward the dessert table at the back of the room.

By then, according to the video taken by my cousin Louise, who wasn't taping my performance so much as recording the whole event for a paper she was doing on community gatherings, the hotel had turned on the piped-in hotel Muzak that was, I think, a loose rendition of the Beatles song "When I'm Sixty-Four."

Mostly what I remember hearing was the telltale *whooshing* in my ears. The pounding of my heart in my chest, which my brain translated to the opening chords of "Mama Mia" by ABBA from the album *ABBA*, released in 1975, not to be confused with *ABBA: The Album*, which came out two years later in 1977.

(I know, right? Was it that they just really liked their name or was it that there were four people in the group and they couldn't agree on an album title so someone, maybe Björn, was like, "Fine we'll just call this one ABBA, too!")

(Yes, my cat is named after the lead singer of ABBA. Surprised?)

Many of the desserts at my grandma's birthday were things guests had made, which they had placed on a set of foldout tables at the back of the conference room. The tables were covered in plastic tablecloths and liberally sprinkled with colored confetti. Not exactly classy, but who says an older person's birthday has to be classy?

Herbert's grandmom, my great-grandmom, was a very interesting lady.

She was the one who bought Lucy her first disco record, the Jacksons' self-titled 1978 album *The Jacksons*. Which is why I knew she would love my performance.

For this birthday, Herbert bought her decorative soaps, just FYI. Who buys someone *soap* as a *present*?

(Herbert. Consistently.)

Okay, so back to the story: So on these tables there were two trays of Rice Krispies Treats, two platters of Jell-O squares, two dozen chocolate-chip cookies, and three cakes, all because everyone ignored Lucy's organizing email with a chart of desserts and just did their own thing. Which is also standard on that side of the family.

Two of the three cakes were store-bought. Which, obviously, I have no judgment on that. Not everyone has time to make a cake (and I don't know how to bake).

The thing about store-bought cakes is they are mostly icing. Like at least an inch, as anyone who has ever pushed her finger into the icing on one of these cakes or dared to try to eat a mostly icing corner piece will tell you. I don't know if that went into my decision, standing in front of that table. I was only standing there a minute. Maybe I picked the big-ass white cake because it was one of the desserts at the front of the table and I could barely reach because I was, as I said, seven.

I remember my thumbs sinking into the icing as I picked up the cake and marched it back to my uncle and my moms. Who were still fighting.

"Herbert. This is a situation we can either choose to be CALM, in the interests of Grandmom's birthday, or we can choose to make this day about conflict—"

"Jesus, LUCY!" Herbert thundered. "You and your fucking feminist politic—"

I remember Millie stepped back when she saw me, I guess out of the corner of her eye. Maybe to see what I was doing or what I was carrying. I gather she figured out what was about to happen just as I heaved Grandmom's birthday cake up and slapped it into my uncle's torso.

Lucy said she *did* think *something* was going on because she could hear my tap shoes as I stalked back over to my uncle from the dessert table.

My grandmom later expressed her relief that it was one of the store-bought cakes.

To this day, whenever I have to go to anything when my uncle Herbert is there, he always holds up his hands by his face when I walk in, like in defense of future cakes.

I could give you a few other examples of me doing this kind of thing.

Like when we lived in Kansas City and I started a hot dog fight at Debbie Smolkum's eleventh birthday party after she made fun of my friend Alice's bathing suit because Alice was wearing her mom's old bathing suit. Debbie said Alice looked like a senior citizen. I told Debbie there's nothing wrong with senior citizens. Debbie told us we couldn't be in the pool because seniors pee themselves (not true) and so I walked over to Debbie and I hit her with a hot dog her dad had just grilled me on the BBQ, which ended up *ruining* the Smolkums' pool because Debbie retaliated and threw a bun at me and it went into the pool filter.

(Which, let's say it, that's on Debbie.)

I will say I've never, like, physically harmed anyone. But overall it's not good. I know it's not good.

So, yeah. Anyway.

BACK TO THE IN-THE-NOW STORY

So, to recap. Tanner was a homophobic, sexist, probably other things, jerk.

I hit Tanner . . . with a pizza.

Still technically hitting.

I'm not exactly clear on how the actual full-on food fight started after I slapped Tanner with the pizza. What I do remember is that as soon as the pepperoni made contact, he basically bounced up from his seat, knocking me back on the ground.

(On my already bruised ass, BTW.)

And by the time I got to my feet, the food fight was in full effect. Food flew, hard and fast like propelled by the winds of a hurricane, until the whole thing came to a crashing end with many angry whistle blasts and me and Tanner getting pulled into the office.

I will say, at least it wasn't a waste of pizza, because the Greenville High cafeteria pizza was and is horrible. Like don't call it pizza if it's actually a soft, barely edible, triangular piece of cardboard covered in red-and-yellow goop. Like, maybe people in Greenville are so mad all the time because they've never had a decent slice. Which I can say I've had in almost every other place I've lived in, including Petaluma, which has a population of 60,000 and at least a dozen great pizzerias.

(Do the math. Greenville could still have at least *one*.)

I gathered that the pizza detail was not something anyone, my mom included, wanted to hear from me as I stood in her office—her new office—an hour later, with her new boss, Principal Lynde, who I will describe as a woman who was tall and made of granite, with impossibly shiny hair piled on top of her head in a perfect silver bun and green wire-frame glasses. A woman with the smallest, angriest mouth I have ever seen on a human.

Principal Lynde was standing in the middle of my mom's office when I arrived. Tanner and who I could only assume were his parents were sitting in the waiting area just outside. The look on my mom's face said that these things were not in any way good things.

"Well then," Lynde snapped, her voice cutting glass, "quite the first impression. Violence. And disorder. And spreading her influence all over the student body. And . . ." Principal Lynde leaned forward and peered over her glasses. "Dressed like a prostitute to boot."

My eyes widened.

"And that hair." Lynde shook her head.

Lucy stepped forward. "Principal Lynde," she cut in. "Anne's clothing and hair are not at issue here, and I would like to be clear—"

"OH!" Principal Lynde swiveled, her body stiff. "So *you* are clear what is and isn't at issue here? Are you? I'm glad you're so experienced with these matters, *Miss* Shirley."

"I am . . ." Lucy snuck a look at me. "I am of course not pleased to have to discipline Anne on the first day, but that falls within *my* responsibilities, and I will make sure I deal with this situation appropriately."

Principal Lynde sniffed the sniff of the unimpressed.

"I see. Well, pardon me if I question your judgment given what your child is wearing and how she has conducted herself since arriving at *my* school." Lynde stepped forward, one step closer into my space than I would have liked. Possibly so she could look down on me like one looks down a cliff at something that has just fallen off that cliff and ended up a splat on the ground.

Or maybe that's just what it felt like.

"I will go and reassure the Spencer family, then." Lynde took another moment to deliver another steely look before gliding across the floor and out the door. "I'm sure they will be *thrilled* to know you have this under control."

As the door closed behind her, I took my first breath in five minutes.

Lucy also took a deep breath, leaning on her desk, which had, I was only then noticing, just *pillars* of paper, precariously perched on every inch of space. It looked like she was conducting an experiment to see how many pieces of paper she could fit on her desk. And the answer was a lot.

It looked like Lucy had also had . . . kind of a day. Her smooth morning hair looked like it had been restyled by an angry horde of kittens. Her suit looked weirdly wrinkled and her sleeves were rolled up to her elbows. I was pretty sure this discussion about me was not my mom's first not-great discussion with Principal Lynde.

"Mom," I said, catching myself.

Lucy stared at me. Then her eyes skipped past me.

Coach Harras, whistleblower extraordinaire, appeared in the doorway.

"Who started it?" Lucy looked at me, then at Harras.

"Your ki—" Harras started.

"I did," I cut in.

Lucy gave me a sharp look. "You're interrupting Coach Harras?"

"I'm sorry," I said, chin to my chest.

"Darn right," Harras mumbled.

"Sorry to whom?" Lucy asked.

I turned toward the doorway. "Sorry, Coach Harras, I shouldn't have interrupted."

"We're fine now, thank you, Coach Harras," Lucy said, with her softest, calmest voice. Coach Harras gave a small huff, then turned and walked away. Lucy closed the door behind her.

"Okay," Lucy said, a few seconds after the door clicked. "Okay." She took another deep breath. "This is hard. This is a new school. This is a town that's not like other towns where we've lived."

"Mom—"

"You can't keep— Anne. Do you understand what it means when

you act this way?" Lucy looked to the door, through which she could see Tanner and his family.

"I—"

"You *cannot* act out this way." Lucy's voice cut sharply. "I say this as a mother *and* as the vice principal of your school, Anne. Do you want to talk about *why* this happened?"

"Not really," I said quietly. I could still hear Tanner's voice shouting the word *dyke* ringing in my ears, but the idea of saying anything about that to my mother in that office at that moment seemed as possible as turning into a bird and flying out the window. Or something.

"Are you sure?"

The phone on her desk started ringing.

"Yeah."

Lucy looked like she wanted to say many things to me. There was a knock on the door.

"Well. We'll revisit this when I get home. Go to class."

And then she stood up, walked over to me, and peeled a pepperoni off the top of my head I legit didn't know was there. She flicked the pepperoni into the trash, opened the door, and walked out of her office and into the room where Tanner and his parents were waiting with Principal Lynde.

"Are you going to talk to her?" Tanner's father barked at Principal Lynde, clearly pointing at me. "Where's that kid going?"

The last thing I heard as I exited into the hall was his booming voice: "DISGUSTING."

Berry had to go to Band practice after school, but she sent me a text of a bunch of pizzas and happy faces. Which, every time I thought about the look on Tanner's face when the pizza hit him, I agreed, but then I got home after school. And then an hour later Lucy got home, and it felt like it was less happy faces and more the face with all the lines on it.

I won't give you the whole thing. But the highlights were as follows.

I was in serious trouble.

Lucy's first day at her new job, which was already going to be really difficult, was a nightmare for reasons that did not need to be described to me in detail in order for me to take them seriously. But needless to say, it wasn't just the students who thought a militant dyke was taking over their precious school.

The PTA, including Tanner's family, had already expressed serious doubts as to Lucy's qualifications. Through a series of emails. And voicemails.

Sitting on the couch, Millie frowned, rubbing Lucy's back. "It's your first day. It's Anne's first day. How can they even presume to judge anything?"

"Right," Lucy sighed. "Well, Lynde said she is considering *this* incident as 'meriting a probationary approach to my job.'"

Millie looked like she wanted to say more, but she gave Lucy a hug instead.

So, Yeah, I guess since there were bigger things going on, in the end, I was not grounded. But they were disappointed.

This is the ultimate lesbian punishment, by the way. *Disappointment.*

After Lucy left to go to her study, Millie took a few minutes to just look at me. Then she stood and went to the kitchen. I followed. Then she looked at me some more, and standing next to a giant bag of cat food that already had a hole in the bottom, she drilled her lesbian laser beams into my brain. Searching. Assessing. Debating. Judging.

"Please say something," I cracked, dropping my head back.

"Say *something*?" Millie mused. "Anything? Why pizza? Why on the first day? That kind of thing?"

"I'm *sorry*," I moaned. "I'm sorry I hit Tanner with pizza and then it started a whole pizza fight."

"Yeah, the problem with that is that it *sounds* funny," Millie said, kicking a stray pebble of cat food across the floor, to Bjorn's delight. "But it's not really funny."

"No."

"You know, when you were a kid, your doing this sort of thing was admittedly *kind of* amusing to me," she said, walking back over to the couch and flopping down. Monty promptly joined her. "And I thought it was good you were standing up for yourself because I knew you were going to have to do that. Probably your whole life, for some reasons that are obvious and many reasons that are not."

"Okay." I sat on the coffee table as Bjorn plopped down and rolled over to show us a belly that suggested he'd been breaking into the cat food on the regular.

"Can you tell me exactly what happened?" Millie asked.

Monty picked up her head from Millie's lap and raised her dog eyebrow at me. Like she knew. Golden retrievers always know.

Damn their adorable dog faces.

"That kid, Tanner, said something shitty." I frowned. "It wasn't . . . I just . . . I couldn't just not do anything, so I did a shitty thing, okay?"

"So two . . . crappy things? How's that working for you?"

"I don't think they're equal," I countered. "If someone says something hateful, that's not the same as a pizza in the face."

"I think it's hard to say what is what, especially when you weren't exactly in control of *your* actions. Right?"

"You don't know what kids here are like."

"Oh yeah, I do," Millie rubbed Monty's ears between her fingers. "Believe that, kid. I *do* know *exactly* what they are like."

"Well, then if you know, you know how crappy it is, and you know how *bad* it can be."

The thing about Millie is, she's stealth. She's observant. She's always right in this way I find really annoying.

"Well, given how bad it is," Millie noted, "it's a good thing you dealt with it in a way that will make everything better for you, and for your mom."

Millie is not a lawyer. Like she does this job that doesn't involve words. I think maybe she takes pictures because if she *did* use her words, she would just eviscerate us all. Like it wouldn't be fair, is what I'm saying.

"It's not that I don't believe, don't *know*, that moving here means there's a ton of not great stuff you have to deal with, Anne. It's that I'm worried maybe you've settled on *one* way of dealing with it, and really, kiddo, that's just not going to fly anymore. Not just because we're living *here*, by the way. But just in general. It doesn't solve any of the legit problems you are having to smack someone in the face with lunch."

She reached over and clicked on the TV, which she likes to watch on mute so she can talk over and about it.

"Okay," I grumbled, "I get it. I will apologize. To Tanner."

Millie nodded. "Sounds like something that could actually make things better."

"Thank you for the life lesson," I mumbled.

"You're most welcome," Millie propped her feet up on the coffee table, lightly tapping me out of her way. "Go do your homework."

"Fine."

I was almost out of the room when she added, "Small towns aren't like the other places we've lived, Anne."

"They don't like *newcomers* here," I said.

"They don't like newcomers? Interesting. I wouldn't go that far," Millie's tone was level. "*They* is an amorphous and not exactly helpful amount of people to describe. As you well know."

"The *people who live here*," I said slow and enunciating. "Don't like newcomers. It's true. Stereotypes can be true."

"I'm just saying you don't know this place yet, and maybe instead of just reacting to it, you could figure it out first," Millie said. "Figure it out *more*."

"Fine."

"Take Monty out before you go up to your room," Millie said as Monty sprang off her lap.

"What about dinner?"

"I'll get dinner later. Walk Monty."

"Okay."

"I love you."

"I love you, too."

"I'm cheering for you in this, by the way. I don't wear the official Mars intergalactic cheerleading outfit, but I am still . . . cheering. For you."

"Great."

Monty still didn't know the lay of the land in Greenville either, which meant getting her to walk any farther than a block from our house was still basically like pulling teeth. I felt like I was torturing her.

"Come on, Montsamillion," I moaned, "help me out here."

In the end, our "walk" was me standing next to Monty while she lay on the sidewalk and looked up at me.

"You look like I feel, Monty o' Mine," I said. "You're annoying and you look like I feel."

Millie was right, I didn't know Greenville.

And maybe I didn't want to.

I was carrying Monty home when I got a text from Berry.

More pizzas. And rainbow emojis. And unicorns. All arranged in patterns around a single sentence.

BERRY
SEE YOU TOMORROW, PIZZA FIGHTER!

SIX

Okay, so my first day at Greenville High, and let's say my general entry into Greenville as a whole, had not gone great.

And that was not entirely my fault, obviously. Like, I think the record will show it wasn't just me. But I had also lost my temper and as a result gotten the cutting and accurate reprimand from Millie.

The next day when Lucy woke up, I had already prepared a stack of (store-bought mix) pancakes for her and made her coffee and packed her lunch with a sandwich and cut-up celery.

Lucy took the lunch bag from me and took a moment to eyeball my outfit. Which was probably my most notable to date. Because it was entirely . . . normal.

"Where did you get those clothes?" she asked, feeling the lunch bag on the sly for leaks because I have, in the past, packed Lucy lunches that leaked.

"My closet," I said, pointing at the bag, "And I wrapped everything in there up, so don't worry. No leaks."

The shirt was actually Millie's shirt, which she got from one of the many art festivals she attended. Most of these deals gave out shirts with logos so big and sticky feeling they were almost unwearable. This shirt, fortunately, was from a minimalist image festival called "I," so the only logo was a tiny *I* on the left sleeve. The jeans were jeans I had originally bought to distress and acid wash, back when I was in a more acid wash phase.

Danny, who received a photo of this outfit before I made breakfast, had kindly taken the time to text me an encouraging message.

DANNY

Have fun giving up your individuality for Greenville's Capitalist Shitheads!!!

Lucy looked me up and down with a tiny, worried frown on her face.

"I'll see you at school!" I chirped.

Lucy, that day, was wearing another women's suit thing, green, with, I would say, not entirely effective gold buttons. Before she took this job, there's no way Lucy would wear a pencil skirt made out of wool. She certainly wouldn't wear that two days back-to-back. Really what she would normally wear was something like what I was wearing, but with khakis. Because that's Lucy's specific gay.

But no, Lucy was wearing an undoubtedly uncomfortable, *not* in character outfit, and she was wearing it for *Greenville*, I'm assuming. To let them know she wasn't a militant feminist. Or that if she *was* a militant feminist, she was at least willing to put in a little effort to blend. (Say this, though, isn't a stiff fabric like the wool in these dress suits kind of similar to what you'd wear in the army? Maybe?) If *Lucy* could wear an ugly woman-suit for Greenville, I could wear white and tragically unadorned denim for Greenville.

Not that I had to explain this to Danny, who clearly wasn't getting the context. I wasn't fitting in or giving up. I was putting up . . . a white flag. I was chilling for a little bit so Lucy and I could get our footing at Greenville High. That's all.

Although I'll say this, who wears white? It's so annoying. Like two seconds after I put it on, I already had a little spot of coffee on the bottom. You know what you can't see coffee stains on? Orange. Blue. Floral patterns. You name it.

Right before I left the house I turned and spotted my reflection in the mirror Millie had just hung in the hallway, normally a mirror I used to take a moment to make a really weird face at before leaving the house. You know, just to keep myself in the practice. My orange hair, which that day had decided to retain a bit of a pouf, fluffed around my face.

I pulled a tie out of my pocket and tied it back into a boring ponytail.

I squinted at my reflection. "You can be normal."

My reflection squinted back. Admittedly the me in the mirror didn't look convincing or familiar.

"White flag," I told myself. "It's going to be fine."

Me in the mirror blinked as if to say, *Sure it is. Nice shirt.*

Roller-skating to school was my one concession, and necessary because Millie had to take Monty to the vet for a checkup. I wore my baby-blue roller skates with the pink stars on the toes for no other reason than the fact that I tripped over them getting out of bed that morning.

(Side note: I really needed to clean up my room.)

By the time I got to Greenville High, I'd almost forgotten about what I was wearing. That is, until, weaving between cars in the parking lot, I almost slammed into Principal Lynde getting out of her massive pickup truck. My toe brakes squealed louder than I wanted them to— and loud enough to fall under Lynde's judgmental icy glare.

"Anne Shirley," she snapped, spinning sharply to face me as I attempted to stay still without putting my hand on her car. "Roller-skating in the parking lot."

"Uh, yes." I looked down. "Mrs. Lynde. Principal Lynde."

Lynde sniffed, like my skates smelled. (They did not.)

"I hardly think those are appropriate for school grounds."

"Right, I just"—I pointed back from where I'd come—"was just . . . getting to school."

Lynde narrowed her eyes as I attempted to stop sweating. Once again, her hair was a pillar of silver. Which made me wonder if Lucy was trying to do a similar helmety type thing with how she was doing *her* hair lately.

"I have spoken to your mother," Lynde continued, raising her eyebrows and lifting her chin as she spoke, "as you know. We had great hopes for her here at Greenville. I'm sure you share your mother's aspirations to make a good start at this school."

"Yes," I said. "Of course."

"Of course." Lynde's gaze fell on my head. "That *hair*." She leaned forward slightly to look at the top of my head, like there was a spider there she wanted to kill. "Why you would debase your body with such a *pointless* effort is beyond me. Given all you have to overcome."

For just a second, I let my gaze narrow. *All I have to overcome*?

Lynde raised an eyebrow. Was I glaring at her? Yes. I dropped my gaze to my skates. "Okay, well."

"Students at Greenville High look their elders in the eye when they are spoken to," Principal Lynde said.

I lifted my chin. Something inside me was ticking like those bombs you see in cartoons.

"Yes."

"I know you are issuing an apology today," Lynde continued. "Please make it a good one."

And with that she pivoted and headed toward the school.

I had a flash image of me putting my skate through Lynde's pristine windshield. The sound of glass breaking and the inevitable shriek of Lynde.

You want to see me overcome? HUH?

WATCH ME OVERCOME THIS GLASS!

Oh, and maybe I didn't dye my hair *brown*, but I did wear ugly clothes to school *on purpose*, and clearly *Lynde* didn't even *care*!

"Hey."

I spun around, and might have put my hand on or possibly through Lynde's passenger window if Berry's hadn't reached out and grabbed my arm before I did a full spill.

"Oh my gosh, I'm so sorry," Berry gushed nervously. "I thought you maybe needed a rescue. From Lynde."

Berry, I noticed, wore a variation of the same thing every day. Coveralls. Green hair. That day she was wearing a green-and-blue tie-dyed shirt under her coveralls with matching socks.

"Hey," I said as she released my arm. "Thanks."

"What did Lynde want?"

"She hates my hair." I sighed, rolling to the front steps with Berry close behind.

I sat on the steps while Greenville High students flooded past, Berry sitting next to me, watching me unlace. Her stare was very intense. Which is maybe why it felt weird. Like, could everyone just back off for a moment?

"Are you okay?" Berry asked quietly.

"I have to go find Tanner," I said, slinging my skates over my shoulder and charging into the school. "And no."

"Oh," Berry said.

Tanner was standing in the hall right next to the door to homeroom, wearing his signature soccer jersey and jeans. Soccer ball in hand. Waiting. He looked up and spotted me, his thick lips curling into a smile. Sarah stood on his left and Gilly leaned against the wall on his right, a book clutched to her chest.

"Well, well," Sarah singsonged as I approached them. "It's Pizza Girl."

Popping the *p* like it was bubble gum.

I pulled my whole body into a fist. Held it tightly. I stopped in front of Tanner. Took a breath. "Tanner. I want to apologize for hitting you with a piece of pizza yesterday."

Tanner's mouth gaped open. "Uh-huh."

"It wasn't appropriate. So I'm sorry."

Tanner nodded, his tongue poked into the back of his bottom lip. "Yeah and."

The fist tightened. What was he getting at? I'd *apologized*. What did he want?

More.

"I won't do it again," I said, my voice small.

Me. Small.

"Yah." Tanner smirked at Sarah, who smirked back. Gilly looked down the hall. Slow, like he was savoring each moment, Tanner draped his arm over Sarah's shoulder. "See you don't. Can't have that kind of behavior around here."

Crying is natural and healthy. Both my moms "have cries" and sometimes Millie even makes us watch sad movies so we will cry, if she feels we all need it. Lucy says it's a natural human filtration system. But in the halls of Greenville, it felt dangerous, opening up my insides like a set of shutters so everyone could see inside my house.

So I *uncried*, which requires kind of disappearing from your body for a moment and going somewhere far away. I used to do it when I was really small, when I got scared. I'd float away. I called it "ballooning."

I just sort of drifted off. And me in jeans and a white shirt floated into homeroom and then floated to Math. Then I floated to Biology, a dotted outline of a person. And that was pretty much me for the rest of the day.

I honestly hadn't even noticed that the day was over until Berry poked me lightly in the shoulder as I was standing in front of my locker and asked if I wanted to skate around the parking lot after school.

"It might, you know"—she searched my face with her hazel eyes— "help to sort of shake the day off."

The more she looked at me, the less I was an outline. It was like she was coloring me in with her eyes.

"I don't know," I said.

I noticed Berry had a freckle on her nose that looked like a heart.

On the left and right of us, kids relished slamming their lockers as loudly as possible.

"Big game tonight," Berry added.

"Yeah," I said, my head in my locker. "Look. I kind of gotta get out of here. Like now."

Groups of kids were gathering outside, stripes of green swiped across their cheeks, green foam hats and fingers. Homemade flags with dragons.

I slammed my locker shut, turned down the hallway.

"DON'T! COME! FOR US!" they chanted. "WE! WILL! DESTROY YOU!"

I ducked under the noise and picked up my pace. It wasn't even a decent chant.

Berry followed me, her skateboard tucked under her arm. "So. What are you going to listen to? Like on your way home?"

I scrolled through my phone. "I think I'm going to start with 'Turn the Beat Around.'"

"Vicki Sue Robinson." Berry nodded. "Good song."

As I pulled my skates on by the edge of the parking lot, I watched Berry drop her skateboard and put her foot, which today for the first time was sneaker clad, on the deck.

"It's really cool that you know all this stuff. About disco."

"My dad." Berry smiled. "He taught me how to skateboard, too. The full education."

"My mom Lucy taught me," I said. "How to skate and everything else."

"It's a good skill set . . . to have," Berry offered. "For surviving in Greenville." She hopped on her board. "I can follow you out. Okay?"

"Sure."

Standing on my skates, for the first time since I'd taken them off that morning, I felt a little bit me. Popping my headphones in, I pressed play on my phone, leaned my head back, and let the drums and violins ring through my body. We rode for a block together, Berry on her skateboard rolling over the asphalt like a surfer, her body calm and steady, hand in pocket, her hair sticking up in a big green sprig like a happy green onion.

The whoops and hollers of Greenville High got smaller and smaller with every pump of my skates.

And the music took over.

At some point, Berry curved left and waved as she disappeared down the road.

I turned right and picked up speed.

A full person again.

It was a crappy day, but at least it was over. And if anything, at least one other person got that being in Greenville, right now, was surviving.

SEVEN

Berry waited for a full week of the white shirt to ask me about it.

To be fair, it was probably starting to look weird. Because it was the same shirt and pants every day for eight consecutive school days. Or maybe that's just weird to me.

Behind the scenes, BTW, I had to wash the shirt *every* night because I got a stain on it *every* day, everything from strawberry ice cream to Monty's paw prints to the orange glow that was constantly creeping around the collar from my hair. Millie took advantage by making sure I did *all of* the laundry every night when I washed my shirt.

"I mean," she noted, plonking the basket of to-be-washed on my floor, "you *are* wearing *my* T-shirt. Again."

I did get a sense that Millie got that me wearing the T-shirt *and* apologizing to Tanner—which somehow everyone knew about, including Millie—was connected. Lucy may have gotten it, too, but it was hard to say because she was buried under the load of her VP duties.

For every school night that I wore the shirt, Millie also, magically, let me pick what we had for dinner. Which, you're welcome, everyone: tacos, lasagna, and spaghetti, and repeat.

This didn't help with stains on my shirt, but whatever.

By the way, on the first weekend of my white-shirt spree I wore only sequins. Like as a cleanse. Danny also suggested I wear only orange to combat the white.

I agreed.

So yes, on day seven of the White Shirt Experiment, Berry found me on the way into class and, first pinning her lips together, inquired.

"So. Like. Not to intrude, but I'm just guessing this, like, whole look you're doing . . . I mean it's cool! Right? It's just, like I'm assuming, from the other stuff you wore before, this is not your standard clothing choice? I mean, I haven't really known you that long but it's pretty clear you're an overdresser at heart."

"Overdresser." I nodded, tugging up my jeans. "Yeah, that's one way to put it."

As we plonked down in our seats, I turned to Berry. "I mean, you wear the same thing every day."

"Yeah." Berry looked down at her coveralls, which today were splattered with blue paint. "I mean, I like these coveralls and I don't like anything else. I have like eight of them."

"They're cool."

Berry reached up and tweaked her ponytail. She did a little side-to-side dance in her chair. Something I noticed she did when she was thinking. "Do you like your outfit, this outfit?"

I pulled out my books for class, noting the students piling in. "No," I admitted quietly. "I'm trying something. I'm blending in," I added. "Temporarily."

"Huh." Berry nodded. *"Blending."*

"I just need to fly under the radar for a bit," I said as Mrs. Sherman strode in through the door with a giant mug of coffee.

Berry looked at the front of the class. "I hope it works."

She didn't sound *super* hopeful.

And to be honest, I wasn't *super* clear if the shirt was working. The fourth day I wore boring clothes (the same boring clothes), I got a brisk nod from Principal Lynde when I passed her in the hallway and nothing else.

I was even covering my hair with a hat that day. And nothing.

Tanner's soccer training or whatever you called it seemed to be picking up for "the big game" (was there one of those every week?), which I knew because he talked about it loudly every day, so possibly I wasn't his main concern.

So maybe, I was kind of riding the fitting-in train . . . ish.

And then . . .

Like right after Berry asked me about the shirt, I walked to English. And spotted . . . it. A piece of green construction paper with a printed sheet with lines on it. And at the top it said AUDITIONS.

My heart softly exploded.

"Auditions," I croaked, like the word jumped out of my throat.

Berry smiled. "School play."

"Right." I could hardly breathe.

"Yeah, I was actually gonna ask you about that the other day," Berry said as we took our seats. "It seemed like something that would be up your alley. I mean, among the many things that are."

Up my alley? How about my *whole street system*? Which is not to say that people who are into music overall are into theater. Being an artist doesn't mean you have to be into all forms of art. And in fact, the one thing I didn't spend a lot of time on was, like, paintings and stuff. I'm into theater because when I was little, it was the first piece of magic I ever got to see. Millie and Lucy took me to see a production of *Cinderella* at this little playhouse. I guess it was in Anchorage, where we were living at the time.

And, of course, to be clear, my moms spent like let's say a solid thirty minutes before and after *Cinderella* talking to me about why this model of heteronormativity, this idea of a princess needing to be *saved* by a prince who somehow loves her even if he's never met her or only met her *once* at *one* dance, is problematic.

"Not that we don't want you to enjoy the play! Or pursue your own concepts of love as they make sense to *you*," Lucy had added as she took my hand and gave our tickets to the older woman at the front of the theater.

"But if you realize that the whole Cinderella story is a *story* and kind of a bullshit story, I don't think that hurts," Millie had concluded.

Turns out, I loved all of it. I loved the velvety seats, the feeling of sitting with all the people kind of squished but not, the moment when the lights came down and then the stage lit up with a whole other world.

Also my parents had nothing to worry about, since all I was really into was the singing turtle this particular production of Cinderella had added for a bit of levity. I didn't like the Cinderella songs and I thought the prince was rude and not a good dancer.

But still. I loved the theater. I begged to go back the next day I loved it so much.

I memorized the turtle song and sang it during breakfast for a month.

Theater is magic and bright lights and people being big and bold and entertaining.

Truly what's not to love?

"What kind of plays does Greenville High usually do?" I asked with entirely faux chill.

"Mostly we do *Our Town*," Berry said, flipping through her textbook.

"*Our Town*'s not so bad."

"It's like ancient history and *everyone* in the town has seen it like a million times." Berry sighed. "But yeah, it's okay."

"It has a lot of parts," I said.

"I guess. Mr. Davidson took over like two years ago, and I know he's kind of dying to mix it up. But you know, Greenville. There was a rumor he was going to do *Grease* a few years ago and the soccer moms lost their minds. And then Lynde stepped in and they did *Sound of Music* instead."

"Davidson wants to do *Grease*?!"

I was freaking out.

"All right." Mr. Davidson pivoted and gave his vest of the day, which was a navy-blue corduroy number, a sharp tug. "Let's get this poetry started."

Only I laughed.

On my way out of class, I very very casually paused to take a closer look at the audition list. There were four names on the list already, at the very top, Gilly Henderson and Sarah Pye, with Tanner's and John's names written in the same pen and handwriting underneath.

Beside me, Berry peeked at the list, unsurprised. "Yeah. It used to be Mark Spencer, who's Tanner's cousin, and his girlfriend, Katie, were the leads every year, but they graduated last year. They were the town *actors*. And they were both Forevers."

I turned and started speed-walking away from the tempting list. Berry followed.

"So it's a question of who's gonna take up the torch?" I asked.

"I'm guessing Sarah's thinking she's getting Katie's spot. Like, all her social media profile photos are headshots she got at the mall."

"Huh."

"Unless." Berry stopped and grabbed my arm, suddenly glowing. "Would *you* sign up?"

A few feet behind us, Gilly and Sarah stood in the doorway to English class. Noticing me. Looking at me.

But possibly, I thought, because of the power of the white shirt, they turned and walked away.

School. Play.

The rest of the day, all I could think of was that sign-up sheet. What play would Davidson pick? Most high school teachers were still solidly in the Shakespearean column *but* a person with his taste in jumpers and a thing for *Grease* could possibly be down with *Mamma Mia!*

A girl could dream.

Mamma Mia! did require a pretty big cast of singers. What about *Guys and Dolls*? Mmmm. Also a big cast. Also you need some solid voices. *Guys and Dolls* is a classic high school musical, which, while sexist, also contains winner numbers like "Fugue for Tinhorns" and "Sit Down, You're Rockin' the Boat."

"Sit Down, You're Rockin' the Boat" was vibing pretty hard with me, for obvious reasons. Was I going to rock the boat I had *literally* just committed to not rocking with a week of normalcy? Although, clearly, if I was taking my plan of normalcy forward, I was going to need more than one white shirt.

Signing up for the auditions was not "weird," but given my short but potent history with Greenville High and its higher-ups, it was clear it *could* be . . . a problem. If I was going to get up on the stage, it was going to get attention. It was going to be a thing.

Because that's theater. The nature of theater is that it is a *thing*.

But already in my head I was putting together a medley of musical numbers, maybe something from *Waiting for Guffman* and then a theatrical monologue? Tony Kusher's untouchable masterpiece, *Angels in America*? I had plenty of time to ruminate on this because the next period we had Gym and we all had to play soccer.

Berry was in the goalie net because Berry can really play soccer.

When she walks out of the locker room, she's a warrior. Like usually she seemed reserved and thoughtful. Like graceful but not like aerobic? But once she was in her gym uniform, she got this stance, this like vaguely aggressive posture. It's like there's, like, killer robot beams coming out of her eyes. Beams that kill soccer balls.

Not because she didn't look like someone who could, but because it hadn't come up, at first I was surprised to find out she was kind of a jock at heart. "Wait. You like soccer?"

"Sure," Berry noted, adjusting her green sweatband, on the field, "I destroy in soccer."

"Then . . . Wait. Then why don't you play on the team?" I asked.

Berry rolled her eyes. Coach Harras tweeted in our direction, mostly I think because that was her only mode of communicating.

TWEEEET!

"Does that tweet mean we start playing?" I asked. "Or is it just an angry whistle?"

"We start playing," Berry said, jogging in place. "And you should be in the play."

"If I should be in the play, then maybe you should be on the soccer team," I said, walking to my spot on the field.

"Forevers only," Berry told me as she backward-jogged.

"So the play isn't Forevers only?" I called back. It seemed like only Forevers had signed up. So far.

TWEEEET!

"It's different." Berry took her place in goal.

I stepped out to what felt like a peaceful and easily avoided corner of the soccer field.

If I was going to audition for the school play—not saying I would—I could also audition with a number from a new piece I'd been working on set to Olivia Newton-John's disco hit "Xanadu" (featuring ELO).

Olivia Newton-John. Australian actor and singer. Mostly popular in the seventies and eighties. A polarizing figure? For some nerds, yes. I mean, she played a teenager in the hit movie *Grease* (1978), Davidson's fave, when she was twenty-nine years old. And yet somehow audience viewers completely accepted her as teen Sandy (the character she played). Maybe because she was appearing alongside actor Stockard Channing, who played the troubled teen, Rizzo, and Stockard was thirty-three years old at the time (and she won a People's Choice for that role).

Technically movie trivia is not my thing, but it was my friend Danny's thing, and this was one of his favorite movie facts.

Maybe, I thought, if you play your part with heart and panache, that's what matters.

Did Olivia Newton-John worry what people would think about her playing a teenager, or did she just do her best to act like a teenager? Although, let's say it, she didn't *look* like a teenager, but she could *sing*!

I can also sing, by the way, something that would come up in my audition, if I auditioned. Oh, I thought, I could do a medley of "Sit Down, You're Rockin' the Boat" and the *Grease* finale, "You're the One That I Want." Both great songs.

But "You're the One That I Want" is a duet between Travolta and Newton-John.

Who would I duet with?

After the game, which was a shutout for our team because, as Berry said, nothing got past her in the goal, I was walking back to the locker room when suddenly Gilly jogged up beside me. She ran in long strides that went with her legs that seemed to be as long as my entire body. Given that most of what I had seen of Gilly up until that point was a person who was leaning or keeping her head down next to her horrible friends, it was strange to see her . . . alone.

Up close, Gilly was tall and thin with a big head, like a balloon on a string. She had large blue eyes and long blond hair that whipped around in the wind like it was its own creature. Her arms were all tanned except for a set of white stripes on her wrists. She looked like someone who spent a lot of time in the sun.

She scooped her hair up into one hand. "Hey . . . Uh. Anne!"

Admittedly I was kind of shocked she knew my name. Also Gilly has kind of a nice voice. I couldn't think who it reminded me of.

"Yeah?"

"So." Gilly looked around. "Were you going to sign up for auditions? For the play? Earlier?"

"Oh." I felt my face flush. "I mean, I don't know. Probably not."

"I was thinking"—Gilly's gaze wandered down the field—"it's probably something you know about? You've lived in bigger cities and you would have something to bring to a Greenville production, right? I mean, Mr. Davidson is great, but it could be interesting to have your . . . perspective."

I turned to see if Sarah or Tanner was anywhere near, feeling suddenly exposed. Like I was standing on top of a hill.

"My perspective?"

Because, like, what else did I want to hear from someone like right at that moment? (Who doesn't want someone to care about their perspective?)

"Yeah." A small smile crept over Gilly's face, revealing what looked like a chipped front tooth. She covered her mouth with her hand.

Okay, like, hello, obviously this was exactly what I wanted to hear. And maybe it was nice to hear it from Gilly, who had a nice smile, but like, maybe they knew I would think it was nice? Or maybe Gilly *was* just being nice? I mean this was my first time talking to her. Maybe she was like the mediator, and this was her, like, reaching out. Like, "Hey, Anne just wore this really ugly plain shirt for us for a week, let's give her a break."

Right? That was possible? Right?

Or was it so possible that it was clearly *not* possible?

"Okay, well, I'll think about it."

"Great." She hopped forward. "I mean, I think you should sign up. If that means anything."

Her hair seemed to leap into the air as she ran off into the school.

I found Berry in the locker room looking sweaty and triumphant. "Hey!"

"HEY," I cheered, offering a high five, which she accepted. "You had a shutdown!"

"Shutout," Berry clarified. "Yes I did."

"Maybe you *should* try out for soccer," I added, speed-undressing and -dressing. "I mean, aren't you as good as the Forevers or the locals or whatever?"

Berry nodded, looking suddenly more like her chill self. "When I was little, I played on the team. For like a minute."

"And?"

"And it wasn't very fun." Berry shook her hair out (an act that practically came with a sound effect, she had so much hair). "It's, like, they want you to be good, but they don't want you to be as good as their kids, or if you are, they want you to play like exactly how they want, but no matter what, you're not them."

Suddenly I could just see little Berry in her adorable soccer uniform, like, sitting alone with her soccer balls and her giant water bottle.

"If you lose, they freak out so bad. Like, someone yelled at my mom once in a grocery store when we lost a game and I was like ten?"

"So, then. If all THAT sucked, why do you think I should do the play? Don't people care about theater here?"

"Yes and no. The play is different. It's not their lifeblood. Like, they care if it's pornography or, like, too gay, but they don't live and die by it." Berry pulled on her boot. "Which is why you could still do it and be, you know, blending. Maybe? A little. Plus, mostly, I think you'd be really good."

"Hmm." I pulled on my white shirt which was, let's say, kind of a mess. How did I get red pen on a shirt when I didn't even own a red pen?

Berry looked up from tying her laces. "What did Gilly want?"

"Gilly," I said, throwing on my not white but very plain sweatshirt, "*also* thinks I should sign up."

I peeked my face out of my sweatshirt in time to catch Berry picking her jaw up off the floor.

"Really?"

I pulled my head out of my shirt. "What?"

"Oh, I just—" Berry's eyes searched for something to look at that wasn't me.

"What? Say it."

"I mean she's pretty tight with Sarah and Tanner and John. You know, she's a Forever."

I sank down to the bench. "Right."

Berry did a little wiggle. She was thinking again.

"Look," she said. "Okay. I don't trust Gilly. Okay. But. I mean, if YOU really want to do the play, you know, you should. And Mr. Davidson is cool. And . . . yeah. Do it, like, because you want to."

My brain felt like a ball pit at a playground. "Why don't you trust Gilly?"

Berry shrugged. "It's a long story. But that doesn't mean you shouldn't try out for the play."

Millie says sometimes when things feel like too much you should try and find the one thing you're sure of.

That one thing was this, if I audition, I would be amazing.

Like, in two weeks at Greenville, that was what I knew; that I could kick *ass* in an audition, even if I didn't get it.

"Can we go *now*?" I asked, standing. "And sign up?"

"Totally." Berry sprang up. She glanced at her watch. "If we run, we can make it to the sign-up sheet before Math."

So we ran, sprinting past classrooms, slowing briefly past Lynde's office and my mom's office, then picking up speed. Berry's boots clomped on the tile as we rounded the corner to what I was pretty sure was my destiny.

I slid a little, rounding the corner to the hall by homeroom, and spotted the sheet, which was still there, taped up on the wall by Mr. Davidson's classroom. Berry, who is fast like the wind, picked up speed and got to the list before I did. She looked triumphant for a half second, before her eye caught the names on the list, and then her face fell. In what felt like slow motion, she stepped toward me, hands out, eyes big, pools of worry.

She caught my shoulder with her hand. "Uh, change of plan."

"Hey!" I laughed. "What's wrong?"

A nervous laugh escaped her lips. "Um. I forgot. I heard this weird rumor Davidson was thinking of doing some modernized musical based on *Jerry Maguire*, so maybe this is a good year to skip theater?"

"What's *Jerry Maguire*?"

Berry dropped her hands, "You know how many albums Donna Summer recorded, but you don't know the movie *Jerry Maguire*?"

"They're totally different things."

Berry was shifting her weight from foot to foot, bobbing her head back and forth, so I couldn't see the list.

"Berry. What are you doing? We're going to miss Math!" I moved my head to see past her. "What is going on?"

"Fine." Berry's face crumpled, and she stepped out from in front of the list.

So I could see.

It was full.

Sarah, Gilly, and Tanner's names were still there. And a few other kids. And then the rest of the twenty spots were . . .

. . . other names.

"'Debbie McDyke,'" I read aloud, "'Harry Homo. Lucy Slut.'"

"Fuck them." Berry put her hand on my arm.

"'Ferris Faggot. Mabel Mustache.'"

At the very bottom of the list, in bright red letters, someone had just written BYE BYE, ANNE! GO HOME! My heart hammered in my chest.

"Did you know they would do this?" I tried to keep my voice from cracking.

"When you said the Gilly thing I was *worried* that something was going on, but also I hate Gilly so that's bias, so I wasn't sure?" Berry looked panicked. "I mean, I thought, maybe they would give you shit somehow but—"

"Need a pen?"

Tanner, Gilly, Sarah, and John all stood in the hallway. Sarah waggled a pink marker in between her thumb and forefinger. She must have busted out of Gym class. She was still in her uniform.

Had they filled out the sheet before Gym? Did they get Gilly to talk to me to stall?

"Dang. Looks like maybe that sign-up sheet is full." Tanner craned his head to see, an exaggerated frown twisting the bottom of his face.

"Can we just go?" Gilly whispered.

Sarah ignored her. "Too bad. I mean, I heard Mr. Davidson was thinking of doing *Miss Saigon*. Which like. So perfect, right? I mean, since we have an actual Saigon now."

"You know it, Anne?" Tanner asked, nonchalant. "*Missss Saigon?*"

"I'm Japanese," I growled. "*Saigon* is Vietnamese."

"Same same?" Tanner chimed.

The next thing I knew I was clawing the list off the wall, storming over to them, shouting. "FUCK YOU AND YOUR FUCKING SCHOOL!" I tossed the crumpled paper and it hit Gilly in the face.

She batted the paper away, clearly stunned. "Screw you, Carrots," she snapped.

"Carrots?" I sneered, stepping up close. "That's what you got? Carrots?"

Gilly looked stunned. Maybe even upset? But I didn't care. I sprinted away, with Berry on my heels.

"KUNG FU PANDA!" Sarah yelled after me. "JACKIE CHAN!"

"That's Chinese," I yelled back as I fled down the hall, the lockers blurring into a streak of forest green.

I heard a door open behind me and a bellow, "WHAT'S GOING ON?"

By then I was bounding down the stairs two at a time. I spent

Math in the bathroom with Berry, who crept in after me and perched on the floor a few feet away from where I sat, sprawled under the sink. What better musical accompaniment for feeling like crap than the leaky sound of a school bathroom sink dripping?

Berry spent the first several minutes of our silence looking at me, then looking away. I spent the first several minutes of our silence thinking about how ignorant racism is. *Miss Saigon*? Like what high school kid even knows *Miss Saigon*? That's, like, nineties racism. But that's the thing with racism. It's so retro, yet so now. So entirely uninformed and uneducated and yet it feels like its scientifically designed to turn you into nothing.

Finally Berry got up onto her knees. "Disco?"

"Now? Like dancing?" I grumbled. "Not really in the mood."

"I just thought if we played something." Berry drummed her fingers on her knees. She had pink paint on her fingertips. "You know it makes you feel better. Music."

I pulled my phone out of my pocket. Pressed the power button. Held it up for Berry to see. "Out of juice."

Berry pulled her phone out of her pocket. Frowned. "Yeah, me too."

"So," I said, then went back to feeling both nothing and so overwhelmingly sad I might melt.

"Okay."

I looked over. Berry had closed her eyes. As I stared, she opened her lips and, after a deep breath, let out the tiniest but heart-fullest tune. . . .

ABBA.

ABBA in the high school bathroom.

"Super Trouper."

Berry opened one eye, trained it on me as she started in on the chorus. She even sang the piano parts.

I sniffed.

We got up off the floor and danced around the bathroom while we sang. I did a little jig and a few spins. Berry did this very classic step-to-the-left, step-to-the-right dance that was just adorable. For just a few minutes the world was sherbet stained and hopeful, and it was just me and Berry and the feeling music gives you when it fills your lungs.

Joy.

"I think you were right," Berry said, when, exhausted and out of breath, I plopped back down on the floor.

"About what specifically?"

"About why you should audition," Berry said, giving a very small wiggle.

"So they have another reason to come for me?"

"Maybe they don't need another reason, maybe there's nothing you can do about them coming for you and it has nothing to do with anything you're actually *doing*." Berry sighed. "I mean, in my experience, I can keep it down but they'll always have *something* to say. But maybe you have something to say, too."

"I mean, I definitely always have something to say. Like so much. To say."

Berry grabbed her stuff. "Plus I think we should go to the next class so they don't tell your mom you're skipping school to sing ABBA songs."

"Good call."

After school, I watched *Jerry Maguire*, even though Berry told me later that it really is a terrible movie and she picked it because it was the first horrible basis for a musical that she could think of. Because every movie with Tom Cruise would make a terrible musical.

I actually think you could make *Mission: Impossible* into a musical if you wanted to.

Speaking of *Mission: Impossible*, was it worse that I believed Gilly when she pulled a high-school-prank-101 on me on the soccer field, or that Gilly thought I was a person who both deserved that and would fall for it?

Plus she called me *Carrots*?

Maybe it wasn't even Gilly's idea. She was kind of an . . . enigma. I ate three bowls of popcorn trying to decide which was worse, them underestimating me, or not caring about me. And decided both options sucked equally.

That night Lucy came home for dinner looking like I felt: like a dishrag that needs to be washed, but people keep using it because it's there.

"How was today?" she asked. "Little better?"

"Sure," I said, because it was weirdly true.

Millie carried the pot roast over to the table and took a moment to look over my shirt. "You were not built to wear white, kid," she said, handing me a napkin.

"Don't worry, it won't happen again," I said. "Me and this T-shirt are breaking up."

"Wash it before you give it back."

That night I just carried Monty on her walk, depositing her by the bushes she seemed inclined to do her business on. Halfway home it started to rain. Like someone in Greenville saw how far away Monty and I were from home and they decided to just turn on the tap.

And it seemed a fitting end to the day.

I mean, yes, I knew I could sing my butt off and kick ass at the audition, and maybe Greenville suspected this and that was why they were all being jerks. But it sucked to have to go to school with people who were being jerks in order to take the stage and to have to prove to them that they were all *wrong* jerks.

"It's a rock and a hard place, Monty," I moaned.

Monty howled in agreement and I carried her wet dog body home.

EIGHT

The next day I woke up and instead of a voice I had a squeak, which I took as a reasonable response to the day before, which clearly was so bad it actually made me sick.

Or maybe it was walking in the rain after singing ABBA in the bathroom.

Let me just say, the problem with being a dramatic person prone to bouts of . . . dramatics, is that it is sometimes hard to indicate to your audience when the whistle coming out of your throat is symbolic and when it's you actually sick.

Also, both Lucy and Millie *never* get sick. Ever. I have no idea why but it's sort of helpful because they accept many things as symptoms of a cold, like itchy fingers, that I think most habitual cold getters would not buy.

This time, though, I was actually sick.

Millie sat on my bed touching my forehead for ten minutes and finally, giving me a bit of a hairy eyeball, told me she needed to go to get some film developed on the other side of town that day so I would be home alone.

I gave her a thumbs-up.

"If you're feeling up to it," Millie said, making her way out of my room through a series of, I'm going to say, well-organized piles of stuff, "maybe you could clean your room and finish unpacking."

I pulled my covers over my head.

"*If* you feel up to it."

I did not feel up to it.

I spent the day watching videos of people disco dancing in the seventies, including several ABBA videos. Let's say it: TV was just way more interesting in the seventies. Like, we need more shows that are just for dancing where people aren't competing for a million dollars.

After lunch, I watched some videos of people dancing at a club called Studio 54, which was kind of a famous disco club in the seventies, where famous singers and actors and dancers and even some really good-looking regular people used to go to dance and do drugs. Every video of Studio 54 looks crowded. It's all flashing lights and people with long fluffy hair bouncing and twirling. I always imagine it hot and sticky, smelling like lipstick and perfume and melting ice in people's drinks. It was the kind of place where people could be themselves, but it was also a place, Millie reminded me once, where there would be a huge line of people at the door waiting to get in.

"And part of what made that place so famous was how few people *could* get in," Millie said.

Even cool disco places from the seventies were mean and excluding (also, drugs).

I was thinking about this and about how I'd have to find the pots and pans my mom still hadn't unpacked if I wanted to make soup, the food of the sick, when I got a text from Berry.

BERRY
Hey you weren't in school (which u prob know)

BERRY

BERRY
⌐?

ANNE

BERRY
 of Greenville?

ANNE

ANNE

BERRY
Are you contagious?

I tested my voice. I already had more of a whisper.

ANNE
Probably not.

BERRY
So you're not doing anything and you're not contagious?

ANNE
Yes and yes.

BERRY
Come downstairs, then.

It shouldn't have surprised me that Berry knew where I lived when even I didn't know my address by heart yet, but she did, and it did. I looked out the window and there she was, standing outside my door, the sun setting behind her plume of green hair. Monty barked her two barks indicating that a person she did not know was near the house. Then she lay back down in the front hall and whined.

"What the heck?" I pushed open the door.

"Are you wearing footie pajamas?" Berry pulled a pair of paint-splattered sunglasses down off her face.

"Yes," I said, kicking up my left foot. "It used to have a unicorn head hood, but Monty chewed it off." I stood back so Berry could see Monty sitting and looking unamused. "My dog."

"Well, that's something I didn't know!" Berry looked around my shoulder. "Moms home?"

I shook my head.

"So, you can leave?" Berry asked. "I mean, the house?"

"I guess." I texted my moms and shoved my phone in my pocket, which on the onesie was actually a pouch. "Do I need to change?"

"People around here are pretty cool with people wearing their pajamas outside."

"I've heard that." I locked the door. "Where are we going and how are we getting there?"

Berry stepped back, holding her hands out like a game show assistant to showcase a giant, boatlike, ancient red station wagon. "Anne, meet Mato. Mato, meet Anne."

"Mato?"

"It was my parents' car when I was little," Berry said, skipping down the front walk to the car and opening the passenger door, which seemed to pop like a dislocated shoulder. She stepped aside with a little flip of her hand. "I thought it looked like a tomato."

"I mean, it does!"

Inside, Mato was door-to-door red velvet, scratchy and plastic. Her seat belts were like thick floppy ribbons and stained dark in various places. Her dashboard was sun bleached to a salmon pink in parts. As I slid onto the seat, the heat rose up into my butt like fire.

"Yeah, she's been baking all day," Berry said. "So she's a little toasty."

Mato smelled like cinnamon, probably because someone had tied a bunch of cinnamon sticks to her rear window.

"She's beautiful." I ran my finger along the dashboard. "Hi, Mato!"

Berry slid into her seat and turned the key. Mato purred. "Mato rules. She's my escape pod."

The air had been hot earlier in the day, when I'd poked my head out to let Monty go for a pee. But now the sky was purple and orange, and the air was soft and cool, like a glass of cold tap water. I rolled down the window and let my fingers dance on the breeze as Berry coasted farther and farther away from town, like we were a ship heading out into the ocean.

"My dad installed the shocks," Berry said, "so they're a little . . . loosey."

I leaned my head back onto the baked potato that was the headrest and felt my body relax for the first time in days. "This is amazing."

A few miles away from the house, Berry turned off the main road, toward what I thought was the parking lot of a burger joint. Which, honestly, I would have been fine with. Like if someone I knew was sad,

I could see taking them to a burger joint. But then she took another left into what looked like an alleyway, past a used car place, to a small yard fenced in by green chain link. And she pulled the car to a stop.

"TA-DA!" She popped out of the car with significant bounce.

"A fence?"

Berry reached into a veil of dried vines and bushes until she found what seemed to be a pretty small opening. After a few minutes of shoving and pulling, she parted the wall of weeds to reveal a small hole in the fence. "Follow me."

I stepped out of the car and followed Berry through a curtain of green.

"My parents used to bring me here when I was a kid," Berry explained, stepping onto the frayed Astroturf. "Then I guess it closed. But I still love it."

It was a dilapidated but still incredibly cool mini putt course. Really a fine example of the twisted logic of most fun parks built before the aughts: a mix of possibly "realistic" and "fantastical," concrete creatures all painted in chipped neons and bright hues. A two-headed dragon loomed over the first hole. A timid giraffe stood stunned over the third hole. A furious lion looked like it was choking on the fifth hole, its left paw cracked to show the metal rods holding the whole circus together.

"It's weird that it's kind of cute," I said.

I stepped toward a bear and suddenly something clicked. The bear's fur was a kaleidoscope of colors, neon blues and oranges I recognized—from Berry's hands.

"You're painting them!"

"Oh." Pink streaks bloomed on Berry's cheeks. "I mean, when i'm stressed, I give them a little touch-up."

I spun around, taking it all in—the giraffe's psychedelic-patterned polka dots, the panda's green spectacles. "It's amazing." I sighed.

"Thanks." Berry held out a rusted putter in one hand and a chewed-up-looking ball in the other. "Madam."

"Thanks," I said, my voice hoarse.

Berry twirled her putter as she walked up to the first hole and dropped her ball by her feet. "Baton lessons," she said, tossing the putter up and catching it with one hand.

"No kidding. Because you wanted to, like, join the marching band?"

"I'm *in* the marching band." Berry grinned.

"Wait. I knew you were in the stage band, but you also *march*? While playing the *tuba*? How did I not know this?!"

"I mean, yeah, you don't know all my talents yet. I play the flute and the sax, and I can spin a baton like no one's business."

"That's legitimately amazing." I made a mental note to ask Berry more questions about herself.

Berry tossed the putter up into the air and, after a wobble, snatched it just before it nailed the sleeping concrete leopard.

I clapped. "Maybe *you* should audition for the play."

"Nah." Berry nudged her ball with her toe.

I took a deep breath. The smell of burgers floated through the air, mixed with what was clearly fresh paint. Berry chipped the ball and it bounced along the edge of the green, zigzagging along the rough terrain. "I was just thinking about why Greenville likes people in pajamas," she said.

"Why?" I dropped my ball.

"It's like when you're a little kid," Berry said. "And you go to parties and stuff, like going to the park to watch the fireworks with your pj's and your sleeping bags. It's like . . . this idea that it's your home. Maybe Greenville likes that, that feeling of home."

"So, it's nostalgia?" I wondered.

"I guess." Berry reached her putter behind her to scratch her back. "Maybe it's just an excuse not to get dressed up."

"*This* place is nice," I said, patting the giraffe and hoping the paint wasn't wet.

"This is my favorite place in Greenville," Berry said, "because when I was a kid it was the only place in Greenville that didn't seem boring. And even though no one else wants to psychedelic mini putt, I still do."

"I'm glad you're keeping it spruced up."

Berry looked around. "It relaxes me. There's a slide and stuff over there, too. Which I'll eventually do in green."

"Well, I'm always down to do a psychedelic paint job," I said, kicking my ball into the hole. "You have my number."

It was like a little Garden of Eden in Greenville. Or . . . no. I guess that doesn't work because you get cast out of the Garden of Eden, right? It was a secret place, a world that Berry made inside of Greenville that was just her world.

Maybe she just wanted me to know it was possible.

"You have every right to hate this town." Berry leaned against the Technicolor panda statue wearing a wizard hat. "But I'm really glad you're here, Anne Shirley."

I wished I could say the same. But at least I was happy right at that moment, in that individual spot in Greenville, which was something. The sun finally set. The lights from some building in the distance flashed on and cast shadows all around the mini putt.

On the tenth hole, Berry finally confessed. "Okay, so, full disclosure. And, like, don't be mad. But I feel like we're going to be friends, so I, like, have to be honest."

My stomach dropped. "What?"

"Don't be mad."

"No promises."

"Like, I know a lot about it but"—Berry pulled her shoulders up—"I actually hate disco."

"YOU WHAT?"

"I mean I'm not all *disco sucks*, obviously." Berry shrugged. "But, like, I think there's better music. And if you ever meet my dad he will tell you I make fun of his disco records. So I felt like I should just be honest with you. So you don't think I'm a big disco liar."

"Disco is the best!"

Berry sighed. "It's repetitive and the lyrics are terrible."

I mock-fainted to the green turf. "This is a blow, Berry, I'm gonna be honest, it's a real blow. Like on today of all days. To hit me with this. Kind of uncool."

Berry snorted.

I sat up. "What do you like?"

"Punk." Berry counted off on her fingers. "Um. Country. I like some old nineties rock?"

I shook my head in exaggerated despair. "Say it isn't so."

Berry stepped up onto the back of a concrete pony with no ears that looked like a dragon. "Can we still be friends?"

I folded my arms over my chest. "Thinking." I couldn't hold it. I let out an embarrassing snort of laughter. Berry gave my butt a light nudge with the boot of her toe.

"Oh, COME ON!"

"Yes! Fine! Geez!" I threw my arms out. "Berry! Of course we can be friends. You're like . . . the best!"

Berry's cheeks turned cherry red. "Okay, well, good."

She pulled her phone out of her pocket. "So, given that this is *your* night out with the concrete animals, I'll spot you one disco track for a decent track and we'll go back and forth, okay?"

"Okay, in all seriousness, what are like your faves?" I asked as I pulled myself up off the ground using the head of a purple turtle.

"Iggy Pop?" Berry flipped through her phone. "Lizzo. Um. The Clash? B-52s?"

"B-52s is kind of disco."

"Ish?"

"Okay." I stood up, walked over to her phone. "How about *you* drove so *you* get first pick."

Berry picked the Iggy Pop classic "Lust for Life," which is actually a very good song.

That night I learned a few of Berry's favorite things. In addition to mini putt, Berry's favorite superhero is Ironman and her favorite surrealist painter is Magritte, although as of recently she'd switched to a love of folk art. Berry liked the idea that it was possible for a person to overcome something really horrible and save the day. And the idea that a person could see the world and then produce an artistic rendering of that world that was totally unexpected. We talked about the things that we liked and didn't like, and we danced around the bear statue and the giraffe and the unicorn with the tail that had fallen off.

And the more we talked, the more I kind of liked being in Greenville.

Right before she dropped me off, Berry snapped her fingers. "Right! I forgot to tell you, Greenville High 101, tomorrow's last Friday of the month."

"Which I knew," I said. "That's not just Greenville BTW, the whole month and days thing. They have it all over the world."

Berry shook her head. "Mmm. Last Friday in Greenville isn't your average Friday."

"What does that mean?"

"School Spirit Day," Berry said, grimly. "Whatever you do, wear green."

NINE

Okay, so I wore green.

But I mean, I *really* wore green. Like, I wore green like it was nobody's business: my sequined emerald-green cheerleader outfit that used to be Danny's with a matching mint-green bomber jacket and lime-green/neon-green-striped tights. Inspired by Berry's giraffe, I painted (yes, "ruining") my white cowboy boots from a vintage place in Arizona with green polka dots.

Even I, looking in the mirror, was like, "Okay, Anne. Wow."

When I got downstairs, Lucy was sitting in the kitchen waiting for the coffee, talking in low, serious tones with Millie, who glanced up and gave me a look of amusement.

"You look like a leprechaun . . . who's feeling better."

"I am. It's Spirit Day," I said, pointing at Lucy's pale pink suit. "Hey, last Friday, you have to wear green!"

Lucy looked down at her outfit. "Oh, shoot," she gasped, and bolted upstairs.

"Well." Millie, who did not have to wear green and was instead sticking with her blue fuzzy robe and pj's, took a long sip of her coffee. "So we're ready for round two, choosing a new tactic I see."

"It's not exactly a tactic," I said, "although I am committing myself to nonconfrontation and assimilation within the bounds of fashion choices I enjoy."

"So they wear green, you wear green. But in a you way." Millie took another long sip. "Sounds like a plan."

"Or a tactic, depending on who you ask."

Lucy bolted down the stairs in what seemed like a hastily assembled ensemble of mismatched greens and ran out the door before I had time to comment, not that I would.

"Do you think it will work?" I asked, grabbing a banana and my skates.

"I think whatever will work will work because of you and not because of them," Millie said.

"I feel like that's a non-answer," I noted, pointing my banana at Millie. "A classic Millie Mom non-answer."

Millie held up her coffee. "Have fun at school!"

On the average day, Greenville High, to me, was a somewhat stressful place full of loud kids who I found somewhat alien and intimidating.

That Friday, aka Spirit Day, it was like that with the volume turned up to eleven.

The halls were a sea of bright green with various lockers covered in green cards that said stuff like DESTROY! and CHAMPIONS.

Like put it this way: My outfit was not really all that out of line.

It was like Greenville was about to send a band of intrepid green adventurers into space or something.

"Are they a good team?" I asked Berry at lunch that day. "This team we're spiriting today?"

Berry lowered her voice. "They're okay. Mostly they win because the other teams in the district aren't so hot. Then they get slammed when they go to state."

"Bummer. So is today Spirit Day just because it's last Friday or is there a game?"

"Um. I mean, today, yes there is a game. Not every Spirit Day is a game. And, um, it would probably be a good thing to make an appearance, then we can go for burgers or something after."

It did seem like me going to the game would not mean open season on me. Tanner had spent the day continuing to apparently not care about me. After English he sailed right past me into a sea of high fives from everyone, including Mr. Davidson, who high-fived all the players on their way out.

And then, as I was the last person out of the classroom, Mr. Davidson complimented my outfit. "What a lovely daiquiri green. That jacket!"

"Thanks! I like your jersey." I squinted. "Is that a Greenville Dragons jersey?"

Mr. Davidson held up his arms. He was actually wearing the ancient soccer jersey over a slightly blousy blouse, which, let's say it, is how they should be worn. "Vintage." He winked. "From back in my power forward days. Enjoy the game!"

By the end of the last class, the hallways were quaking with students cheering and hammering on the lockers in an a-rhythmic but compelling beat that exploded out into the quad as students and teachers and parents piled into the bleachers. Lucy and Millie were seated in the center square, so to speak. Millie was wearing a green sweater and had looped a green sparkly collar around Monty's neck. Berry and I crept into the stands by the goalie net, which was Berry's favorite spot.

"John's a shit goalie," Berry said, popping open a bag of pretzels, "but he's getting better."

As Tanner and the team ran onto the field, the crowd stood up and cheered. Tanner ran backward and waved at the stands, doing a few extra leaps. It was weird to see the guy who wore his soccer jersey every day finally on the field, actually playing soccer.

It was like all the pieces were in place. He grinned and raised his arms in the air, holding up two fingers, like . . . peace signs?

Okay.

Suddenly there was a sharp bark from the crowd, which I legitimately thought was Monty.

"TANNER!"

Berry and I looked over at the same time to see Tanner's father—who I recognized from Pizza Fight Day—pointing a meaty finger at Tanner on the field. Tanner's dad looked like Tanner, but with more concrete in his jaw. He wore a button-down shirt and jeans, both of which seemed to barely contain the man wearing them. His hands were like steaks.

"TANNER! GET YOUR HEAD IN THE GAME!"

"Yikes." I looked at Berry.

"Seeerious business." Berry popped a pretzel in her mouth and chewed.

I'm sure there's two levels to enjoy sports on. One of them is understanding why people are doing what they're doing. The other is just watching who wins without understanding why. It seemed like the Dragons were fast. Tanner was *very* fast, and he could move around people with a kind of sharp speed that made me think he practiced at home with some sort of system with cones.

He scored three goals in the first . . . quarter. Thing.

The other team scored two.

Anytime Tanner did anything, his dad got up and started yelling about what Tanner had just done. Which seemed to cut through the cheers like . . . a hammer. I guess hammers don't really cut, but you get it. It was like someone slamming on the door. Only it was just for Tanner. I could see his eyes darting up to the stands.

I will say, while it looked like most of the crowd were having fun, after a few minutes of yelling, it didn't look like Tanner was having any.

At some point the teams took a break, or it was halftime or something. Berry went looking for more snacks, and parents swarmed my moms so that all I could see was Monty's tail wagging from inside the crowd.

I looked out over the sea of green. The whole thing felt weirdly buoying but also connecting. Like everyone on that side of the stands was feeling the same thing, in such a big way? And then suddenly the sun on my shoulders disappeared, and I looked up and it was the tall meat tree that was Tanner Spencer's father.

His hands twitched by his side, flipping the giant gold watch on his wrist around his wrist.

"You must be Anne," he said in a thick voice.

"Yes. Hello." I shielded my eyes. The sun crested from behind Mr. Spencer's giant Easter Island statue head.

"Vice Principal Shirley's daughter," he said, sucking on a tooth, "that right? You take that name? Anne Shirley? Since you got two moms? Is that how you do that? Just pick a name?"

"I go by Shirley, sir," I said.

The air on my face felt prickly. Hot. The sequins on my cheerleader outfit stuck into my thighs. Did he really just ask me if I got to *pick* a *name*?

"Right, right. Anne Shirley." He thumbed his nose. "I'm Michael Spencer. Tanner's father."

He tilted his head toward the field as if the field were Tanner.

"Right." The man who may or may not have called me "disgusting" outside my mom's office.

"Seems like you're still adjusting to things around here. Causing a little trouble."

My stomach squeezed. "Yes, I mean. No," I said, "I, uh, did and I apologized to Tanner, for the pizza fight. I am sorry." This was not easy to say. But I said it.

"I heard that. Heard that." Mr. Spencer stood still as a statue. "Well, we are of course happy to welcome you and your mother to our community. Hopefully you'll learn a little respect for it. For the community."

Berry jumped down into the seat next to me, "Mr. Spencer." She pushed a bag of popcorn under my nose. "Popcorn?"

"It was nice meeting you," I said to Tanner's father, holding out my hand. "Thank you for, uh, introducing yourself."

He raised an eyebrow before he shook my hand, which disappeared into his like a nugget into a hamburger bun. I could swear my hand was a little smaller when he let go. With that, Michael Spencer disappeared into the swaying sea of green as the game started up again.

"Thanks," I whispered to Berry, grabbing a handful of popcorn.

I spotted Millie in the distance, waving, and waved back with a big smile. I squeezed the popcorn in my hand until the kernels bit into the insides of my fingers.

The game had started again. Players scattered.

"Hey," Berry said. "You just going to hold on to that popcorn?"

"Oh yeah." I looked down at my hand, greasy and full of wilted kernels. I slid my palm down my side and brushed them off on the seat.

"Want to get in Mato and ride?" Berry asked.

Suddenly there was a gasp. Some tall kid on the other team, the Princeville Kings, kicked the ball up the field, moving at a clip.

"NO!" someone below us screamed.

"STOP HIM!" someone else bellowed.

Tanner sprinted after him, but another player from Princeville ran ahead and cut in front of Tanner. Tanner tried to sneak around him and tripped, pirouetting to the ground.

Mr. Spencer stood up and started screaming at the coach, "YOU GONNA JUST SIT THERE? GODDAMMIT!"

How could anyone do anything? The kid from the other team scooted right past John and scored a goal.

"Crap," Berry mumbled.

Tanner hopped up under a rain of horrified hollers from the stands and the sound of his dad yelling at him about his feet.

"What ya got, six left feet, son? What is wrong with you?!"

The game ended in a tie. Which I guess for the Dragons was like a loss? How does that even work? Everything went from grass swaying in the stiff breeze of victory to grass that had been trampled and squished by a thousand heavy feet.

"Hey there." Millie walked over to us at the end of the game with Monty in tow. "Ready to go?"

"Where's Mom?"

"She's talking to a few parents," Millie said. "She'll probably be a while. Who's this?"

"This is my friend, the one and only Berry." I held my hand out not unlike the way Berry held her hands out when she introduced Mato. "Berry is awesome. And an artist."

"Clearly." Millie smiled. "You need a ride, Berry?"

Berry shook her head. "My mom is around here somewhere."

Lucy had her car, so I rode with Millie and Monty, who, the whole way home, panted like she was finishing up a marathon.

"Did she eat something weird?" I asked.

"Mmmm." Millie frowned. "Nothing I gave her . . ."

That night a bunch of things happened, none of which were fun.

First of all let me say, Monty is one of those dogs you *think* is chill and then she goes and does something cracked like eat all your shoes. She's a mystery. She's a quagmire. She's a golden retriever. And everyone loves a golden retriever. My guess is that maybe there were a few parents who came to say hello and they slipped her a little hot dog butt.

Or two, or three. Or ten.

So she trotted into the house when we got home, sat down on the rug, relaxed and content, and then she barfed up a stream of vomit that settled into the size of a small wading pool. Just as Lucy walked into the door.

So we didn't really have time to talk about anything other than dog vomit and the fact that we were basically going to have to burn the rug it was deposited on. We spent all night either walking Monty outside and trying to get her to drink water or scrubbing and rinsing.

So I didn't have a chance to tell Lucy and Millie about my conversation with Mr. Spencer. We just lit as many lavender and citrus candles as we could find, and I collapsed on the couch with a newly shampooed, still-wet dog. I promptly passed out into a dream about a sea of tall grass.

I didn't hear a thing. Not a truck. Not a whisper. I didn't hear anything until I looked out the window and saw Greenville had left us a message.

TEN

GO HOME, DYKE.

That's what they wrote.

Actually, I think they wrote something else, but then they maybe weren't sure on the spelling, because there was some stuff crossed out. But then they wrote GO HOME, DYKE.

In black spray paint.

On our front lawn.

Luckily I was the first person to spot it out the window, and I tore outside as quietly as possible, speed-calling Berry as I zipped out the front door and onto the grass. The paint was only just dry, sticky on the individual blades of grass, which were already wet with dew. The black rubbed off on my fingers as I listened to the phone click and Berry's sleepy voice. "WHA? ANNE? What time is—"

"BERRY! I need you to do me a favor, like FAST. Do you have spray paint?"

"Have? What?" I could hear Berry getting out of bed, thumping around her room. "What do you need spray paint for at . . ."

There was a pause. A rustling sound.

"Holy cow, seven a.m.!"

"Berry—"

There was a thump. "Wait. Are you okay?"

"I need to paint over something," I said, looking back at what I hoped was my still-sleeping house. "Like. Now. Or I need to like blow-torch. But I think paint—"

"I'm coming now."

Fortunately for me, Lucy wasn't exactly bursting out of bed that morning, and Millie never liked to get out of bed until after noon if she could help it. I zipped into the kitchen and made coffee and grabbed two muffins out of the fridge and put everything on a tray with some sliced oranges and brought it up to their room.

Knocking first.

"Come in!"

Millie sat up in bed, which was already covered in books and maga-zines. Lucy was watching the news.

"We'll be down in a minute," Millie said.

I held up the tray, "I brought you breakfast. For the bed in break-fast. Which you will eat now."

"You brought us . . . breakfast?" Lucy sat up.

"I always knew we raised you right," Millie joked, taking a mug. "Does the living room still smell like dog barf?"

"Only faintly," I noted, handing Lucy her mug and muffin. "The garage smells more because the rug is in there."

"Well, we'll get to that this afternoon," Lucy said, putting her muffin on a stack of books about education. "I wanted to talk to you—"

"Actually I've got some stuff to do," I cut in. "So enjoy your breakfast and . . . I'll see you in a bit!"

Millie sipped her coffee. "Mmmm. Hey, isn't tennis on?"

"I think so!" I called back as I tore down the stairs into the laundry room to grab our beach towels.

Plan B.

Berry screeched up to our curb in Mato thirty minutes later, and, not even breaking a sweat, vaulted out of the car with an armful of spray paint. "I brought black and green and blue and orange and yellow and pink. And purple!" She stepped up toward the letters on the grass and frowned. "Fuck."

"Yeah." I sighed. "Fuck. You think this was because they didn't win the game? Like somehow the tie is my fault?"

"I mean, it could be anything, but yeah, the game probably didn't help." Berry straightened her shoulders, dropping the rest of the cans on the grass. "Okay, what's the plan?"

Shaking the can of pink paint, I stepped up to the lawn and began drawing a pink square around the letters. Then I divided that square into thirds. And thirds again.

"Tic-tac-toe," Berry asked, shaking the can of green.

"Even better," I said. "*Saturday Night Fever.*"

Saturday Night Fever, another film starring John Travolta, released in 1977, about New York discotheques. Featuring several key hits by the ultimate disco band, the Bee Gees, an Australian group who wrote three mega hits for the movie including: "Stayin' Alive," "Night Fever," and "How Deep Is Your Love."

And "We Should Be Dancing." The best.

I pulled up the image I was thinking of on my phone, which was also the poster for the movie. On it, Travolta, in an iconic white polyester suit and black shirt, stands on a lit-up dance floor, a square platform of lights, his hand up in the air pointing at . . . the stars possibly, maybe at a tech who was standing on a ladder.

I looked at Berry, my heart an exaggerated bass line. Because we didn't have much time. Because at any moment my parents could decide that it *was* indeed weird that I was all like, *Here's a muffin in bed.* Because I basically yanked Berry out of bed on a Saturday, precious Saturday, and made her bring me all her paint and at any moment she could just get in her magical red car and drive away. I really didn't know what I was going to do if she did that. Or if she said anything about my Plan A being more like an actual Plan H or W.

"Let's do it." Berry nodded, shaking the can and, with expert flair, filling in the top corner square.

Technically the *real* floor in the movie was an LED floor that changed with the music. But this was kind of an emergency rendition. More of an "inspired by" than a direct copy.

Even though she was not a fan of disco, and had made it clear to me that she would never see the movie, Berry was impressed with the final product. Which looked more like a quilt of many colors on the lawn than a dance floor, but you know what? It wasn't *terrible*.

"What now?" she asked, tossing her can in the cardboard box.

"Wardrobe change," I said. Grabbing my favorite sequined two-piece suit from where I'd left it on the porch, I pulled it on over my shorts and shirt and slipped on my gross white sneakers because I knew they'd be ruined. The suit was a light pink instead of white, but with my black shirt it looked pretty Saturday night.

Berry pulled out her phone. "Awesome."

I started playing "Stayin' Alive."

"All right." Berry stepped back, "So. Um. Strike a pose!"

I stepped onto the still-sticky grass, which immediately dyed my sneakers a rainbow of colors. Somewhere under my toe was the faded outline of the word *Go*.

I pressed my toe into the paint, imagining Tanner's face getting squished under my shoe. George Herbert was a poet and the first person, I think, to say, "Living well is the best revenge," in 1640. People still say it, centuries later. I held up my one finger, pointed at the sky, and put my other hand on my hip. I pursed my lips as Berry clicked the photo.

Which is about when Monty started barking her head off and I heard the front door squeak open.

"What the—"

"ANNE!"

Lucy and Millie, still in sleepy robes, holding empty coffee mugs, stood on the front steps. Mouths *open*.

"What the heck?" Millie gasped.

"You painted the LAWN?!" Lucy stepped forward and bent down to look at the grass, inspecting the damage.

In fairness, it wasn't as bad as a rug of dog barf. I didn't say that, but I definitely thought it. I don't know what Lucy was thinking as she rubbed the paint between her fingers and stared at my suit.

Berry took a huge step back. Awkward.

"Why would you do this?" Lucy asked.

You're going to say, of all the people that would understand why I would want to cover someone's hate message on the lawn, Lucy and Millie would be two people who would get it. Also, let's say, covering the lawn with spray paint is not hitting someone with a piece of pizza.

But I didn't want them to see it. I didn't want to see it. I wished I hadn't seen it. And I didn't want that to be in their brains like it was in mine. Even if it wasn't *new*, I didn't want one more for Millie or for Lucy. I just didn't. It was easier for them to be pissed at me, for some reason, than to have them feeling sad with me.

Or that's what I thought, I guess.

"There was a hole in the grass," I lied. "So I figured I'd take advantage of it. Make some art. Then I could fix the whole thing."

Berry dropped her phone by her side and looked at me.

Monty, who had sprinted out of the house after my moms, did a zoom across the front lawn, apparently feeling much better. With great

dog zeal, she charged through the painted square. Her paws were immediately soaked in paint.

"GAH! MONTY!"

Lucy shook her head. "I can't deal with this right now." And she
walked back inside. I think she was talking to herself because she was
making angry gestures with her hands.

Millie took a long sip from her coffee, thinking. "What would make
you think that it was even *remotely* okay to cover the grass with paint?"

"I just thought . . . it would look cool. Like an installation piece." I
dropped my hands by my side. "I mean, it's our property, and you can
just replace grass."

"*I* can?" I could feel Millie searching my eyes for a hint of something. Millie can read my eyes like a book. I tried to look indifferent:
the green of the lawn at the edge of the pink, my ruined sneakers,
Monty's now dyed paws.

"I'm sorry," I said. "I guess it was a bad idea."

"I guess so." Millie looked at Berry, who was frozen in place, which
is what I would have done. "Well, looks like you're going to be grounded
for the next week. And *you* can spend the rest of *your* weekend resodding our lawn."

I assumed resodding meant putting more sod on there. Because sod
is grass, right? Probably not a great time to ask, I reasoned.

"Okay," I said.

Millie turned and went back inside, and Berry released a very loud
sigh of relief.

"That was intense."

"Yeah," I said, dropping to the ground, just shy of the paint that would have ruined my suit on top of my day.

"My parents would have grounded me for a month."

"I mean, we live in Greenville . . ." I held my palms up. "I'm pretty grounded as is."

The sun was out by then. A big ball of heat seeping through my polyester jumpsuit and turning my skin into something that felt like a cooked egg.

"Why did you lie?" Berry asked.

"Because I didn't want my moms to spend their weekend thinking that someone left a hate message on their lawn." I squinted.

Berry looked at her phone. "You think it's for them or for you?"

I scrambled to my feet. "Good question."

"Maybe both," Berry said. But she didn't sound sure.

The sun was starting to cook my skull. "Maybe it's all the same thing."

"So." Berry stretched. "You want to change or are we resodding the lawn with you in polyester?"

"You already drove a buttload of spray paint to my house," I said. "I don't want to put you out. You know. Again."

Berry shrugged. "What else do I have to do in Greenville on a Saturday?"

Something about Berry's tone . . . it was kind of lonely, just at that moment. Like it felt the same as when I pictured Berry alone with her soccer equipment when she was little. Suddenly I realized maybe Berry didn't have anyone else but a bunch of concrete animals to hang out with? Because Greenville sucked?

I don't know, maybe that made me feel worse for being the new friend that needed . . . help.

Maybe I was also not that fond of wanting help.

Maybe I was standing there in silence, looking at the lawn, and Berry bent down a little to catch my eye.

"Sodding is actually really cool," she said, with a grin.

"It's not." I grinned back. "But thanks. For being here. And helping."

"When it's my lawn." Berry tossed her keys in the air and caught them. "You'll sod me."

So we drove to the nursery. And Berry, who somehow knew something about grass (on top of knowing how to play like four instruments and how to play soccer), helped me load six sushi rolls of dirt and grass into the trunk. Then we went to the burger place for breakfast and looked at the pictures from that morning on her phone while I shoved fries in my face.

"You look hilarious," Berry said, turning the phone sideways. "What do you want to do with these?"

"Photoshop. Then I'm going to post it tonight," I said, pointing at her phone, "Can you send me that one?"

"Photoshop what?"

"You'll see." I slurped up the last of my shake.

"Sending in a message now," Berry said, and sipped on her soda.

"Got it."

We spotted Tanner and Sarah in Tanner's Jeep pulling into the burger place as we pulled out. Sarah stuck her tongue out at me and laughed. Berry, staring ahead, didn't see. And I didn't know what to say, so I just looked at my photos on my phone. I wonder what people did with horrible moments before they had phones?

I wouldn't let Berry help me actually sod. Like, I just couldn't and I also didn't want her to get any more cold glares from my moms, who were definitely going to be lurking. I got her to explain it to me and did it myself. Killing at least one of the sushi rolls in the process. And getting mud everywhere. It was kind of like repairing a hole in my pants but with more dirt.

I was about a quarter through and heading back from the garage, with a pitchfork and a dream, when I heard a clip-clop coming up the road. I looked over and spotted a shadow—a tall four-legged shadow on top of which was what I thought was someone saluting.

So apparently there are people in Greenville who have horses? That they ride? On the street?

And apparently one of those people is Gilly Henderson. On top of a big black horse with a big white stripe on its nose. Gilly sat with one hand on her hip, the other shielding her eyes under her helmet. Which was pink with a pom-pom on the top.

I didn't know helmets came with pom-poms.

But then apparently there were a lot of things I didn't know.

I froze, pitchfork in hand. For some reason I didn't want Gilly Henderson to see me working my sod. Not just because I was pretty sure I was doing it wrong and it was possible Gilly knew the right way to fix a lawn.

The horse stopped in front of the house. Gilly stood up in the stirrups. She was looking at the grass. She looked confused.

The horse shuffled forward and Gilly pulled back on the reins. Then she reached into her pocket and pulled out her phone.

Taking a picture of the lawn? For what? To show her friends. The friends who probably, maybe even with Gilly, *sent* this message?

"Hey!" I yelled out, stepping forward. "HELLO! HEY! GILLY!"

Apparently you have to be very careful not to scare horses. A good way to do that would be to hold up a pitchfork and approach them, shouting.

Spotting me, the horse skittered backward, startling Gilly and me. "WHOA!" Gilly cried.

"Ah!" I dropped the pitchfork. "Sorry. I just. I didn't mean to pitchfork at you."

Her hair was spilling down her back from under her helmet. She looked weirdly glamorous for someone on a horse in what looked like track pants and a T-shirt. She reached down and ran her hand over the horse's neck. "Just chill," she whispered. "Chill, man."

"Hey, uh," I stuttered, suddenly a dangerous combination of embarrassed and mad. "What are you doing here?"

"I'm just riding," Gilly pressed her lips together. "What are you doing here?"

"Uh, I LIVE here and it seems pretty obvious that I'm cleaning up *your* mess," I seethed.

Making a mess in the process, yes, but let's stay on point.

"My what?" The horse started walking backward, and Gilly dug her heels in his sides to push him forward. "What are you talking about?"

"Next time you want to leave a message," I spat, "send a text."

Gilly blinked. "*What* are you talking about?"

Okay, in my head that sounded like a much more scathing reprimand instead of just like a request for courtesy.

Could you send a hate email next time?

"Your friends? My lawn?" I pointed. " 'Go home, dyke'?"

Gilly shook her head. "I didn't do anything to your lawn. I didn't even know you lived here."

"Right." I frowned, turning back to my mud-and-sod hole. "Well, I'm pretty busy, so bye."

I didn't see Gilly leave, but I heard her horse's hooves clopping away. Like I was going to buy her crap a second time? Don't think so.

I waited till she was gone to resume my sod stomping and poking on grass I basically spent three months of allowance on. When I was done, I sent a picture to Berry and she sent a laughing emoji.

BERRY
What did you do to that poor grass?

ANNE
GAH! Did I kill it???

BERRY
No but I take it back. You are never sodding my lawn.

That night, my parents went out for pizza. I'm assuming I wasn't invited because of the lawn, although really the last thing I wanted to do was go out into the lion's den of Greenville.

I assumed the Spencer family also ate pizza.

Instead, I got to work on Photoshop, which was one of my skills of choice, which I learned when I was six, which is what happens when your mom's a photographer. Which is not as fun as glitter but serves its purpose.

Berry had taken a pretty solid photo. I sort of wished I'd styled my hair, but I realized I could also just Photoshop a nice Travolta pompadour on there.

On top of the photo, in the classic *Saturday Night Fever* font, a blast of silver blue, I put the text, "STAYIN' RIGHT HERE."

I posted it and went downstairs to clean off Monty's paws and add some lavender candles to the garage.

ELEVEN

I don't spend a lot of time online.

That's not a judgment of the internet, or social media, or whatever. Not that any of those things cares what I think, but mostly a result of me being the kid of parents who both intensely value my freedom of expression and have intense opinions of their own about what will limit that freedom of expression.

Aka the internet.

Lucy believes, I think I'm getting this right, that the internet is a playpen of unchecked, unregulated, often uninformed opinions and anonymous, often toxic content. She doesn't trust the internet and thinks other people should also not trust it.

Millie sees the web as some sort of strange board game that she believes is mostly boring and uncool.

I have a Pic-o-gram account where I post art type things, but I only have like fifty followers: an accumulation of people I went to school with, including Danny, and a few of my moms' artist friends, and my grandma on Millie's side, who is a bit of a harsh critic and rarely likes things I post.

So I wasn't all that surprised to wake up on Sunday and find forty smiley faces on my picture. I also wasn't *terribly* surprised to see that Greenville had also weighed in, but it was a little . . . much. You can't *unlike* a picture on Pic-o-gram. But you can make fun of it and the person who posted it.

Mostly Greenville responded in my comments by telling me I was a) fat or b) ugly or c) some version of a *bitch*. A few people didn't get the reference and thought my *Saturday Night Fever* tribute was a salute. There were *a lot* of barfing emojis.

DRAGONSRULE9824: Wow this fat bitch needs to do more cardio!
FIGHTFORDRAGONS23: HAHAHA disgusting!!!
DRAGONBBABYGGGIRL: Someone needs some anorexia

I didn't recognize all the names or profile pics, but pretty much all of the comments, suggesting a lack of originality, had dragon names.

I also noticed that DRAGONBALL88 had the most to say.

DRAGONBALL88: I thought they told you to GO HOME.

I stared at my phone as the barf emojis continued to populate. It felt like someone was wiping their cleats on my stomach.

At about six a.m., Danny (mostmagicalD aka MOSTMAGICALD) popped into the comments.

MOSTMAGICALD: Oh look! A bunch of straight people with no imagination commenting on something they know nothing about! Cool.
DRAGONPINKQUEEN: 👆
MOSTMAGICALD: Oh wow! Vigorous intellectual debate. Greenville seems like tons of fun!
DRAGONPINKQUEEN: Don't care if you have fun here asshole.
DRAGONBALL88: / 💩
MOSTMAGICALD: #tackybitcheswithlotstosay
DRAGONPINKQUEEN: Maybe fuck off?
MOSTMAGICALD: Um do you know your name sounds like dragon vagina?

A few seconds later my phone buzzed.

DANNY

Hey. RU ok? Do you want me to come and
slay some dragons for you?

ANNE

No. I'm just sitting here in the middle of
nowhere seriously debating getting on a bus
back to Petaluma.

DANNY

Then things must REALLY be bad.

Danny lives in Chicago and thinks anywhere that is not Chicago sucks.

I flipped over to Pic-o-gram on my phone and deleted the photo. Which I instantly regretted. Because it's like they somehow convinced me to erase myself.

FYI, the choice between being yourself and being shit on is not mine alone, but it universally sucks.

So there I was, Sunday morning, drowning in a special formula of self-loathing and regret when Millie knocked on the door.

"Hey," she said, pointedly walking around my still-unpacked boxes and piles of clothes. "I need you to come with me to a shoot today. Are you free?"

"Today?" I flopped back in my bed, hoping to convey with that one word that I was overwhelmed with life and in no position to be of any help to anyone. "It's SUNday. And I'm grounded."

"Yes, it is, and yes, you are, but you will be under my supervision, and you don't want to do it, so it's still sort of a punishment." Millie nodded briskly, taking one last look. "Come on, I'll buy you a probably subpar breakfast burrito."

It was pretty subpar. (What is up with Greenville and normally tasty takeout foods?) But it was definitely more satisfying than cold cereal and sitting in my room feeling like crap.

The shoot was for one of Millie's portraits for her series on aging, at a location just outside Greenville, a little town called Avonlee. Avonlee might be the most adorable place I've ever been; it's a hamlet behind a curtain of trees with tiny little flowers. Driving there was like entering a snow globe of petals.

"So," Millie asked, flicking on the windshield wipers to brush the floral confetti off the windshield, "should we talk about your photoshoot yesterday?"

"You saw it on my photos?"

"You're shocked your moms are lurking on your social media? The only reason I use any of those apps is to spy on your life. Plus my mom said I should take a look." Millie raised an eyebrow. "The comments seemed . . . pretty rough."

"I mean, it sucks, but it's fine." I stared at the petals twisting in the wind. "I'm just getting the feeling . . . like . . . nothing I am or like or do is going to be okay with Greenville."

Millie took a last bite out of her burrito. "It is entirely possible that Greenville will never get you," she said. "But at some point, it's not about them."

I must have sighed one of those sighs that's bigger than you mean it to be. Like, a more honest breath than you expect coming out of your body.

"Which is not to say you can't talk to me and your mom about *why* it sucks." Millie's eyes darted my way. "I mean, that was really a lot of barfing emojis."

"Rain check," I said hopefully.

"Always," Millie said. "Just check in with my assistant, I'm always around."

Our destination was at the top of a road that wound up a green hill like some sort of fairy tale. At the tippity-top was a pink house that looked like it could open up like a dollhouse. It was the most magical thing I had seen since arriving in Greenville. Crisp white molding flashing in the sun. Little gold-looking triangles perched on each roof peak.

"Damn."

"Here we are." Millie shoved on the parking brake. "I think you're going to like this lady."

This lady, when she opened the pink door with an emphatic and almost dramatic *whoosh*, was a tall woman, like even taller than Millie, who looked to be about a hundred, with long silver hair she wore in a braid that trickled down her right shoulder, and two distinct, but not necessarily overly garish, circles of rouge on her cheeks. She looked like a fairy princess if fairy princesses wore long multilayered velvet muu-muus. And sandals. And smelled like cookies.

Actually, those all seem like they could be legit fairy princess things.

"Good morning," the woman called out, in a voice that was almost operatic. "How lovely to finally meet you in person, Millie!"

Millie reached out to shake the woman's hand, which was covered in layers of silver and gold rings. "Thank you so much for agreeing to take part in this."

"Well, I'm a fan of your work!" the woman boomed. "Aside from some BBC tonight, this will be the highlight of my day."

"Anne." Millie held her hand out in a gesture of introduction. "This is Beverly Lynde."

Lynde?

My breath caught in my throat. Mrs. Lynde? Like the mother (or aunt, possibly) of the imposing, very judgmental, often disdainful Principal Rachel Lynde? A person who hates me?

I shot Millie a look that read, *You brought me to the enemies' house, on a* Sunday?

Millie missed this look, as she was busy getting her bags of equipment through the door.

On cue, this older, possibly cooler Lynde, heretofore known by me as Lynde Senior, rested her watery blue but also very sharp eyes on me. "*The* Anne. I have heard about you. I have also been anxious to make *your* acquaintance."

I stiffened. Spotted. Spied on? Probably.

Of course she knew everything!

I still hadn't gotten those curtains up!

Was Principal Lynde her source? I searched her face.

Play it cool, Anne, I told myself.

"Okay," I sort of shouted. "It's very nice to meet you."

Lynde Senior smiled, revealing a gold canine tooth. "No need to shout, dear. The knees are out, but the ears work fine."

"Sorry."

She winked. "Goodness, I love your hair," she said. "And that sweater! What a fascinating color story! Please come in."

Okay, unexpected points to Beverly because I *was* in fact wearing a color story consisting of a neon-yellow sweater, pink jeans, and green Crocs, which with my orange hair constructed a story I had mentally titled "Citrus Fantasy." Looking at Beverly Lynde some more, I realized *her* outfit *also* told a color story, which I would title "Ancient Moonlight Velvet Witch Lullaby."

I stepped over the threshold into the world of Beverly Lynde. Which was full, *full* of stuff. Every wall was covered in paintings and portraits of all different styles. There were black-and-white photographs of austere-looking men and a few of some less-than-austere-looking men. And many *many* photographs of various pretty sexy-looking Beverlys.

This was not her first photoshoot.

There were walls and walls of bookshelves and books stacked on every surface and on almost every step of the white winding double staircase that led up from the front hall. Every piece of furniture looked less like a piece of furniture and more like a houseguest, dressed in some sort of fabric, scarf, or sweater. Chairs lolled in the hallways and couches cut off doorways. Lynde led us through, weaving adeptly and moving at a solid clip despite her knees.

"*Don't* excuse the mess," she joked as she directed us through the maze of stuff, her robes billowing. "It's part of my charm."

She pointed at a back room, a sort of sunroom full of plants and even more books.

"I think," she mused, "the light will be best in here."

There was a giant blue-and-yellow stuffed bird perched on a large branch that stretched across the room. Its left wing was spread out to reveal delicate layers of various shades of blue feathers. Its eyes looked like they were made of some sort of ancient precious jewel.

"Just ignore *him*." Lynde Senior waved at the bird dismissively. "That's Waldo. His spirit is strong but not destructive."

"Got it." Millie nodded. "Anne, gimme a hand?"

Millie is a fan of a no-fuss-no-muss approach to photography. We quickly secured a chair, setting it just in front of Waldo, and set up the tripod for the camera. Lynde Senior chatted away about the weather and the art of photography as she carted in snacks on tiny plates, perching them on various books.

Beverly was a fan of art, period. She liked mixed medium work. But adored portraits. She loved textile work. And sculpture so long as it wasn't too big on itself. She wanted to be delighted, she said, and sometimes even challenged.

Once there was a snack balancing on every surface, Lynde Senior took her seat and Millie got behind the camera.

"This is perfect," Millie said. "Just relax and talk to Anne; I don't want you too stiff."

"Not yet, at least." Lynde Senior winked.

!!!

"Well, then. Where on earth did you get that lovely sweater, Anne?" Beverly Lynde clapped her hands together.

"It's vintage." I held up the belled sleeves. "I got it at a place in Petaluma, where we used to live."

Millie's camera clicked.

"It's gorgeous. Bright colors don't appeal to my pallor but I adore them." Lynde Senior turned her head slightly. "Now, Anne, how are you finding Greenville? You've only just arrived, correct? A few weeks? How does it measure up?"

"Oh, um." I snatched a cookie off the plate. "It's great. I love it here."

I was mid-munch when Beverly Lynde, I shit you not, snorted. Millie chuckled, snapping another picture.

"What's so funny?" I wiped the crumbs off my sweater.

"My dear girl. Greenville, do not get me wrong, is a lovely, beautiful place. Picturesque even." She adjusted her layers. "But it is a well-known fact that its residents have very old, well-worn sticks up their butts!"

I shock-coughed so hard a little piece of cookie actually shot out of my nose.

"Well, then." Millie chuckled as she rummaged in her bag for a different lens.

"Greenville is not good with the new on any level, so I am hard pressed to imagine them being receptive to a multidimensional daisy like yourself," Lynde Senior finished, adjusting her robes.

Mental note: I am a multidimensional daisy.

"I mean," I said, cautious, "I would say they seem a little . . . like . . . traditional. Here."

Lynde Senior, aka My Favorite Lynde, reached forward and snatched a cookie off a nearby plate, popping it into her mouth whole. "My family has been here for generations, my girl, so I say this from experience. Greenville is a city that has always rewarded and housed the small-minded."

My Favorite Lynde adjusted in her seat, tossing her braid over her shoulder. "I was the first woman in my family, and the town, to practice law *and* to choose a career over marriage. And what did they do? In light of my successes?"

I shook my head, legitimately curious to hear what she was going to say next.

She tossed her hands up in the air. "Pandemonium! They lost their buttons! They set me aside and adrift. As though I had set the town on fire for refusing to be another stone in the road."

Millie snapped in her new lens, but not before tossing a meaningful look my way.

"Yeah, I can see that happening," I responded quietly.

"And do you know what I did when they showed me their spots?" Lynde leaned forward, her eyes twinkling.

"You didn't care?"

"Well, I did care at first," Lynde said, swiftly snatching yet another cookie, "but then I had a lot of sex and made a lot of money and I traveled the big and beautiful world . . . and then I didn't care so much."

This time it was Millie's turn to choke on a cookie.

"Well." Millie coughed. "Wise words if ever I heard them."

"I'm taking notes," I told her.

"You do that, my dear, and you'll be better for it." Lynde took a moment to give me another wink. I wanted to vault over the two couches between me and her and throw my arms around her.

Millie snapped a final picture. "I think we have it, Beverly."

"Call me Bev." Bev stretched. "All my friends do."

Just then there was the soft crackle and pop of tires over gravel.

"Ah, dear." Bev raised a finger. "That will be my less enjoyable appointment for the day," she grumbled.

"Do you need us to clear out?" Millie asked, reaching for her bag.

"Heavens no! You may take your time," Bev sighed, "but you'll likely *want* to leave when you see who my next guest is."

As we hustled our gear out of the house, I got her meaning. There in the driveway was the Other Lynde, aka My Least Favorite Lynde, aka The Lynde who *didn't* think I was a multidimensional daisy. Or didn't *like* daisies. Or both.

Principal Lynde was wearing what I guessed were her "Sunday Clothes," which consisted of a plain T-shirt (white. Who'd she get *that* idea from?) and a pair of let's call them gray pants? This version of Principal Lynde was a little less intimidating, but still, I got a solid flood of back sweat as her gaze met mine.

Principal Lynde gave Millie a sharp nod. "Mrs. Shirley."

"It's just Millie, thanks," Millie said, popping open the trunk. "Principal Lynde."

Principal Lynde's narrow gaze settled on me. "*Miss* Shirley." Her voice sliced through the air. "I see we have abandoned the decorum of appearance you *briefly* displayed at school not long ago. Where did that girl who knew how to conduct herself in public go? I wonder."

Sweat. Dripping. Down my back. "Uh. Hello, Principal Lynde. Good Sunday to you."

"Good gracious, Rachel." Bev floated toward us. "These people are my guests and I'll thank you for keeping your fashion tastes to yourself. Especially given the circumstances of you having *no taste*."

A small fire flared in Principal Lynde's eyes. "I beg your pardon, Auntie."

"You heard me." Bev's eyes narrowed. "If you don't have anything nice to say to my very special guests, you can keep your trap shut. Now what was it you came here for?"

BATTLE OF THE LYNDES! (Guess whose side I was on?)

It was over pretty quickly, actually, as Principal Lynde huffed past Bev and into the house. "I'm *just* here to pick up some files from Uncle Mackenzie's office, Auntie. I'll be gone in a minute."

Millie and I hopped in the car, which I was expecting to be the end of it, but as Millie shoved her keys in the ignition, there was a tap on the glass next to my head. Bev waited patiently for me to roll down the window.

"I can tell you're a smart bird," she said. "Because I'm a smart bird, too."

Noting that the other bird in this scenario was stuffed and in her sunroom.

"Well. Thanks."

"Don't let them get you down." She waggled a finger at me. "This town is too small to push you down a hill."

And with that she flicked her braid over her shoulder and headed into the house on wings of velvet.

"Well," Millie said, backing out of the driveway. "I thought that would be quite something."

"And it was," I finished, breathless.

Look. I'm not saying I think it was the best pep talk ever. What hill and how does a town as a collective push you down said hill? Hard to say. But I thought a lot about Beverly after that meeting. So much that later that night I dreamed I was a giant green bird with gray feathers on its head, flying over Greenville.

The next day, inspired by Beverly, I wore a velvet batwing gold-and-pink-tie-dyed poncho top that I like to imagine once belonged to a magician. Or an art teacher. Paired with my pink jeans now cut into shorts and my gold sparkly high-heeled boots that I had sparkled myself.

I left a trail of glitter from the front door of the school to homeroom. Which Berry said looked like some sort of Wizard of Oz yellow glitter road.

I caught the looks of Tanner and Sarah as I took my seat in English class first period, but I didn't let them bother me.

At the end of class, Mr. Davidson, in a powder-blue vest, held up a crisp new sign-up sheet for the school play auditions.

"Not sure what happened to the last list," he said, surveying the crowd for signs of guilt. "But this new one is going up now. If anyone would like to sign up for auditions, please put your name here by the end of the day."

Berry snuck a look at me from behind her textbook.

I raised my hand. "I can put it up in the hall," I offered.

Mr. Davidson handed me the sheet with a flourish. "Thank you, Anne."

The bell rang just as I was pressing the last piece of tape onto the wall. I wrote my name on the top line.

"So, I don't GET it." Sarah stepped up behind me, her whole face a pinch. "You think because you dress like a freak you can, like, act or something?"

I swiveled on my glittery heel. "What did you say?"

"I SAID"—Sarah looked around, maybe not expecting a request for a clarification—"you think just because you dress like a freak you can act?"

"I guess we'll find out," I said. "Won't we?" I held out my pen. "You signing up, too?"

Gilly and Tanner stepped into the hallway. Tanner walked up next to Sarah while Gilly leaned on a locker, looking in the other direction.

Sarah stared at my pen like it was a worm. "Uh, no. Thanks."

"New girl bothering you?" Tanner asked, putting a protective arm around Sarah's shoulder.

"Yes." Sarah pouted. "She IS."

My heart started beating in my throat.

I am a smart bird, I told myself. *I am multidimensional.*

"You know"—I twirled my pen around my thumb—"freaks *invented* theater. It was like the weirdest job you could have, like in England when Shakespeare was around, it was *the* weird job. And only freaks could do it. The grand history of theater is not a history of normal people. It's of people who are willing to take *risks.*"

Berry emerged from class.

"See you at auditions." I waved.

Greenville didn't have room for me? I would *make* room.

Too small to push me down a hill? Was that what she said?

Like maybe it was about seeing your own weight and size, to see how much bigger you are than someone else's small ideas.

"All good?" Berry asked, leaning into me as we exited, past Gilly, who glowered at me from lowered lids.

"All good," I said.

After a celebratory high five, Berry split for band practice, and I skipped all the way home from school.

All the way home, I kept having this feeling, which I get from time to time. A feeling like a sparkly balloon in my chest. A slightly nervous but also good feeling.

Like something was about to happen.

TWELVE

In my up-to-then high school theatrical career, I had been in six school plays. Generally I am not the lead. But there are, as theater people know, no small parts, only small actors.

My first role was as Sneezy, the sixth of the seven Dwarfs in my kindergarten production of *Snow White* (where the *teacher* gave herself the role of Snow White). Millie noted I had a very believable sneeze, which I learned from Lucy's allergies and a lot of practicing.

I was the Nurse in *Romeo and Juliet* in fifth grade, I was a townsperson in *The Crucible* a year later (I switched schools halfway through the term that year); ditto *Our Town* a year later. I was Nick Bottom in

A Midsummer Night's Dream because there weren't enough boys that year and I was the only girl who wasn't confined by gender roles.

My dream roles include: the Butler in *Clue* and Dorothy in *The Wizard of Oz.*

But really, I'll play anything.

I think that's kind of key to being an artist. That level of flexibility.

Millie told me once that the stage is an example of a liminal space. Which is a space that's between, not one thing or another. It's the real world because it's real people and it's actually in the real world, not in say, space.

But it's also a magical space. Where anything can happen. Where you can take a box and say it's a spaceship and then it's a spaceship, or take a kid who's sixteen and from New Jersey and say they're an ancient wizard.

On the stage, when the lights are on me, I can be whatever I want to be.

To prepare for an audition, when possible, I like to pretend I'm in a dressing room at a fancy Broadway theater, sitting in front of one of those mirrors with the lights all around, a bouquet of roses on my dressing table as I prep my makeup and run my lines. Obviously the bathroom on the second floor at Greenville High, the one with the door that doesn't close and only one sink that works, is a poor substitute, but you work with what you got.

For the purpose of my stage debut at Greenville, I wore my signature orange in multiple shades of . . . orange: a set of blood-orange bell-bottom pants with heart patches on the knees, a sorbet turtleneck, and a neon-orange blazer that the salesperson at the used place where I bought it told me was once owned by a girl who worked for Lucille Ball (star of *I Love Lucy* and comedic genius).

Since Lucille Ball was around way before neon was chic, I was pretty sure it was a lie, but I appreciated the effort and the magic.

I'd re-dyed my hair Tangerine Madness, christening our new tub with an orange glow.

Millie said I looked like a really aggressive extra from *The Mary Tyler Moore Show*. Which is a retro reference that is curiously outside of my wheelhouse.

I read an article once that said an actor should have two auditions prepared in case someone else has the same piece ready, also so you can read the room and do whatever feels the most appropriate at that time. I had "Don't Rain on My Parade" from *Funny Girl* and I had the "I Don't Tip" speech from *Reservoir Dogs* memorized, which could be a controversial choice but a surprising one, I think.

Keep them on their toes.

I snapped my compact closed and moved my face closer to the mirror over the sink.

"It's opening night," I said, pulling an orange hair off my face. "It's opening night and it's time to put on a SHOW."

The whole way to my audition I sang "Don't Rain on my Parade" under my breath, infusing it into my system. I wasn't expecting to turn the corner and run into Tanner. But there he was, standing outside the auditorium in his soccer jersey and jeans, grinning like he was holding a package for me.

Special delivery.

"Anne Shirley." He smiled wide. "How can I help you this fine morning?"

I reached for the door. "I'm here for the auditions, Tanner Spencer. Please move."

"Oh ho no." Tanner moved slightly so he bumped my arm out of the way. "Just hold on a minute."

"Tanner," I said evenly. "Move. Now."

"Guess you've never auditioned for a play in Greenville before." Tanner crossed his arms over his chest. "You got your audition ready?"

I buttoned my lips together.

"You got your outfit." He nodded at my pants. "Got the password?"

"What password?"

"Oh, if you're going to audition for a play here, you got to have a password. If you don't . . ." Tanner held up his hands. "What can I do?"

His face bobbed in front of me, swimming on a sea of psychic steam that was clearly pouring out of my ears. He had a zit on the tip of his chin.

"You know what? I'm going to give you two guesses." Tanner's teeth flashed.

"Tanner."

"Three guesses. For the new girl."

My face was getting hot, not helped by the fact that I was wearing a turtleneck, which was funneling all my body heat into my cheeks.

"Tanner." My voice burned. I looked down the hall, which was empty.

"You think the password is *Tanner?*"

I visualized my fist connecting with Tanner's jaw, cracking that smile off his face. The vision was powerful. But I also knew I was a hallway away from my mom's office.

But still, it was a *very satisfying idea* and Tanner was being a jerk.

"How about *zit?*" I said. "Is *ZIT* the password?"

I rubbed my chin with my middle finger.

"You know what, new girl?" Tanner leaned forward. "I feel like we've told you a few times now that no one here likes your shit, like, no one wants you here. And you need to get that message. Soon." He pushed his face up closer to mine. "What do you say about *that*, Anne Shirley?"

He wanted me to hit him.

And I was definitely considering it—when suddenly there was a bump from behind the door, and a scuffling sound, followed by a muffled, "Who is that?"

Tanner hop-stumbled forward, almost falling into me, as the door pitched open, revealing Mr. Davidson in a turtleneck (white) with a confused look on his face.

"Tanner?" Mr. Davidson looked back and forth between Tanner and me. "What's going on?"

My face was the angriest red balloon.

"Just waiting for auditions, Mr. Davidson." Tanner lolled, stepping back so he was standing next to me. "Me and Anne."

"Anne and I," I corrected. Not that I care about grammar but because I hated Tanner and could not punch him.

Mr. Davidson looked at me for a long second. Then he nodded crisply. "I like your turtleneck."

The red balloon became my face again. "Thanks."

He stepped back, holding open the door. "Well, I'm very much looking forward to seeing both your acting chops," he said.

"Okay," I said, stepping through Davidson and Tanner into the auditorium.

Where I could breathe.

"Let's go, Tanner," I heard Davidson say.

Inside, the auditorium lights were lowered except for three spots of light on the stage. Which seemed like a kind of gift really as I took a seat in one of the back rows and enjoyed a moment in the dark to hold my hands till they stopped shaking. Mr. Davidson walked to the front of the room, and the stage, which was lit up with lights, to talk to the rest of the people in the auditorium.

"Right, so we all know—well, most of us know—the routine. We'll do the auditions in groups of two or singles. Your choice. We're just looking for emotion here, for some personality, some stage presence, so don't worry about memorizing."

"Are we doing a Shakespeare play?" someone asked in the dark.

"Uh, no." Mr. Davidson looked at his sheet. "We're still in negotiations as to what our play will be. Any other questions?"

The room was quiet, just bodies in the dark, murmuring.

"I know you'll all do your best and be wonderful." Mr. Davidson looked out at each face. "Just take a deep breath."

Sarah, Tanner, Gilly, and John sat in a cluster of seats in the front row.

"Let's start with Sarah." Mr. Davidson looked up from his clipboard at the front of the stage. "Sarah, are you here?"

"Yes!" Sarah pulled Tanner up by his arm. "Tanner and I are going to do *Our Town*."

"Sounds good." Mr. Davidson waved them up onto the stage. "Get on up there."

Sarah and Tanner marched up to the front of the stage. Gilly's head seemed to scoot down in her seat. Maybe she didn't want to be there?

As Sarah got up onstage I noted that she was wearing a long blue dress with a white collar, her hair brushed into a soft blond swirl that fell around her neck.

She looked really nice. She looked . . . like she was in costume.

Sarah stepped up to the front of the stage and gazed out into the audience, purposefully wistful. I mean I'm not a huge fan of *Our Town*, but Sarah did look like Emily, and when she held her hand to her heart and delivered her lines, she sounded like Emily.

Mr. Davidson, who had walked backward up the aisle as she and Tanner delivered their lines, clapped loudly as they finished. Sarah took a very deep and graceful bow and Tanner did a little short one and then they hopped off the stage and took seats on the other side of the aisle.

Okay, so Sarah and Tanner had some chops. The world is a surprising place.

"Very well done," Mr. Davidson boomed, "Very well done."

He turned, pointed at me with his clipboard. "Anne, you're next."

I stood up abruptly, my knee knocking the seats as I scooted out of my row. I deep-breathed calm into my body as I headed down the aisle. I was a few steps from the stage, walking toward Mr. Davidson, when suddenly I felt something hard hit my foot, coordinated with someone calling out:

"Whoops!"

I flew forward into the dark, catching sight of Mr. Davidson's horrified face as he leaped forward to grab me before I took a total header. My wrist got the hard end of his clipboard as we both struggled to get to our feet, while snickers rolled over the audience behind us. A somewhat familiar, hissing voice cut through it all.

"Tanner! What the fuck?"

"Shut the fuck up!" Tanner snapped. "I didn't do anything."

Mr. Davidson managed to get his footing and haul me to my feet, a human bag of flustered.

"Are you all right, Anne?" he asked, looking up. "What happened?"

Gilly was standing in front of her seat. She looked at me, and then at Tanner, who threw his hands up.

"I don't know! She must have tripped," he said.

Sarah stood. "I saw it," she said. "Anne just tripped on her shoe or something."

I tugged my turtleneck back into place and tried to wipe the sweat out of my eyes. Mr. Davidson tightened his grip on my hand. "Do you need a moment, Anne?"

"No."

I roller-skate and I have taken part in my share of performance art. You need to do a little more than stick your foot out to get in my way, Tanner Spencer.

But my legs were wobbly as Mr. Davidson gave me a pat on the arm before letting go.

"Okay, then," he whispered. "You'll do great."

I looked up. Gilly's eyes darted over to Tanner and Sarah before settling on me.

"*Are* you okay?" she whispered.

"Yeah, I'm good," I said, walking toward the stage.

The auditorium stage was shallow, and the floor looked like the same floor as the basketball court. My knees felt soft and shaky as I stepped up to the edge, the edge of the light and the line between real and make-believe.

"I'm doing, um . . ." I'd forgotten. "I'm starting with, um, the song, uh, 'Don't Rain on My Parade.'"

"Lovely!" Mr. Davidson took his seat. "When you're ready, Barbra."

A small snort echoed through the room.

I walked to the center of the stage, shook my hands out, they were so sweaty. I faced my audience, tried to feel the rest of my body. My feet, my legs. My voice, which was somehow gone. Or hiding somewhere in my chest. Fluttering around in the dark where I couldn't find it. Where I couldn't touch it with my fingers outstretched. I closed my eyes.

My singing voice sounded strangled, like someone was holding it by the tail. Suddenly there was a low gutter-rumbling cough.

I stopped.

Mr. Davidson looked around the room, then back at me, nodding. "Take your time, Anne."

I started again, did my best to channel my inner Funny Girl.

This time it was two coughs. One low and one high. Followed by whispers. And a laugh. I knew where it was coming from. But it was also spreading. Little coughs. Someone clearing their throat. Snickering.

The coughing continued, getting louder and louder with every second. Louder as I sang louder.

So I stopped. My breath stopped too. Everything stopped. On the stage.

I dropped my head. Everything froze. Including the coughing.

I lifted my head. Felt the light on my face.

Come on, Anne, I thought. *You love this. This is your fucking thing. Don't let them take it away.*

I opened my mouth and let the first thing to come out of it, come out.

I was not surprised that it was "I Will Survive" by Gloria Gaynor, released 1978, with a roller-skating video that's maybe the coolest thing on the internet, that was the first thing past my lips.

And it's a song about not giving up.

And I wasn't giving up.

I threw my arms up in the air, glared out into the audience as I belted out the chorus.

"Heck yeah," Mr. Davidson cheered.

I did once have a routine I used to do to this song when I was twelve, which I knitted into my a cappella rendition for my audition. It included a set of splits on the second chorus, which I think surprised everyone in the room.

But not as much as the backflip I saved for the final move.

Yeah, that's right, Greenville. I can backflip.

After that I went right into my monologue, which I switched up as well. I did Romeo's monologue from *Romeo and Juliet*. Why that was in my brain, I don't know. But "But soft, what light from yonder window breaks," just seemed like a legit follow-up to Gloria Gaynor.

The whole thing was like this beautiful carousel ride. I didn't have to think at all. I just let everything come out. I was completely and totally me in Greenville.

Miracle.

Mr. Davidson's applause boomed out over the auditorium again as I blinked and realized it was over. "Very nice, Anne. *Very* interesting choices. Bravo!" He looked at his notes. "Gilly? You're up next."

I floated off the stage like a tiny disco cloud, bumping into Gilly on my way up.

"You were awesome," she said quietly.

"Thanks." I beamed. "Break a leg!"

Gilly looked really nervous. On the stage, she shifted around like she was trying to get out of the light.

"I'm going to, um, also read, um, a scene from, um, *Romeo and Juliet*. The Juliet part. I'm not singing. Because I don't want to sing. If that's okay."

"Sounds good." Mr. Davidson nodded. "Whenever you're ready."

She turned her face away from the light. And let out a long sigh as she tilted her head. She clasped her hands together. Then she closed her eyes and lifted her chin. "O Romeo, Romeo! Wherefore art thou Romeo?"

There was something about her, standing in the spotlight. Maybe because Gilly was always turning her head away, or looking down, there was something about seeing her whole face lit up. Like she was suddenly there. Like I could see how scared she was, but she was hanging in there.

Like how Juliet is standing there, hoping for this impossible thing to happen in the play. Even if that thing she hopes will happen will be the end of a part of her that used to feel safe.

It was really good!

I leaned forward in my seat.

Her hands fluttered by her sides till she held them together. Like she was steadying a creature. Her voice trembled, but her eyes were wide and searching.

And then, I could swear, she looked right at me.

"Romeo, doff thy name, and for that name, which is no part of thee, Take all myself."

I mean. Maybe because we were doing two parts from the same play? Or?

But, yeah, I'm 99 percent sure she looked right at me. But then she looked up across the field of seats, and suddenly I was having a heart attack?

"Lovely!" Mr. Davidson hollered when Gilly lowered her head on her last line. "Just lovely, Gilly. Thank you."

In a flash, like she'd been released, Gilly hopped off the stage and disappeared out the door to the hall, her hair swishing behind her.

And just like that, my very strange heart did a little twirl in my chest. For the *one* person it should not be doing any moves for whatsoever, Gilly.

I will say Greenville High had way more solid theater performers than I would have originally thought, which is my prejudice, obviously. There was a kid named Taylor Mackenzie who brought his drum from marching band up onstage, and he was amazing. There was a girl named Minnie, who, did I detect some excessive artful eyeliner? Who requested to be a "non-human part if possible." And a kid named Brandon, who was at least six foot two who did a solid bit from *Glengarry Glen Ross* and requested the part of an old man if there was one.

Such interesting choices!

I sat ruminating on this awesomeness until the theater was empty except for me and Mr. Davidson. Just the two turtlenecks.

"Anne." Mr. Davidson smiled in the dark. "Lovely job today."

"Thanks." I grabbed my bag and spotted Berry at the back of the room, waving jubilantly. Had she snuck in to see my audition? Aw!

"Gloria Gaynor." Mr. Davidson put his hands on his hips. "Are you a disco fan?"

"Sort of," I admitted, turning back to smile at Mr. Davidson. "In that it's kind of my life."

Davidson tapped his clipboard. "I do have a thought, about the play, I'd like to run by you."

"Okay."

"How do you feel about flying?"

THIRTEEN

My first crush was on the wicked stepmother in the original animated *Snow White* movie.

Not the direction you thought this was going?

Yeah, obviously my moms were pretty devastated when they learned that my obsession with watching the movie over and over was not because of the stereotypical heartthrob that is the Prince guy or Snow White (either of which would have been fine with them).

I remember distinctly Millie leaning forward and pressing pause on the DVD as I sat on my blanket, eyes an inch from the screen. "Wait," she gasped. "Who did you say is 'nice'?"

I pointed. "The lady with the hat."

Actually, it was a cowl.

"Well, that's fine," Lucy said, sitting back on the couch and patting Millie's hand, "she can like the . . . mother."

"Wicked witch, huh?" Millie shook her head. "Good luck with that."

The character's name was *Lucille*, and she took my little six-year-old heart captive even as she plotted to *kill* Snow White because she was so jealous of her stepchild's youth and beauty.

I think when my crush didn't pass, like months later when I was still insisting on watching and rewinding that part of the movie, Lucy started feeling like maybe it was a smudge on their parenting record. Millie finally banned the movie from movie night. So I broke the DVD out of the liquor cabinet where they'd stashed it and watched it on my computer in my room.

The heart wants what it wants.

I can't really explain it myself. Even now. I just thought she was beautiful. The whole cowl thing. The ruby-red lips. Maybe I also thought I could change her.

Like if there's a version of *Snow White* where she meets this really charming young waif in the woods (with orange hair) and their falling in love shows Lucille the error of her ways and she leaves that stupid mirror and castle behind and she and the waif live in the woods happily ever after?

Yeah. I guess it's pretty weird. Never mind. Let's never make that movie.

After that I fell in love with Katie Simpson, who was in my Girl

Scout troop in fourth grade. Which didn't really lead to anything but an extra year of scouts when I was about to quit. Then I fell head over heels for Darla Hammersmith, who sat in the seat in front of me in fifth grade when we lived in Ohio. Darla Hammersmith, who never knew who I was despite the fact that her smile haunted my dreams and I bought her a multitool for her birthday that her parents later confiscated because, apparently, it's really just a bunch of small knives.

I changed what I ate for breakfast for a year because I saw Darla Hammersmith eating a granola bar once on the way to school and tried to eat the same granola bar instead of toast like a normal person because I had this idea one day we would walk in the door at the same time together and I would point at her bar and say, "Hey, same bar!"

It never happened.

Granola bars suck.

Millie says I fall in love with unattainable girls with long hair.

"Not a great idea," she says, every time it happens. "Not the long hair bit, obviously. You know what I mean."

My first kiss was with a girl I met at camp who had long hair, but was also really cool and her name was Zoey. She had long red hair and freckles and we used to canoe together. And then on the last day of camp I worked up the nerve to tell her I liked her in the boathouse. And she kissed me. And then she went home to Idaho and fell in love with this girl she played soccer with. Which she emailed me about.

We still write actually, Zoey's really cool.

Look.

I have no current interest in the evil witch of my youthful desires. I get that being someone who only talks to mirrors that are forced to be complimentary to you, and plotting to destroy your stepchildren with apples are terrible (criminal) qualities.

I don't want to like people who are not good people.

I feel like I've said this already, but really what I want is my true true. Okay? I want someone I like who gets me, and who likes me back and gets *me*. All of it.

I was almost 100 percent certain that wasn't going to happen in Greenville.

Or with Gilly.

Consider the evidence for the prosecution. Gilly was best friends with people who had been actively, like, racist and sexist against me. Like her friends had basically, in her presence, gone out of their way to do and say really shitty things to me. Things that she had helped make happen (see exhibit A of her coming up to me on the soccer field and encouraging me to sign up for auditions)!

Evidence for the defense? I *thought* it was *possible* that when she was giving her *Romeo and Juliet* audition monologue, she looked at me in the audience. Like I was her Romeo. And she said something nice to me after her friend tripped me.

But (the prosecution butts in rudely) she *didn't* speak up and tell Mr. Davidson that it was *Tanner* who tripped me when he clearly did.

The prosecution rests.

So of course, the *first* person I walk *right* into on my way into school the next day is Gilly. Like I opened the door and started looking left and right to avoid Gilly and then I literally *slammed* right into her so hard I knocked her down like a tree. It must have looked on purpose because Gilly looked at me from the ground like I'd KO'd her in a boxing ring.

"Um, OW." She frowned, pulling herself up.

"HOLY CRAP I'M SO SORRY!" I gushed.

Gilly's face turned beet red. "It's okay," she mumbled, grabbing her bag and unfolding herself so she could stand.

I wasn't sure if that meant, like, "help me up" or "go away," so I just stood there like a true Romeo and watched her get to her feet, at which point she jetted off like a rocket just in time for Berry to walk up behind me and scare the crap out of me.

"Anne—"

"AH!"

"AH!" Berry tensed up in a coil. "What's going on?"

"I just hit Gilly. I mean," I sputtered. "Gilly was here and I rammed her. I mean. Bumped. Into her. By accident. I walked up—I mean into. Gilly."

"Oh." Berry pulled her knapsack up on her shoulder. "Okay. Um. Well. Is she okay?"

"She is! I think." I looked down the hallway. "It was an accident."

My brain followed Gilly down the hall. Was she okay? Did she think that I hit her on purpose because of the Tanner thing?

Was she even thinking about me?

"Okay," Berry said. Waiting for me to turn on to an actual subject of conversation possibly. "So. Any more word on the audition?"

"Not yet." I shrugged, still looking down the hallway.

Probably Gilly was okay, right?

"What do you think Davidson meant when he asked how you felt about flying?"

"I mean it's not exactly a standard post-audition question. . . ."

Berry tried to follow my gaze to nowhere. "I mean I wonder if he'll just do *Our Town* again. It's kind of the safer choice although there's no flying in it," she said.

"I guess," I said.

Did Gilly think I was an asshole? was probably more the question.

"Okay, well, so!" Berry raised a finger. "Speaking of flight! This weekend. I was thinking superhero movie marathon. Since you said you hadn't watched any Marvel movies, which is insane."

I mean, was I an asshole?

"Sure," I said. "I may have watched ONE of them. I think. I saw *Wonder Woman.*"

"That's not Marvel." Berry frowned.

"Okay, well, whatever." I started walking to homeroom. "We can watch whatever."

Like right now, I thought, am I being an asshole right now? Thinking about Gilly? Why am I thinking about Gilly??? In front of Berry. Who was talking to me. About what, exactly, I'd already lost track of.

Berry stepped in front of me, suddenly serious. "Marvel is the X-Men, it's the Avengers. Superman, Wonder Woman, Batman, that's DC. Got it?"

"Sure." I tried to look interested. "Right. Got it."

I watched the corners of Berry's lips turn down. "Okay, well, whatever." She turned and continued down the hall. "Or we can watch an old movie. If you want."

I shook my head. Like seriously, here was a person who was actually trying to be nice to me. But I couldn't think straight enough to come up with something to say, so instead I just said, "Sure."

Inside homeroom, Tanner spun his soccer ball on the desk, letting it cusp the edge before pulling it back with the tips of his fingers. Gilly's eyes flickered upward when I walked into the room, but then settled on the book on her desk. Her hair pooled next to her fingers on the pages.

I almost missed my chair when I went to sit down, but I saved it with a sort of dramatic arms-out move that only Berry noticed.

"Are you okay?"

"You ask me that a lot," I said, before I thought about what that would sound like.

Berry's eyebrows went up. "Okay. Sorry."

"Crap." I frowned. "Sorry. I'm just like, not myself today. For different reasons than usual. Like not white T-shirt reasons?"

Berry nodded, somehow understanding a phrase like "white T-shirt reasons."

That day my outfit was mostly purple, because I'd realized in all my orange-and-green Spirit Day enthusiasm I'd completely ignored my lilac-and-orange vibes. So I was wearing a purple corduroy jumper with a very puffy vintage orange blouse, baby-blue leggings and gold boots. I looked like a backup dancer from a seventies kids show. Which was just for me to appreciate.

Gilly, absorbed in her book, reached up and started twisting her hair around her finger.

"Anne?!" Berry looked at me from her seat. "I asked you. A question?"

"Right," I said, embarrassed. "What was—uh, the question?"

"Geez, never mind." Berry frowned, picking up her books. Her hands were covered in yellow spots of paint. "I'll see you later."

"Where are you going?"

"Dentist?" Berry's lips pressed into a hard line. "I just told you?"

Right.

For the rest of the day half my brain argued about Gilly and half my brain did its best to get me through the day. Which did not work out great. Apparently high school requires a whole brain.

Highlights included:

1. Spending most of English class with my math textbooks open on my desk.
2. Walking into the wrong classroom for second period.
3. Writing on the whiteboard in regular marker in Biology.

You're like, "Oh that's not so bad."

But wait. There's more.

In History, because we were moving desks around and changing seats, I reached to grab a chair . . .

And yanked said chair right out from under Gilly's butt.

Like I had some sort of vendetta. Against Gilly's butt.

She went down like a bag of bricks, if a bag of bricks could fall on its ass.

Gilly looked up with wide eyes. This time like actually thinking maybe I was out to destroy her. This time I *did* reach down.

"Oh my CRAP, Gilly, I'm so sorry."

"What the FUCK?" A hand grabbed me by the back of my jumper. It was Sarah. Who I weirdly hadn't even noticed until that class. "What the fuck are you doing??"

"It was an . . . an accident," I stammered, wrenching myself free as Gilly struggled to her feet once again. "I was trying to get a chair!"

"All right," Mr. Keeper, who looked like a teakettle, stepped in with his arms out like a plow. "Everyone take their seats. Or a seat."

"She grabbed Gilly's chair!" Sarah screeched. "Gilly is, like, *fallen*."

"It was an accident!" I screeched back.

"TAKE! YOUR! SEATS!" Keeper bellowed. "NOW!"

It probably wasn't possible to mess up the day any worse, but I was considering skipping Chemistry, which was my last period. I thought it was entirely possible that if I went anywhere near something flammable, I might blow up myself—possibly Gilly, and possibly the school.

Not on purpose obviously. This isn't *Heathers*.

I kept turning to my right to say something to Berry, but she wasn't there. Damn dentist.

Also, who goes to the dentist after homeroom? Medical appointments are designed for allowing teenagers to skip school.

But then maybe it was good she wasn't there, because clearly I was on a destructive path and who knew who else would end up on their ass before I was through?

My plan for second-to-last period, Gym, was to fake a cramp in the first five minutes and then spend the rest of the period on the sidelines.

Which was a great plan.

And apparently Gilly's plan as well, as I walked up into the bleachers to find her already sitting there, arms wrapped around her stomach in the universal sign for "I don't feel well." She was sitting slightly askew, so she was leaning more on her left cheek.

Because, clearly, she'd taken a pretty solid hit to her right cheek. Care of me.

Maybe I was the villain in this crush situation. Don't villains happen when people fall for people who don't actually like them?

Is that what was happening? Crush? Me?

"Hey!" I looked around. "Uh. Hi."

Great opener, Anne.

"Hey." Gilly shifted so she was sitting straight. But it was clearly not comfortable.

"Is it okay if I sit there?" I pointed at the row behind her.

Gilly looked around the entirely empty bleachers. "Sure. Free bleachers."

I took a seat behind and to the right of Gilly, because sitting right behind someone in a huge set of seats is clearly *very weird*. But I could still look at her back, which I obviously did in a cool no-one-else-would-notice kind of way.

Gilly has a long, straight back. She sat still and straight for most of the class, I assume watching the other students running circles. Her hair stuck to her shirt, which had a little rip in the neck. Also she has a long neck. It's, like, a graceful neck, actually.

Okay, stop.

I tried to think of the perfect and appropriate thing to say to Gilly. The thing that would encapsulate all my concerns and arguments and thoughts and theories. A thing I could say that would stop the Ferris wheel of a day I was having.

"Sorry I made you fall on your butt," I finally managed.

"Twice," Gilly said, not turning around.

"Yeah. Twice," I noted. "So. Sorry twice, I, like, Wile E. Coyote'd you."

I thought I heard a tiny snort from Gilly, but it could have been the crack of someone kicking the soccer ball on the field. A cool breeze blew up the stands, sending the smell of what I guessed was Gilly's shampoo up into my face.

"Hey," she said.

"Yeah?"

"I'm sorry about that thing in the soccer field. And—"

The stands bounced as Tanner strode over, a long loping stride designed for maximum bleacher jostle. His soccer jersey clung to his chest. He must have run over.

"Hey! Gilly! Your mom's here to take you home," he hollered.

"Oh." Gilly swiveled. "Okay. Thanks."

She sounded annoyed.

Tanner stormed closer. "I *said*—"

"I got it, Tanner." Gilly stood up.

Tanner jogged closer. Put his foot up on the end of the bench I was sitting on. Gave it a shake.

"Watch your back. You got New Girl on a revenge streak now." Tanner squinted at me. "You hurt my friend again, New Girl, I'll break you in two."

"Shut up, Tanner," Gilly hissed, storming past him. "Come on."

Tanner gave the bleachers another bounce for good measure before following Gilly.

Evidence for the prosecution?

Gilly is friends with Tanner.

As I changed back into regular clothes, my phone started buzzing like it was about to explode.

BERRY
ANNNNNEEEE

ANNE
HEY! Have you been at the dentist this whole time?

BERRY
I just got back!

ANNE
Next time you should skip the whole day!

I mean, truly, if Berry did not understand the joy of a legit reason to skip school, it was at least my job as a friend to explain. . . .

BERRY
THE LIST!

BERRY
THE LIST IS UP!

ANNE
WHERE R U?!

BERRY
EAST WING!!!

I stepped out into the hallway, where I was greeted by what I was pretty sure was a shriek from Sarah Pye echoing down the hall like a fire alarm.

"ANNE!" Berry ran toward me, eyes wide. She grabbed my hand. "LET'S GO!"

There was a serious hubbub coming from a bundle of students all packed around a small spot on the wall next to Mr. Davidson's door. The entire hubbub of students turned as we got close to Davidson's classroom.

"WHAT THE HELL?!" Sarah screamed as she shoved her way out of the group, looking like a cartoon bull with her tiny ponytails and clear fury; she stormed right up to me till she was, I would say, an inch from my face. Close enough that I could tell Sarah was heated and she'd had PBJ for lunch.

(Also how did she always get out of Gym so fast?)

"FUCK YOU!"

"WHOA," someone from the group behind her weighed in.

"Fuck me for what?" I snapped.

"You think you can just come here. And just. COME IN HERE AND—" And then she turned and ran down the hallway, her ponytails bobbing behind her. "FUCK YOU, ANNE SHIRLEY!"

By then, Berry was pulling me into the lump of teenagers till we were close enough to see the heart of the matter. The list of the cast for the upcoming Greenville High production of *Peter Pan*.

Peter Pan!

"Huh."

I legit thought it would be *Our Town*. Maybe because Berry was dreading it.

"Anne," Berry squeaked. "Look at the top! Look at the NAMES!"

There it was, my name, at the top.

"It's me," I gasped. "I'm . . . Peter? I'm Peter Pan?"

"I knew you could do it!" Berry's eyes grew wide as she grabbed me by the shoulders. "You're the LEAD!"

"Anne is the lead?" someone in the group exclaimed.

"Anne is the lead." A face poked out of the crowd. It was Minnie, the girl who wanted to be a non-human, gushing, "And I'm TINKER BELL!"

"I'm the DOG!" The guy with the drums from auditions did a fist pump.

"ANNE IS PETER PAN!" Berry cheered.

So wishes were just coming true all over.

FOURTEEN

Berry and I celebrated by watching what I thought was a fairly okay movie about Iron Man that still needed way more women in it. Berry agreed and said it was only her third favorite series.

Millie helped us celebrate by ordering us Chinese food and specifically ordering me my very own pork fried rice, which I would proceed to consume in small doses for the next several days.

"Way to go, kid," she said, handing me a set of chopsticks.

"I'm Pan!"

"I mean, yes, *you are*." Millie nodded.

"Like, perfect role for a spritely person like myself."

"I was just thinking that."

Lucy eventually got home from school and came up to my room to congratulate me.

"Mr. Davidson said you stole the show," she said, giving me a squeeze.

"I sang Gloria Gaynor."

"Did you?" Lucy sat back on the bed. "You know who loved that song? Your grandma."

"You know who *else* loves that song? You and Millie. It's a great song."

"You know we played that song at our wedding."

"I hadn't heard that," I added, mocking. Because of course I'd heard that story a thousand times. Maybe more times than I'd even heard the song.

"Stop." Lucy gave me a light shove and I flopped back onto the bed. She scooched down on the quilt, where Bjorn was curled up and snoozing. "This is pretty hard, huh? This Greenville."

"It's not easy," I agreed.

"Too hard?" Lucy's voice got smaller. "Anne?"

"No." I sat up. "Just hard enough. So far. Too hard for you?"

"Well, let's say Principal Lynde isn't exactly *my* fan either, and the PTA wants a constant update on every email and memo I send, and they're all convinced I'm going to cancel soccer and turn the whole school into a pornographic art gallery." Lucy took a breath. "But no. Not too hard."

"Good." I nodded. "Did I tell you I get to be Peter Pan?"

"You did." Lucy gave me a serious face. "Anne. We'll tell each other if it gets too hard, right?"

"Right," I said, not that I was sure what "too hard" would mean.

Was Greenville getting harder? Maybe not. Was it getting *better*?

I mean I had a part doing the one thing I loved more than almost anything except my dog, my parents, roller-skating, and disco. I did not expect everyone to be happy for me and my accomplishment of pulling off what was obviously a pretty stunning audition.

At the same time, getting the part meant spending more time with the Forevers. Sarah, Tanner, Gilly, and John had all gotten parts. Sarah was cast as Wendy, a part she could probably wear her *Our Town* dress for. Tanner was Captain Hook, which was a juicier part than he deserved, but then again he did have a pretty decent audition. John was going to be Smee, which, again, is a pretty solid role, and his audition was okay too. Gilly was one of the Lost Kids (aka the Lost Boys in the original).

The next day I felt a weird static in the air as soon as I opened my locker and noticed that Sarah and Tanner were looking at me from the other side of the hallway.

"Hey!" Berry bounced up to me. "What's going on?"

"Just checking out the salt-and-pepper harbingers of *doom*," I answered.

Berry looked over her shoulder, not entirely covertly. "Ugh."

In homeroom, Mrs. Sherman showed up in a turtleneck that made me rethink *my* turtleneck. It really is such a precarious thing, the turtleneck. Mrs. Sherman looked like an actual turtle in hers, partly because it was a kind of avocado-green puttylike color that didn't go with her skin tone.

That's not me judging, although Lucy would say it sort of was.

It was English class when the static source was finally revealed— Sarah put up her hand and, before Mr. Davidson could call her name, rose from her seat.

"I have something to say, Mr. Davidson."

"Is it about the poem we're reading?" Mr. Davidson leaned on his desk. He was wearing cowboy boots that day. Also an interesting choice.

"No," Sarah said, holding up her chin. "It's about . . . the play."

"Well." Mr. Davidson put his book down on the desk. "Perhaps we can make it quick, then, or talk about it after cla—"

"I wanted to say"—Sarah placed her hands on the desk, then on her hips—"I wanted to say that I think that it's inappropriate, the play you chose."

"*Peter Pan?*" Mr. Davidson lowered his chin to peer at Sarah over his glasses. "You think *Peter Pan* is inappropriate?"

"I think, we normally do plays that are about, like, us, and *our town*, and who we are. And now, for like no reason, it's like you're doing this gay play."

Just as an aside. Growing up with queer moms, I know about almost all LGBTQIA things. And J. M. Barrie, who wrote *Peter Pan*, wasn't gay. I don't know if that's what qualifies something *as* a gay play, but he wasn't.

"*Peter Pan*"—Mr. Davidson cleared his throat—"is not a gay play, Sarah. I mean, there is nothing wrong obviously, with a gay—"

"A girl is playing the lead," Sarah said, "which is supposed to be a boy."

Mr. Davidson straightened. A teachable moment.

"In the tradition of theater, in fact if you see most of the broadcast productions of *Peter Pan*, the part of Peter is played by men and women."

And could be played by anyone in between, FYI, but I could see Mr. Davidson was trying to make a singular point.

"This town"—Sarah's voice got high and reedy—"this town has always been— We have always done, like, traditional plays and now, like, just because Mrs. Shirley's the vice principal, and Anne is here, it's like—"

Sarah's eyes flickered in my direction. "It's like there's an agenda now."

"Well." Mr. Davidson stood and picked up his book with a sharp flick. "I understand that those are your thoughts. There *is* no agenda obviously—"

"Well." Sarah's chin shifted up a notch. "I am going to lodge a complaint."

A long slow sigh expelled from Berry's lips.

I realized my hands were clenched under my desk so tight they were starting to cramp.

An agenda complaint???

"Of course, you are free to do so." Mr. Davidson nodded. "Thank you, Sarah."

Sarah looked around the classroom, her eyes skimming over my (probably very red) face, and primly lowered herself into her seat. Tanner gave her a punch in the shoulder and she smiled. Gilly looked at her desk.

I made sure to be the first out the door when the bell rang, with Berry close behind. Not that she said anything. Maybe because my body was ticking like a time bomb.

I changed, like, lightning fast and took as isolated a position as I could on the soccer field.

Sarah Pye.

Was an ignorant asshole.

Who wanted to be the lead in a school play more than anything else in the world, clearly, but also knew nothing about theater!

As the game wore on, I watched her jogging around the field, her twin pigtails bouncing next to her face. She looked like she was dancing around the grass with joy.

The joy of being a jerk, I fumed.

Was she really going to complain? I jogged over toward the goalie net.

"Hey." Berry waved from her post. "Surviving?"

"What do you think about getting in your car and just driving really really far away from here?" I offered.

"Yeah?"

"Yeah."

"Where are we going?"

"The ocean? Shopping? Something? Broadway?"

"For how long are we going?" Berry asked, her eyes darting between me and the action on the field. "Broadway is pretty far."

"We could be gone anywhere between the next three hours and forever." I sighed.

Before she could answer, the ball came rolling up the field and I had to get out of the way to let Berry do her thing.

I was, albeit maybe kind of strangely, strolling away from the net when I felt what felt like a bomb go off at the back of my head. And the next thing I knew I had a mouthful of grass and there was the sound of footsteps thundering on the ground.

I opened my eyes and saw a giant blur of black and white only inches from my face. I reached out and poked the blur with my finger. It rolled away.

"ANNE!" Berry screamed.

Suddenly I was surrounded by a hive of voices, including Coach Harras, bless her, who decided the best way to deal with the situation was to blow her whistle an inch from my ear. "ALL RIGHT, WHAT'S GOING ON?!"

"Anne?" I felt a hand on my arm. Looked and saw a splatter of pink paint. "Oh my gosh. Anne. Crap!"

Finally Harras spat out her whistle, possibly because by then the whole class had circled around me like we were about to do some sort of trust game, while Berry tried to help me to my feet.

"What happened?" Coach Harras spat.

"The ball came right for her head!" Berry fumed as my body wobbled, and I thought about spitting the grass in my mouth out. "*Someone* kicked it right at her head."

"Who?" Harras picked up her whistle and pinched it between her fingers. "Who kicked the ball?"

Suddenly Gilly's face swam into view, like a balloon on a summer breeze.

"Sarah," Gilly said. "It was Sarah."

Sarah stormed up to Gilly. "WHAT?!"

Berry looked from Gilly to me, her heart beating so hard I could feel it in her arms as she held me up and tighter. My brain was still bumping around in my skull.

"I saw it." Gilly looked at me.

"FUCK YOU, GILLY!"

"Sarah!" Harras blew her whistle, entirely unnecessarily, for the umpteenth time. I was ready to throw a soccer ball at *her* head, TBH.

"I didn't do anything," Sarah spat back. "I didn't even see Anne was there, *Gilly*."

Something was tickling my chin. I reached up and touched it, thinking it would be a blade of grass. But it . . . was not.

"Blood." The word slipped out of my lips.

It glistened in the sun. My blood. Ruby. Red.

I looked down and watched it drip onto the toe of my sneaker. Red. And . . .

"What?" Berry leaned in.

"Blooooo—"

I grabbed Berry's hand so she would have the privilege of being pulled down to the ground with me as I passed out.

The next thing I remember was sitting in the nurse's office. Which looked like every nurse's office I'd ever seen except there were lots of pictures of border collies on the wall. Six. Six is a lot. Not too many, though. Let's say that.

The nurse was a nice woman with a pile of white hair on her head, sitting next to me and smiling and holding a juice box.

"Not so great with blood?" she asked.

"Not amazing," I said.

"I'm Nurse Denim," she said, "but you can call me Sissy."

"Hi, Sissy," I said. My lips still tasted like blood, making me swoon a little. "I'm Anne. I'm not good with blood."

"So you say." Sissy smiled. "You're Vice Principal Lucy's girl."

"That's me."

"I'm going to get you a cold compress for your lip, but it's a pretty small split," Sissy said. "You stay put. I think your mother will be coming to check on you."

There was a clicking in the hallway followed by the rush of Lucy in her suit flying into the room. "Anne!"

"She's fine," Sissy called from the other room. "Just a little cut! The mouth heals very quickly!"

"Soccer injury." My smile was mostly lip and mostly numb. "My first!"

Lucy frowned. "I heard, from Mr. Davidson, what happened. That a student complained."

"Yeah." I tapped my toes. "Well. I guess not everyone is a fan of *Peter Pan*."

"It's." Lucy's voice was steel. "It's ridiculous. *Peter Pan* is a classic and the casting of the school play is his purview."

"I think they think it's like a gay agenda," I tapped my toes some more. "I mean she said agenda. So I figure. Gay."

"Well, that's . . ." Lucy pulled the front of her suit down. "As if any of us has time for an agenda these days. I've spoken with Mr. Davidson. He said you did a very professional audition, and he's very excited for your performance."

"If I survive to opening day," I noted.

I could feel Lucy's eyes taking me in, like she was reading me. But also I could feel her keeping track of Sissy, who was now hovering in the doorway.

"Ice," Sissy said, holding up the pack and a small cup. "And something for the swelling."

"Thank you, Sissy," Lucy said, taking the cup.

She waited for Sissy to leave the room before turning back to me and my lip.

"Oh, Anne." Lucy handed me the cup. "Do I take you out of the school? Do I . . . Do I bring all the parents in? Do I . . ."

I wanted to ask her what she thought. If she thought I should just walk away. If she loved her job so much even though the people here clearly didn't like her so much all the time either. I wanted to ask her what to do.

But, you know, I didn't.

We didn't, clearly, know what to do.

"No," I said.

Lucy gave me another hug. "Okay."

I smiled and felt my lip throb. "Everything will be fine."

Everything will be fine is both a very comforting thing to say and a thing that anyone who says it must know isn't true.

Everything is an impossible thing.

Sissy made me stay for a few more minutes after Lucy left, then declared me "fit as a fiddle" and kicked me out just after the bell.

I looked for Berry, but she was gone.

BERRY
I have to go home to help my dad with a job!

BERRY
Hope you're ok

BERRY
That was bonkers

Then she must have taken a solid few minutes to send me a text that was a field of soccer balls with a little surprised face in the middle.

ANNE
Yeah I'm ok. Split 👄

ANNE
Did you see Sarah kick the ball at my head?

BERRY
No

ANNE
That's what Gilly said

BERRY
Yeah

There was a space of three dots appearing and disappearing as I walked down the hall.

BERRY
I mean, first she sets u up with the sign up list,
then this.

ANNE
Yeah

BERRY
Seems weird

ANNE
Yeah

ANNE
Maybe she's just sick of her terrible friends

More dots appeared and disappeared.

BERRY
Maybe

BERRY
You believe her?

ANNE
I don't know????

I collapsed on the steps.

ANNE
Going home for a hundred aspirin

BERRY
OK!

Did Berry not believe Gilly? *Would Gilly lie?* I wondered as I strapped on my skates.

BERRY

If you feel faint when ur skating, pull over and I'll come and get u

ANNE

OK!

ANNE

What if I just feel really cool?

BERRY

Then go with it 😎

When I coasted out of the parking lot that day, there was another ring of people in the lot, what looked like moms in shorts and sandals, their heads tipped together.

FIFTEEN

On Saturday, Berry texted that she had to help her dad clean the garage, so she couldn't come over and watch movies.

Which felt like a weirdly fake excuse, but then maybe cleaning the garage is a big thing in Greenville. I technically had to help my moms unpack the kitchen, since there were still boxes all over the place.

Hey, we all had stuff to do, okay?

Then Lucy ended up having to be at the school all day, and Millie had errands to run for a photoshoot she was planning.

And suddenly I was alone in the house.

So of course I got on the phone and called all my friends and I was like, "KEG PARTY AT MY HOUSE, EVERYBODY! YAAASSSS!"

Ha-ha. No.

Can you imagine? No.

No. I went disco roller-skating.

Which, let's be clear, I'd learned my lesson at that point. I knew Greenville wasn't interested in seeing me perform disco classics of the seventies downtown. I knew there were *many* things Greenville didn't want to watch me do: sing, dance, have joy. But that didn't mean I couldn't enjoy some tunes in the privacy of my own headphones in concert with the wind blowing through my hair.

It was a day to be my own bird, so to speak.

And since I was in the mood, and no one was home, I thought I'd make it a whole occasion.

Which meant fashion.

Which meant it was time to pull out my fringe.

Fringe is not essential for disco skating. It's probably not even recommended because it's kind of a pain to maintain (you basically lose about a hundred strands of fringe every time you put anything with fringe on, especially if it's a garment made in the actual seventies, as mine all are). But if you happen to have a full fringe orange silk jacket and green sequin leggings and you've already done your English homework?

Why not?

After I fed Monty and Bjorn, I strapped on my skates and headphones, tied my roller-skating scarf (pink with yellow flowers) around my neck, clicked play on my favorite skate track, "You Make Me Feel (Mighty Real)" by Sylvester, the B-side to his 1978 hit, "Dance (Disco Heat)," and sailed out the door.

Sylvester—who I think would have loved this jacket—was briefly a member of the San Francisco drag troupe the Cockettes, a group of performance artists who dabbled in gender play and regular play, before leaving to pursue (and achieve) a stellar career as a recording artist.

"You Make Me Feel (Mighty Real)" is the best song ever. Maybe. I think. Probably. The rhythms thumped through my body right to my fingertips as I shot out the driveway and turned down the road. With a few solid pumps, I picked up speed. I spread my arms out in the wind, feeling the strands of my fringe wings dance in the air.

I slipped past Greenville residents watering their lawns. A man in shorts behind a lawn mower stopped to take off his hat and get a good stare in as I shot past. I did a little shoot the duck past two girls sitting on their front steps.

Why not?

The music switched to "Do You Wanna Funk?" by Patrick Cowley featuring Sylvester.

I did want to funk. Who doesn't?

I could see the sun sparkling on the gold-sequined wristbands I'd added as a last-minute costume embellishment.

There are people who say you should take off one thing before you leave the house, outfit-wise. First of all, what kind of vague suggestion is that? One thing? So take off your pants? What if you just take off one shoe?

Be more specific!

Second of all, I think that's advice for people who are afraid of being too much. And on that day, I was by myself, skating, and happy to be too much.

I wasn't in school. There was no Principal Lynde, no Tanner or Sarah, around to say otherwise.

So I was going to be Very Anne that day.

And I was happy about it.

Millie has a theory that if you *think* about someone not being there, it kind of summons them into existence. Like if you're waiting for the bus and you realize you need to grab something at home and you think, *Oh, I hope the bus doesn't come yet*, it's sure to arrive.

And so, it was not surprising that just after I had that thought, I heard, under the amazing beats of music in my ears, a horn blasting behind me.

I looked over my shoulder and spotted a blue pickup truck, its chrome nose blinking in the sun, a cloud of dust kicking up beneath its wheels. I was about to slow down when I saw the head of the person in the passenger's side, leaning out the window.

Even from a distance I could see it was Tanner, his hands cupped around his mouth, like he was yelling something.

At me.

What he was yelling I couldn't hear over the music, but I could guess.

I pushed my headphones off my ears and the roar of the truck's engine got much, *much* louder. The road stretched out in front of me, with nothing but empty fields on either side, except for a ways ahead where there was a tree line.

I bent my knees, feeling the wobble of my wheels as I tried to pick up as much speed as I could on Greenville's pothole-ridden roads. All I could hear now was the pop of stones under rubber, the scratch and grate of my vinyl wheels on the road.

Unfortunately a truck is always going to beat roller skates in the rock-paper-scissors of who's faster.

Before I could catch my breath, the truck blasted past me so close I felt the spray sting of gravel on my legs, and the *whoosh* of something else sailing past my ears. What felt like it could have been a hand, reaching toward me.

Without thinking, I dove off the side of the road, into a set of what I suppose were bushes—very prickly green things that were more stick than leaf. I rolled, I would say athletically (but maybe not), onto my side and scrambled to unlace my skates as I heard the burning noise of a truck screeching to a stop on the road.

I picked up a skate in each hand and, carrying them like boxing mitts, tore off in my stockinged feet into the trees.

I ran until my heart exploded, past trees and shrubs and through some tall grass, until the ground started squinching under my socks and I heard, over the sound of my gasping breaths, the trickle of what must have been a creek.

At some point my heart popped out of my chest and I stopped, because you want to stop when that happens.

I turned to face my pursuers. And they weren't there.

"Well, fuck," I gasped, sinking to the ground. Which was surprisingly lush, like some sort of fairy garden type thing, mossy and pillowy.

"They wanted to scare me," I panted, talking to no one. "I'm okay. They just wanted to scare me."

Mission accomplished.

I lifted my feet. My socks were torn to shreds, but my feet were shockingly intact, if throbbing and distinctly pink in hue. The trickle of water was clearly coming from somewhere on my left. In the interests of a soothing foot bath, I hobbled in that direction with my skates slung over my shoulder, until I found the tiny stream of water winding its way through a road of slimy green rocks.

I sank down on the edge, peeled off my now full-of-holes socks, and lowered my feet to the cool water with an audible sigh of relief only the crows in the trees heard. After a few minutes of the water swirling around my toes, my heart was finally beating a reasonable number of beats per minute. I peeled my wrist cuffs off and shoved them in my pocket. Lowered my fingers to dangle in the water along with my feet, which had started to pulse.

"Okay, Greenville," I grumbled, "I have to say. Like, don't be mad because I don't think I can take any more of your wrath, but, okay, I'll admit it, I'm starting to give up on you."

I looked up to the sky through the trees. "Don't tell anyone else this, like don't tell Lucy or Millie or Berry, but I'm, like, just up to *here* with trying to get you to not hate me and feeling like every good thing I get comes with something horrible. Like. I feel like you owe me some sort of sign."

I clarified. "A *good* sign."

I paused. "Okay, I mean this creek is nice. Don't get me wrong. The world needs water to live, I get that. But at this point I feel like it needs to be something bigger than just water for my aching feet. You know? Like I need something that's a reason to keep trying. I don't want to ask for a miracle but—"

There was, I-swear-to-disco, a perfectly timed loud splash, and suddenly there it was, over my left shoulder.

A horse.

Is that a miracle?

No. Obviously. Horses, like rivers, are naturally occurring phenomenona. But there is something poetic about seeing a horse staring at you with its big brown eyes. . . .

Until you see the saddle hanging off its side like an awkward fanny pack for a horse if horses wore fanny packs.

I held out a tentative hand.

"Hey, buddy," I said, not knowing to whom I was speaking.

The horse bowed its head, stepping through the water and gently pressing its nose into my palm. Which had never happened to me before.

Now I had my miracle.

I just needed to find the rider.

And I was pretty sure I knew who that was.

SIXTEEN

Horses are not like dogs in ways that are both obvious and kind of annoying.

Like if it *was* a dog, I feel pretty sure you could ask it, "Hey, where's your mom/dad/owner? Please take me to them." Although I don't know if Monty would take you to *me*, if you found her somewhere wandering on her own. I think Monty would just wag her tail and look at you expectantly and then walk in a circle and lie down.

As soon as I reached up to take hold of the reins, the horse jerked its head like I'd insulted its favorite band and let out an angry whinny.

"Okay, okay. Uh, easy. I'm not going to hurt you."

As I took another step forward, the horse stumbled backward again like I was waving a firecracker in its face. At which point I realized I was kind of dressed like a glittery flag.

"I get it," I said, my voice calm and quiet. "I'm dressed up. It's fringe. Not everyone likes fringe."

I lowered my arms and stood quiet and still for what felt like hours, until finally, I think looking for an apple, the horse stretched its head out toward me. Slowly I reached out my hand and closed my fingers around the reins.

I was a girl with a pair of roller skates and a horse and nowhere to go.

At which point I realized, because I'd been calling out for good signs, that while this horse felt a little fortuitous for me, it was also, very possibly, a bad sign for whoever was riding him before I found him in the river.

Wait. Him?

I looked.

Yep. Him.

"Hey, friend." I put my palm on his neck, which was sweaty. "Are you Gilly's horse? You look like Gilly's horse. You wouldn't happen to know where she is, would you?"

It was very difficult to tell if the look I got back was a murderous look or a disinterested one. Like when Monty does something even *slightly* bad, you can see it in her eyes immediately. I guess horses are like cats, that way; cats being the most duplicitous and hard-to-read creatures on the planet. (Bjorn comes and demands pats just minutes after barfing on my bed, and you can't tell at all that he's done something wrong.)

I took hold of the saddle, increasingly off-kilter as it continued to slide around the horse's . . . waist? So it was almost under his belly. Upon closer inspection, one stirrup was unbuckled and looked like it had been . . . pulled.

Lending a little bit more than a bit of worry to the situation.

"Where is Gilly? Huh, buddy? You remember? Is she okay?"

As if on cue, the horse, aka Buddy, turned and started charging through the woods, yanking me along with him. As I tried to keep up and not get trampled, a million images flashed through my brain, none of them good. What if Gilly was lying on the ground with a broken neck or something? I mean, I thought this as someone whose mother (or one of them) is convinced that roller-skating means at *some point* I'm going to end up brained on the side of the road.

Which I'd always thought—until today—was an overreaction.

I scanned the distance for signs of a reason for alarm.

Clearing the thicker trees, we broke out into a field of tall grass. At which point I spotted the first clue; a lone riding boot in the mud.

Crap.

I cupped my hands to my mouth, "GILLY!"

The horse picked up the pace, basically dragging me over the grass as I ran next to him, my heart beating as I searched.

"GIL-LY! GIIIIIIIIIIILLY!"

A distant voice carried over the breeze. "Hello?"

My feet sinking into the mud, I yanked on the horse's reins, which apparently you shouldn't do because he gave me a really dirty look, but still . . .

"Gilly?"

"Uh, yeah?" a small voice called back. "I'm here! Can you see me?"

At first she was just a little blond bump on the horizon that, as we got closer, became a person sitting on the ground, like a doll that had been dropped there.

She was covered in dirt; it was in her hair and on her face and caked on her clothes. She had her helmet, also covered in mud, in her lap, her legs stretched out; one sock, one boot (to match the one in my hand). Her eyes peered out from the mud, two lights of brilliant blue.

"Hey!"

"Hey!"

"It's Anne," I said, because I am the most awkward.

"Uh." Gilly smiled a dirt-covered tired smile. "Yeah, I know."

"Um." I held up the horse's reins. "I found your horse."

Gilly smiled bigger. "I see that. Thanks."

(I just want to pause here really quickly to say that I don't buy into damsel-in-distress tropes. Okay? I was raised by two queer women.

I know that the notion of a woman needing to be saved as a motivator for the protagonist is really just contributing to the romanticization of women as victims, and the whole thing takes away from women's, or really anyone other than a cis white male protagonist's, agency.

I get that.)

Anyway! I just didn't want you to think I was, like, all happy to be *rescuing* Gilly.

Except that I was clearly feeling just really elated, not just that she was okay, but that I was standing there and she needed my help.

Don't tell Millie and Lucy.

"He fricking slipped in a puddle and took off right past the fence." Gilly threw her hands up, revealing palms also caked in mud. "I fell out of the saddle and I couldn't get my foot out of the stirrup, so he basically just dragged me through the mud for like thirty feet."

"Oh my gosh! Does that happen, like, a *lot*?"

Why do people ride horses if *that* can happen?

"Yeah, I mean, it can." Gilly pulled a twig out of her hair. "I lost my phone too, so I'm really glad you came along. You're kind of a lifesaver."

I leaned down next to her and watched with alarm as she winced. "Are you, like, hurt? Like broken bones or anything?"

"I think my ankle's sprained." Gilly leaned back. "And I scratched my leg pretty good."

That's when I saw.

Blood.

A huge spot of blood on Gilly's pant leg.

Hurk!

A swell of familiar nausea washed over me.

Gilly's eyes popped open in alarm. "Are *you* okay?"

"Oh, I, uh." I attempted to take a deep breath. I closed my eyes and tilted my head toward the sky, like someone trying to surface from a very deep dive.

Please, oh please, Anne, do not pass out. Not in the middle of this possibly heroic moment. Not that it has to be heroic or that that means Gilly is a victim—

"You look, like, not okay." Gilly leaned forward to touch my shoulder. "You look kind of green."

The dissonance between the feeling of Gilly touching my arm and the feeling of deep vertigo was *Alice in Wonderland*-ian.

"Really?" I took shallow breaths. A wave of cold washed over my face. "Um, sorry I, just a second, just."

"Oh!" I heard Gilly shift. "Oh, are you, like, scared of blood?"

Yes.

"Um. A little? I'm so sorry; that's so super embarrassing."

Please don't barf, please don't barf on Gilly, Anne, I beg you.

"What? Ah!" Gilly cried. "Okay. Just, um, just hold on a second." There was some scuffling. "Hold on."

"Holding."

"Um."

"Once again, I'm so sorry about this." I could feel myself listing to the left. "This is obviously not cool. I mean, *you* are in need, and I am kind of not being helpful right now and I get that."

There were some more indecipherable noises then. "Okay. You can look now."

I opened my eyes, cautiously. There was Gilly Henderson. In her bra. With her T-shirt covering her bloody ankle. Looking like a little nervous and . . .

HO. LEE. SHIT. SHE WAS IN HER BRA.

I actually stumbled backward, like someone hit me with a pillow. Or. Something. I could feel myself blushing like mad. "Oh, uh. Yes. Um. Yes, that's fine."

And of course because I was being so cool, let's be honest, I'd been cool this whole time, but now, like, epically cool, then GILLY felt awkward.

She crossed her arms over her chest. "Is this a problem?"

"*No*, not it's not—"

"Do you need me to put my shirt back on?" Gilly looked around.

Just then the horse let out a *massive*, loud . . . neigh? Like this guttural metallic horse scream.

"Oh, shut up, *George*, you ridiculous nightmare horse!" Gilly cut him off. "This is all your fault!"

George responded with something like a wet sneeze that, if it were a word, would be spelled, "PBBTBTBTBTBTBTBBTBTTT!"

"PAH!" I couldn't help myself. I started to laugh.

It was like the dam broke. For five minutes after that, we were just sitting in the dirt, laughing our asses off.

"Oh my God, I am so weird," Gilly moaned. "No wonder my horse is such a weirdo."

"What?"

"This whole day is ridiculous!" Gilly's shoulders curled forward. "I just took my *shirt* off!"

"So? It was so I wouldn't throw up on you!" I said. "Who's awkward there? Hello? Me?"

"You're like the opposite of awkward." Gilly sighed.

"Well, you're one of the few people who thinks so," I said, getting to my feet. "Can I help you back to your house or something?"

"Yeah. I mean, thanks."

"Do you have someone you can call?" I asked.

Gilly held up her empty palm. "I lost my phone?"

"Oh, right! Duh. You said." I pulled mine out of my pocket. Dead. "Okay, well, that's not going to work."

Gilly looked up at me with those blue eyes. Which had flecks of gold in them. Just saying.

"Do you think you can manage the walk?" I asked. "If I help you?"

"Yes."

It took a few minutes to get Gilly up off the ground, and another twenty minutes of a three-legged crawl to get back to her house, with George trailing, unimpressed, behind us. For most of it, Gilly was surprisingly quiet, which I took to mean that she was in pain, but as we got closer to her house, I felt her eyes on me.

"What? Are you okay?"

"I just— I can't believe you're helping me," she said quietly.

"Why wouldn't I help you?"

"Because," Gilly said, mostly to her stomach, "they were terrible to you. I mean, *we* were terrible. The sign-up sheet? I honestly didn't know what they wrote. But I knew they were doing something. I shouldn't have, you know, helped them."

I didn't want to say, "Yes, you were mean," because I didn't want

Gilly to feel bad, but I didn't want to say "No," because it wasn't true. I didn't know what to say, so I said, "This is your place?"

It was a ranch just beyond the meadow. The house was big and beige and had a paddock and a barn in the front, with loads of different machines parked, and maybe forgotten, on the front lawn. There was one of those lawn mowers you ride. Two bicycles. A wading pool that was cracked up the center.

"That's all my little brothers' stuff," Gilly said. "They're at some sports thing."

George moseyed past the house and through another gate toward what looked like a barn.

"He okay?"

Gilly sucked in a sliver of air. "He's fine for now. I'll get my dad to—"

Oh, right, my caution sensors clicked on. A *dad*.

On cue, as we opened the door, a big voice boomed from inside, "GILLY?!"

Gilly's dad was a giant silver-haired man in a flannel shirt. He bounded over, eyes filled with worry, a dishrag in one hand. "Where have you been? What happened?"

As he stood in front of us, I had to actually tilt my head back to take him in. He looked like a muscular Santa. He was as wide as Gilly was thin, with hands like baseball mitts. The cloud of silver hair on the top of his head was distinct from the mostly cropped hair I'd seen on other men in Greenville.

"George bolted," Gilly explained as her father paused to, I imagine, take in the fact that Gilly was in her bra. I smiled a smile I hoped communicated that I was not necessarily (although I was) responsible for the lack of shirt. "Also this is . . . Anne. She found George in the woods and basically saved me."

"Hi." I waved. "I mean. I *found* Gilly. I wouldn't say *saved*."

"That *damn horse*!" her father boomed. Then, resetting, he turned to me and said, "Thank you, Anne, for saving my daughter from her horse, who I'm going to go shoot."

"Dad! That's not funny," Gilly huffed.

"Not meant to be," her father said as he reached out to take his daughter's arm.

"Also don't let Anne see the blood on my leg," Gilly noted.

"Or I'll barf," I added.

Gilly's father's gaze darted between me and his daughter. "Right," he said finally, carefully putting Gilly's arm over his shoulder. "Well, why don't we get you on the couch and then I'll get that damn horse back in his stall before he breaks his neck."

We got Gilly to a sofa in a living room full of big stuffed couches and a television bigger than any television I'd ever seen in my whole life. Like a wall of TV. Her father brought her a bag of frozen peas and a stool and then ran out the door. I grabbed a stray sweatshirt on a chair and handed it to Gilly.

"Do you"—I looked over my shoulder to give her privacy and to see if her dad was going to bound back in the door—"want me to go?"

"OH," Gilly said. "Do you want to stay for, like, a snack or something? Or will your moms worry?"

"No. I can stay." I pulled out my cell. "Can I charge my phone?"

It was entirely possible Lucy was home and wondering if I was sitting in the woods with a sprained ankle.

"Yes." Gilly brightened. "You can charge your phone and then possibly have a snack?"

"Do you have, like, awesome snacks?" I teased. "I feel like you keep pushing the snacks."

"Hospitality." Gilly pointed at a chair. "Have a seat. My dad will get us something when he gets back. My father is also very into snacks."

He was. As soon as he got back, he made us both root beer floats in mugs I initially mistook for pitchers. Also, whose idea was it to put ice cream in root beer? It's genius!

"Thanks, sir," I said as I took the glass.

"Just call me Bob," he said, moving toward the doorway. "You kids relax. I'm going to call the doctor."

So there I was, on a Saturday, in the living room of Gilly Henderson, getting a pretty solid ice cream headache.

I didn't want to move because I thought if I moved the whole thing would turn out to be a very weird but amazing dream. Although, as soon as I got a wisp of a charge I sent my parents a quick "I AM OK" message.

"So." Gilly took a long slurp. "I just wanted to tell you. I thought your audition was really compelling."

"Really?"

"Oh yes," Gilly gasped. "Your singing, the acting. It was amazing. It was just very professional."

"Wow."

"Now, I'm just blathering on." Gilly looked down at the couch.

"What? No. That's all really nice things to say," I said. "I was going to tell you that you did really great too!"

"Thanks." Gilly sloshed the last bits of ice cream around in her mug. "I liked the song too. The one you sang. What was it?"

" 'I Will Survive.' "

"Really?" Gilly looked momentarily confused. "It didn't . . . sound like 'Survive'?"

"Possibly you're thinking of the Destiny's Child song 'Survivor'?"

Gilly dropped her forehead into her hand and groaned.

"It's okay!" I leaned forward, sloshing root beer on my leg. "Lots of people mix those two up . . . I bet."

I mean no, but.

"I'm ridiculous."

"You're really not. And, actually, in my house I get in, like, deep shit for saying stuff like that, so, yeah. You are *not*."

There was a light knock on the door as Gilly's father stepped in. "Doctor says he can see you in twenty. All right?"

He turned to me. "You need a ride home, um, Anne?"

"Oh sure." I stood up and took Gilly's mug. "I'll just put this stuff away?"

As I walked to the kitchen, I felt Gilly's father hovering. I moved to the sink to deposit our formerly frosty glasses.

This is it, I thought, *this is where the whole thing turns and now that Gilly's safe he's going to say something crappy.* Or something.

My brain flashed to an angry email to Lucy: "THAT GIRL TOOK OFF MY DAUGHTER'S SHIRT AND ALMOST BARFED ON HER LEG!"

"I don't need a ride if you need to get to the hospital," I offered, spinning around and leaning, somewhat defensively, against the counter. "I can walk. It's totally fine. Or I can call my moms."

He was holding out a pair of purple rubber Crocs. "I just thought you'd like something on your feet," he said. "Don't want your moms thinking I'd let a kid out there with no shoes."

"Oh." I took the offering. "Sorry. Defensive. That was weird."

Gilly's father rubbed his beard as I slipped the Crocs over my totally trashed socks.

"Thank you," he said. "Thank you for bringing her home."

"No problem."

"Right." He clapped his hands and turned to leave the room. "Okay, Gilly! Let's get you loaded up!"

Gilly's dad had a massive black truck that Gilly could sprawl out in the back of. I sat up front once I'd managed to climb up into the seat.

"Hey! What were you doing out in the woods when you found George?" Gilly called forward once we were on the road.

"Skating," I said, "I mean, I was skating. Then I . . ." I looked in the rearview mirror. "I had a little detour."

"Oh." Gilly twiddled her fingers. "Like how? Did you get lost?"

"Not exactly."

We were quiet for a while. I looked off and out the window as we coasted up to my front door.

Maybe Gilly didn't want to hear what I had to say about who I thought ran me off the road.

Her friends.

Like even with the apology, only coming from her BTW, she was still their friend.

"Thanks for the ride, uh, Mr., uh, Bob." I opened the door.

"Nothing doing." Gilly's father put the truck in park. "Thanks for saving my kid, Miss Anne."

Gilly rolled down her window as I stepped onto the lawn.

"Thanks," Gilly said, resting her chin on the window ledge. "For everything. Thanks."

"Nothing doing." I gave a little bow.

A wisp of her hair swooped over her face as another tendril floated up and out of the window like a kite string.

Gilly waved. "Bye!"

"BYE!"

And they drove off. And I headed up the walk to the sound of Monty barking her head off and my heart beating out of my chest.

I had a bunch of messages on my phone, which I'd completely forgotten I'd charged. Two were from Millie, wondering where I was and asking me to clean my room. Two were from Lucy, a little more frantic and wondering where I was and why I wasn't answering my phone.

The rest were from Berry.

BERRY
Hey!

BERRY

Sorry was being weird earlier.

BERRY

About when Gilly stood up for you?

BERRY

I have kind of a weird history with her?

BERRY

It's fine though

BERRY

Do you want to come over?

Weird history with Gilly? Geez, was nothing in Greenville simple?

SEVENTEEN

Millie and Lucy came out in the eighties, which Millie has often pointed out to me was an easier time to be gay than previous decades, but it was also when it was still entirely possible that if you thought a girl liked you, and you were a girl, it could be, as Millie said, "complicated."

Like Millie actually got beat up once for liking a girl, by the girl's two older brothers. I mean, she still dated the girl, in high school, but that part clearly sucked.

So, obviously, in some sociopolitical ways, liking someone of the same gender (let alone having a gender that doesn't neatly fit into the binary) is easier now than it used to be. And in other ways it's just endlessly complicated. Because no matter what decade you're in, it's still HIGH SCHOOL.

High school goes out of its way to live up to its reputation of being a place that makes everything miserable, in my humble opinion. Every choice in high school feels like you're in a horrible reality game show.

Like all night, after I apologized to Millie and Lucy and then explained what happened and then took Monty for a walk, I was wrecked with indecision about what to do next. I mean, was I supposed to text Gilly after she and her dad dropped me off? Or was that whole thing her saying that she and me were friends? Like maybe she liked me in a way that we might end up being friends because that's what happens when people go through strange and awkward situations together?

I mean, Danny and I became friends when I accidentally superglued myself to his desk. Maybe that's not the same thing.

I did tell Danny what happened and *he* said I should text Gilly, but I don't think either gay male or Chicago rules apply to any relationships in Greenville.

Then I started and erased two texts to Gilly which said something along the lines of: *Hey! It's Anne! Hope your ankle is okay. Would be totally cool to hang out. Do you want to?*

Plus there was the whole Berry thing. What did Berry mean? What was complicated? Was Berry, like, with . . . Gilly at some point?

Was that just me projecting? Should I definitely not say anything to Berry about "rescuing" Gilly?

The next morning Gilly wasn't in class.

Berry showed up in a set of coveralls solidly splattered in pink, with pink paint in her hair and on her nose.

"Were you painting this morning?" I asked.

"Oh." Berry looked at her arms. "Yeah."

"You paint in the mornings? At the mini putt?"

Berry nodded, then, with a little furrow of her brow, changed the subject. "I heard you saved Gilly from the woods yesterday after she fell off her horse and sprained her ankle."

I plopped my books down on my desk. "HOW do you know that?" She sprained her ankle? My stomach flipped. Was she okay?

"Small town," Berry noted. "I also heard you were in your socks."

"Okay, that is super detailed."

"So, what happened?" Berry slid into her seat.

"It's actually a long story." I pulled out my geography book, "It was a whole horse thing."

"George?"

"Yes! How do you know her horse's name?"

"That's what she always names her pets," Berry said just as Mr. Hempher stepped to the front of the class and started writing our assignments on the board.

"All right, everyone, pipe down," he warned.

Berry opened her book and began turning the pages with great concentration and precision.

Curiously Tanner and Sarah were also both absent, which honestly was a kind of magical blessing. Maybe they were helping out Gilly with her sprained ankle? Maybe they were no longer needed to be the villains of my story now that I had taken my place in Greenville High Broadway fame?

No. Obviously.

But it was nice to at least have a lunch in peace. I lingered over the pizza in the cafeteria line, but chose yogurt instead because I'm not a fool. Once we'd settled into a lunch spot on the steps, I slipped in *my* big, curious question. "So, uh. What was complicated? With you and Gilly?"

Berry was sitting cross-legged on the steps with her skateboard on her lap, wheels up, a bag of chips in one hand. She spun the plastic wheels on her board as she munched.

"We were friends, I guess." The wheels spun under her fingers. "When we were little. Like grade two and up. We used to hang out and stuff. I used to horseback ride too, and we had lessons together."

Gilly and Berry used to . . . ride together?!

"Then she started being friends with Tanner and Sarah, that whole crew. And we just kind of . . . stopped being friends."

"Wait, what? Why didn't you say that? Like earlier."

"I mean, isn't it kind of obvious I had some friends when I was a kid?" Berry crumpled her chip bag and shoved it in her pocket. "I told you what they're like."

She snuck a gauging glance my way. I think my mouth was hanging open.

"Whatever," she said hurriedly as she scrambled to her feet, "it's fine."

"Sounds like it sucked, though." I tried to catch Berry's eye. She bent down to tie her bootlace.

"Yeah, well, a bad friend isn't a friend, right?" Berry straightened and tossed her skateboard on the walk in front of the steps. Then she hopped down the steps two at a time and leaped onto the board in a flow of motion. With a solid pump and a flick of her foot, she zinged around a flock of stray cheerleaders before looping back.

"That sucks," I said, picking up where we left off.

"Yeah," Berry said, kicking her board up into her hands. "I mean, we were twelve or whatever. It's just, like, weird. I guess. So." She spun her board on its nose. "Do you still want to hang out or . . . ?"

I jumped to my feet. "Berry! Oh my gosh of *course* I want to hang out. I mean. Of. *Course.*"

Berry let her board drop to the ground. "Sure."

Suddenly I wanted to give Berry a hug. But she picked up her board and held it across the front of her body. Like maybe she didn't want one.

I shoved my lunch stuff in a bag. "Let's hang out tomorrow, okay?"

The bell rang. "Sounds good." Berry waved as she headed off to band practice. "Break a leg!"

"You're saying that to someone who will probably be in a flying apparatus."

"I know."

The fact that it was first day of rehearsals, to me, explained Mr. Davidson's formal attire, which I had been admiring since I spotted him in the hall that morning; a waistcoat with matching blue coat and pants, and cowboy boots. I thought he looked pretty impressive, and honestly, I was sad I hadn't gone for my green A-line go-go dress with matching tights (which would have been more Peter Pan).

The rehearsal was in the music room, a big wooden room shaped like a shell that smelled like sweat and reed. I was there early, because that's my deal, and the rest of the cast trickled in as the minutes ticked by after last bell, everyone looking nervous. I did notice that Minnie Delain, the girl who was going to play Tinker Bell, arrived at rehearsal with her own wings, which she carried under her arm and then, gently, placed on the seat next to her.

"Wow! Those are really cool," I cooed, transfixed by their rainbow glow.

"I made them myself," she said, touching one of the gossamer edges with a finger.

"Coat hangers?"

"Craft wire." She turned. "You think coat hangers will hold better?"

"I mean—"

"Hello! Hello!" Mr. Davidson strode in with a tray of green sparkly treats, holding them up on his shoulder like a fancy waiter. "I assume everyone is ready to participate in the magical art of live theater?"

Clearly.

By the time we all had a treat and a copy of our scripts, we were still about five cast members short. Mr. Davidson looked at his watch.

"Well," he said, grabbing his clipboard, "where are our Wendy and Hook? I wonder. Who else are we missing?"

I was going to suggest that maybe Gilly was out because of her ankle, when the door opened. Tanner, Sarah, and John, and another kid I recognized from the auditions stood in the doorway.

"Mr. Davidson?"

Mr. Davidson stood. He made a move to his plate of treats then pulled his hands back. He turned and took in the group standing at the door.

"You're late," he said, looking at his watch again.

Sarah stepped forward. She was wearing her *Our Town* dress. Which to me was a weird choice, but maybe to Sarah in that moment it wasn't an *Our Town* dress. "We're protesting. The play."

"Shit," Minnie whispered.

The other kids squirmed in their seats.

"Okay." Mr. Davidson tapped the toe of his boot on the floor. "I'm not clear as to exactly what that means."

"We are not participating in rehearsals until the"—Sarah paused and looked up at the ceiling like something was written there—"inequity of this situation is addressed."

Mr. Davidson sighed. Like the air was coming out of his suit a little. "Are you all *quitting* the play?"

"No." Tanner had maybe the first serious look I had ever seen on his face. "We're just protesting. So. We're not quitting."

This made me legit wonder if Tanner really did want to play Hook.

"Well, then." Mr. Davidson gave a nod. "Thank you for letting us know, Sarah, your group's intentions." He moved to see who else was in the hallway. "You may all go."

Tanner and Sarah exchanged glances. Sarah pressed her lips together.

"Mr. Davidson?"

"Yes, Sarah."

"We will have our demands to you shortly."

"Very well." Mr. Davidson let out another sigh. "Thank you."

As they disappeared down the hallway, the rest of us were finally free to quietly freak out, since we'd all been sitting there frozen for the past five minutes.

Mr. Davidson dropped into his chair, unbuttoning his top button. "All right." He tapped the copy of the script with his finger. "Go home and memorize your lines and we'll be ready to go for our next rehearsal. Okay? We'll figure it out."

Chairs shuffled and squeaked. Minnie picked up her wings and tucked them back under her arm.

"Bye, um, Anne?"

"Yeah, bye, Minnie?"

"Yeah."

I felt cemented into my chair. I'd grabbed a treat earlier and now it was melting in my sweaty palm.

I mean, with all that was happening, what was I wondering?

I was wondering if Gilly knew about this and why she hadn't texted me.

"Anne?" Mr. Davidson's boots clicked across the floor. "You all right?"

"Oh, I'm just . . ." I pulled out my skates. "It's just too bad."

"Well," Mr. Davidson muttered as he rewrapped his treats. "That's Greenville for you, isn't it?"

"Is it?"

Mr. Davidson shook his head, like he'd suddenly remembered who I was. He put on a warm smile. "It will be fine. Just a little fuss."

"Protest is an important part of any democracy," I said as I pulled my skate lace tight.

"Well then, Greenville is very democratic today." And with that, he scooted his treats into a canvas bag along with his scripts.

As I got to my feet, he turned in the doorway. "Don't let Lynde see you on those in the hall."

"I won't."

"And tell your mother I said, 'Hang in there.' Tell her I said Greenville's bark is worse than its bite. Tell her I say that as a queer who's lived here all his life."

I didn't know what that meant until I got home, where I found Lucy and Millie were on the receiving end of democracy at work.

"What's happening?"

Lucy was sitting with her laptop on her lap, a glass of wine in one hand, half-empty. "Don't worry about it," she said, swirling her wine.

"Tell her." Millie got up and pointed me to the seat next to Lucy.

"This is school business," Lucy said, lowering the cover on her laptop.

"It's her school too," Millie said, guiding my shoulder. "Show her."

I sat down on the couch. Lucy drained her wine and then opened her laptop. "I'm not reading you who wrote these," she said. "This is confidential."

I didn't need to see the emails to know who they were from.

EIGHTEEN

There were a lot of emails, and they all started the same.

"First we want to welcome you and your family to Greenville and congratulate you on your new position at Greenville High School."

Like laying out the carpet at the entrance of a torture chamber. A "Welcome" carpet to go with the wreaths on every Greenville front door, wreaths like the one Lucy had added to our door a day earlier—one with a little tiny birdhouse on it.

Then the tone took a hard right into terse.

"It is with great consternation that I, [insert name of parent here], am writing. I am greatly concerned that since your arrival there has been a shift in values at Greenville. The citizens at Greenville are citizens who value traditions and history. The choice of school play, along with many other choices made under your purview, have all been made in discrimination against the people who have lived in this community for many years. And if this does not change, we will have no choice but to notify the school board."

"It's *PETER PAN*!" I fumed, bolting up from the couch, lightly tripping over a napping Monty's tail and then gathering my footing in time to not crash into the coffee table.

Lucy drained her wine.

"They're just being homophobic and stupid," I hollered. "What, so just because Sarah can't act in anything but *Our Town* no one gets to do anything?! So she gets to say *she's* being discriminated against and then she gets her way?"

"This isn't just about a play." Millie dropped into the love seat.

"I read you the letter so you would know what's going on," Lucy said, clicking her laptop shut, "because this is your school too. But this is my job, and I am going to deal with it."

"How are you even responsible for the play?" I charged.

"School arts is something I look after as part of my administration's duties," Lucy clarified, after a sip of wine. "Under Principal Lynde, of course."

"Can Lynde cancel the play?" I asked.

"I truly have no idea right now what Principal Lynde will do." Lucy looked over at me. She had dark circles under her eyes. "But I will talk to her. And *you*, in the meantime, will focus on school. All right?"

"What about—"

Millie pulled herself out of her chair. "Nope. That's it. For right now. You let your mom handle this. For now . . ." She whistled and Monty popped up like a popped popcorn. "Let's get some burgers."

"Good idea," Lucy said.

"Okay." My insides felt like a knot.

"It's going to be okay," Lucy whispered as she leaned over and grabbed me in a hug.

"Okay," I said, pressing the two tears that came out into Lucy's sleeve.

"HEY! Burgers! Let's go!"

The burger stand was thumping with music and Greenville teenagers by the time we got there. So Vice Principal Shirley and Peter Pan Shirley opted to stay in the car while Millie, who was also the hungriest, went and ordered the burgers and shakes from the counter.

"Mr. Davidson said to say, 'Hang in there,'" I told Lucy, while Monty panted hot dog breath into my face.

"Mr. Davidson is pretty great," Lucy said. "He's lived here his whole life."

"He's a local," I said, "but he has flair."

"Other locals don't have flair?" Lucy mused.

There was a soft tap on the window.

Berry waved on the other side of the glass.

I rolled down the window, shoving Monty back. "Hey!"

"Hey," Berry said. "Uh, hey. Vice Principal Shirley."

"Berry." Lucy put on her cordial principal voice. "Nice to see you."

"Yeah, uh." Berry stepped back, slightly shrinking into her coveralls. "My parents want to say hello. So, here we go." She turned to address the very tall, very hip-looking adults standing behind her. "Okay, say hi and that's *it*."

Berry's father wore faded coveralls. He had a friendly face and the same hair as Berry, only not tied up and green. Berry's mom was a little more Greenville standard in khaki shorts and a Greenville sweatshirt.

"Hello." They waved in sync.

"I'm Harry." Berry's father pointed at his chest. "This is Sophie."

"It's so lovely to meet you *finally*," Sophie gushed, causing Berry to cringe. "We've heard so much about you, Anne!"

I stuck my head farther out the window, which was a little squished because Monty was doing the same. "So much! You don't say!" I waggled my eyebrows at Berry. "Well, that's pretty cool!"

Berry rolled her eyes.

"I know Anne feels the same," Lucy confided, out loud, to everyone within earshot. "She's very lucky to have a friend like Berry."

"I mean, after all she's been through with those other girls." Sophie put a hand on Berry's back, which might have very well been made of fire from the expression on Berry's face. "I was just saying to Harry the other day—"

Millie returned with a tray of burgers, giving Berry time to slip away from her mother's hand and give me a look of solid mortification. I returned the look with a psychic message acknowledging that sometimes we don't want our moms to speak the things they speak.

Other girls. Like Gilly, I assumed.

And then a thin thread of Monty drool dropped onto my shoulder and I pinwheeled back into the car. "GAH! MONT-STER! OH MY GOD, THAT'S SO GROSS!"

"We'll let you enjoy your supper," I heard Harry say as I desperately wiped the pool of drool off my neck with the front of my shirt.

"What a nice family," Lucy sighed. "You're very fortunate to find a friend here so fast."

I nodded, shoving my burger in my mouth before Monty got a chance to slobber on it.

I think the world is a little easier to deal with after you've eaten.

When we got home, Lucy holed up with her computer in the living room, and I pulled out my script for *Peter Pan*. As far as I knew, the show was still on. Mr. Davidson didn't seem like he was giving up, yet.

A few pages in, I started getting a string of very embarrassed texts from Berry.

BERRY
I think we should all thank my mom for making sure our first meeting was as awkward as possible

ANNE
I wasn't embarrassed!

ANNE
Finally I got to meet the only other person in Greenville with any musical taste!

BERRY
Yeah u guys didn't get to compare notes

ANNE
Next time

BERRY
I heard about Sarah's protest!!!

ANNE
Yeah

BERRY
And the emails

BERRY
FYI my mom didn't send one.

ANNE
Good

ANNE
My mom is dealing w it

BERRY
Good

I rolled over on my back into a pile of what could have been either cat or dog hair, which I then had to peel off my body while my phone buzzed.

With a phone call.

A phone call?

"Hey." The voice on the other end of the phone was soft, almost a whisper.

"Hello?"

"It's Gilly."

"Oh! Hey!" My stomach did a nervous flip.

"Is now okay? To talk?"

"Oh. Yeah. Sure." I looked around. Bjorn looked up at me from his spot on my bed. It was that solid cat look of *You are bothering me by just existing.* "Um. How's your ankle?"

"Oh. Sprained. Not too bad, though. So I'll be back in a few days. Just got a little boot cast."

"Great. I mean, it's good it's not broken. Right?"

Then there was literally a one-minute pause where I wondered if Gilly had hung up after giving me an update on her cast.

"I heard about . . . Sarah's protest. About the play?"

"Yeah. That kind of sucked."

There was a shuffling sound in the background, making me wonder if Gilly was alone. "I just think, maybe, like, if you could talk to Sarah, it might change her mind."

My stomach took a pause from flopping around in my insides to drop into my ankles. Like how much did this sound like Gilly's *last* idea, that I should sign up for the play? A suggestion that led me straight into a deluge of homophobic slurs?

"Um." I bit my lip. "Yeah, I don't know. Gilly. I think. I don't think me talking to Sarah is a great idea."

"I just thought—" I could hear Gilly's lips get closer to the phone. Or I was picturing it. "If you talked to her, face-to-face, that it could be different?"

This time it was my turn to sit in silence.

"I mean, it doesn't have to be all bad. You know? If she knew you, instead of just having this idea of you? I mean, I talked to you and I think you're really great. And you're so nice. They don't know that . . . about you."

"Gilly . . ."

"Tanner's having a party, tomorrow, at his house. You could come. I'm inviting you, and then maybe you guys could all talk at the party? Just talk it out outside of school? Or if you don't want to talk, that's also fine. And we could all just hang out together."

So here's the thing. Like, by high school rules and based on my Greenville High experience, there was no way in heck this would work. Sarah Pye and Tanner Spencer were not people who were going to have their minds changed by one of my witty party jokes (although I do have some good ones). But. *But.* If I *could* do this. If it *could* work.

Then wouldn't that fix everything? And make Lucy's life better? And the show would go on? And maybe I could show Berry that Gilly had changed? And maybe she had? Because the person I met a few days earlier in the woods covered in mud was really nice and I liked that person?

And she just said I was "great."

"Hello?"

"Yeah. Okay. Maybe." I shifted slightly in my spot on the bed, sending Bjorn running off in disgust. "Can I bring Berry?"

"Sure."

I couldn't tell if she was happy or not. "Okay. Well. I'll see you tomorrow. At the party?"

"Yeah! I'll text you the address!"

"Okay. Bye."

"Bye!"

Possibly, if you are reading this, you are thinking something along the lines of what Millie says all the time. Which is, just because you have a logic for your actions and can explain that logic at length, doesn't mean that action *is* logical.

Damn Millie and her insights that I can only ever appreciate in hindsight.

So yes, this whole party thing, you are possibly thinking, was a terrible idea.

ANNE
Hey! What are you doing tomorrow?

BERRY
Nothing. Why?

ANNE
Do you want to come to a party with me?

BERRY
A Greenville Party?

ANNE
Yes.

BERRY
Whose?

ANNE
Tanner's?

You would not be alone in that thinking.

NINETEEN

Berry picked me up at my house an hour before the party, arriving just as I was debating whether or not I should wear my velvet tuxedo, which, to me did not seem that dressy. But as it turned out even Berry, who was mostly up for any combination of clothing I could dream up, was wearing what looked like a pretty functional wool sweater over her coveralls and she did not think the tux was a good idea.

"It's already cold out," she said. "The party's probably outside."

"Oh." I looked at the tux. It was velvet but probably not really suitable for outdoors. "Okay, hold on."

Berry sat on the bed and looked around my room. "So Gilly thought you should go to this party and talk to Sarah?"

I pulled my sweater out of my closet. "Yes."

"And does Sarah know you're going to talk to her?"

"I don't know," I admitted, peeling off my tux jacket and yanking the sweater over my head. "But Gilly will be there. Maybe she'll be like a liaison, kind of."

"Right." Berry sounded entirely unconvinced.

"I mean, we go, if Sarah won't talk to us, how much worse can things be than they are now?"

As soon as I said it, I realized it was a ridiculous thing to say.

"We could talk to Sarah and Tanner at school? In your mom's office or something? Like, official?" Berry added, a legitimately good idea.

"Yeah, but Lucy is already, like, dealing with this and if I do it *this* way, then I'm taking it off her plate," I summarized.

"I just think— I mean going to Tanner's house. Like I know you went to Gilly's house. But." Berry stuck her finger into the hole on the thigh of her coveralls. "I don't know, Anne. You know?"

"Hey!" I shoved my foot into a sparkle-covered platinum boot and looked up. "Do you not want to go?"

"Are *you* going?" Berry shifted on the bed.

Bjorn, who was slumbering on my pillow, did not move.

"Yes, I mean, I said I would."

"Then we're going." Berry stood up.

In the car, she clicked on a Tegan and Sara track and turned the volume up. Blasting music as Mato wound through the various roads that got thinner and thinner for every mile we got closer to Tanner's house. When we were almost there, she turned down the music with a click.

And then she was just staring at the driveway as it got closer and closer, like it was a lion's open jaws.

"Hey." I turned in my seat to face her. "Do you want to turn around?"

"Do *you* want to turn around?"

I pulled my hands into my sweater sleeves, already cold. Like, really, it didn't look like a thing that anyone would want to do, drive through that set of tall iron gates.

But I said I would.

And Gilly said she would be there.

"We'll just stay for a few minutes," I offered. "Just to see what it's like, right? Show-of-good-faith kind of thing."

"Sure," Berry said, turning the wheel and passing through the gates. "Few minutes."

At the end of a very winding driveway, Tanner's house appeared, a green-and-white mini mansion surrounded by manicured, well-placed trees. The front of the property was stacked with cars and trucks. Even before we pulled up, I could hear the music blasting outside the window.

"Why are they doing this on a *Tuesday*?" I mused.

"Because there's a big card game that happens at John's parents' house every Tuesday," Berry said, pulling the keys out of the ignition and tucking them in her pocket. "All the Forevers' parents go. And they stay out late."

"OH!"

"Yeah." Berry threw open the door. "Okay, let's go."

Out back, behind the house, the yard was set up with lights and various firepits, with circles of teenagers all gathered in clumps. A giant set of speakers was set up on a big patio table, blasting music with enough bass to plug or unplug your ears.

I looked around, staring at each group I could see from where we were standing, for a girl with crutches and long hair, who I hoped would be there. But was not.

"What should we do?" I asked.

"How should I know? This was YOUR idea," Berry said, shoving her hands in her pockets.

"Why don't we just get the party feel?" I said. "Then we can find Gilly and Sarah and Tanner."

Berry held out her hand. "After you."

Okay, so walking around a backyard full of bad music and people who don't like you or don't know you (although probably they knew me by reputation) was about as fun as you would think. Most of the kids were drunk or drinking, and laughing that loud laugh you do when you're wasted.

And, of course, at the end of the rainbow was Tanner, who was standing with Sarah, a beer in hand, scowling at us as we rounded the corner.

"Hey!" a familiar voice called over my shoulder.

Gilly was wearing a big puffy jacket and a pair of jeans, one leg of which was rolled up to make room for a big gray medical robotic-looking boot. She was on crutches, which I could see were sinking into the dirt as she made her way toward us.

"Hey!" I called back, sounding more chipper than I meant to.

I felt Berry give me a look. "Hey," she said.

"Hey, Berry!" Gilly was out of breath by the time she got to us. She leaned on her crutches. "So, you came! That's great!" She looked over her shoulder. "Okay."

"Yeah," I said. "So should we talk to Sarah?"

Suddenly, behind us, someone let out a long, low burp, which wafted through the air and set the tone for the rest of our conversation.

Gilly's face seemed to freeze as she looked at the source of the burp behind me. "Hey."

"What are you guys doing here?"

I turned, Berry plastered against my side.

"Hey, Tanner. Sarah. Great party." I could feel my cheeks getting stiff as my lips pulled into a nervous smile.

Tanner was wearing (shocker) a soccer jersey and pants. Sarah was wearing a shiny pink coat with little hearts on it. They were both, clearly, kind of wasted.

"So, Sarah," Gilly's voice hiccupped. "Anne actually wanted to talk to you. About the play?"

Anne wanted to talk to you?

Sarah squinted.

"How nice." Sarah's jacket zipped up to her chin in a way that to me looked uncomfortable. "What, so now that it looks like you're not going to get your little play, you want to talk?"

I could hear Berry swallow.

"Ah, no." My eyes flickered toward Gilly. "I just thought maybe we could talk? Since it seems like there's a lot of conflict? Maybe we could deal with it . . . here?"

"Okay." Sarah folded her arms. "So talk."

"Okaaaay." I pressed my arms down by my sides to try and look less defensive despite the *flame of self-defensiveness* coursing through my body. "I know it's maybe weird to have someone new here? In Greenville? And maybe that's part of what's been going on?"

Tanner snorted.

I gritted my teeth. "I'm just *thinking*. We haven't really had a chance to talk through the things we don't get along about? So maybe we're both going off impressions of each other instead of getting to know who we each actually are?"

"What does that mean?" Sarah took a slug of beer.

"Like, you don't really know me," I said.

"Oh my God!" Sarah howled. "What*ever*. Have you ever thought that maybe *you* are the one who's prejudiced against *us*? Like, it *is* possible to be prejudiced against white people, by the way."

Yikes. HUGE YIKES.

The flame blossomed into a roaring inferno.

"I don't think that's exactly what we're talking about here? Look, I just thought"—I could hear the conviction funneling out of my voice—"we could talk instead of bringing our parents into this."

"By 'parents' you mean your mom the so-called vice principal. Who only got her job because she's gay," Tanner added.

Gilly shifted on her crutches. "You don't know that."

Sarah snapped around to face Gilly. "Oh my God, Gilly. Shut the fuck up."

Gilly's face seemed to crumble.

Sarah turned back to face me, holding up a finger in my face. "I am so sick of all this, like, bullshit around like how I'm supposed to treat *you*. As if, like, everyone isn't going out of their way to make you feel special when really you're just a weirdo who dresses weird? Who sings gay songs and so you get the part in the play even though you clearly suck? Like you somehow deserve to be treated special because you're adopted from like China or whatever."

"FUCK YOU!" Berry stepped forward.

I grabbed her arm just as she was about to lunge.

Tanner chuckled, taking a swig of his beer. "Oh right, now Berry has something to say. No one gives a fuck what you have to say, *Blueberry*."

"I give a fuck," I spat. "Come on, Berry. This party sucks ass. Nice firepits."

"Right, I didn't invite you," Tanner slurred, taking another swig from his beer. "So you should probably fuck off now."

I took a step back. "Yeah, I already said we were leaving. Way to swing ahead of the curve."

Without looking, we marched *away*, not *out*. But actually to the edge of Tanner's property, to the edge of an abyss of country-style blackout dark. My legs felt like jelly.

"I'm so sorry," Berry said. "Oh my God, I am so so sorry, Anne."

"Why are *you* sorry?" My heart dropped. "I brought you here. Because I'm clearly a party genius who can tell what parties will be good for negotiating not being an asshole. Like, I'm a complete empty-brain nightmare. And I dragged *you* into it."

Tears streaked down my cheeks. I felt Berry's hand on my arm. Like a cat's paw.

"You know the last time I was here," she said, "it was for Tanner's, like, tenth birthday party? And they had a pony? And it shit everywhere. And Tanner wore a little cowboy outfit. And the pony bit him twice. Once in the back."

"You were here? For his birthday?"

"Back when everyone was invited to birthday parties." Berry looked around. "Yah."

"Did you have to bring a present?" I asked.

"Price of admission." Berry nodded. "I think I brought a puzzle. My dad is big on them."

"Your dad is so cool," I sniffed.

"Sometimes," Berry conceded.

I could feel my heartbeat starting to slow to something less than a frantic marching band.

"Did you ever get a loot bag?"

"A loot bag?" Berry's forehead crinkled. "Like stealing?"

"No! A *loot* bag. Is that what you call it? Like a present you get for going to someone's party," I said.

"I don't think so." Berry tapped her lip. "I think Tanner's mom used to give everyone scented candles to take home."

"And yet, somehow, *I'm* the weird one."

Berry smirked. "I think I might have barfed because I ate too much cake."

"I, as you know, am well acquainted with inappropriate feelings of nausea."

Somewhere behind us a girl started screaming as she was picked up and slung over someone else's shoulder. "LET ME GO! HAHAHAH! YOU DICK!"

"You know who I bet throws good parties," I thought out loud, "I bet you Mr. Davidson throws really interesting parties." I pulled my hands into the sleeves. The air was starting to chill my nose to the temperature of a glass of ice water.

"Because he wears turtlenecks."

"Well, I don't think the fact that he wears turtlenecks means he *doesn't* throw a good party," I said. "I mean, Tanner probably doesn't own a turtleneck, and this party . . ."

"Sucks," Berry finished. "Okay. Look. I'm going in to use the bathroom and then we're getting the heck out of here and go someplace way less horrible. Okay?"

I nodded. "I'm sorry I—"

"Never mind." She grabbed my sleeve, "But you have to come with me."

"Yeah," I said. "You're not going in Tanner Spencer's house alone."

There was a strange gray emptiness to the Spencer house, and not just because everyone was outside. The walls were all white and covered in posed photos of the family in various stiff positions. All the flowers in vases were dried, calcified stiff. It smelled like vanilla the way a house that's forced to smell like vanilla smells like vanilla.

Scented candles, probably, I thought, making my way through the hallways as carefully as possible.

"This place makes me nervous," I said, looking around.

"Imagine coming here when you were six."

"Yikes."

"At least it means I know where the guest bathroom is," Berry mumbled. "I think."

She found the bathroom.

"Okay." Berry ducked through a door. "Don't leave."

I stared at gray furniture accented with pops of bright red that reminded me of blood.

"I won't leave."

Outside the shouting rose and fell like waves. The girl who was screaming earlier was still screaming, and now there were other shouts. Not happy shouts.

Other shouts.

I craned to see out the window at the end of the hall. The yelling was getting louder.

"Berry!" I pressed my face against the door.

"GAH! You scared the shit out of me!"

"Something is happening! Outside."

There was the sudden slap of a screen door being thrown open and footsteps rumbling through the halls.

"There's a fire!" someone shouted. "We can't get it out. Yeah. Spencer place. Yeah. Quick!"

"Tell them to stop pouring booze on it," someone else shouted.

"Berry." I hammered not calmly on the door. *Berry!* It's a fire."

Berry burst out of the door like a superhero about to take flight. "Come on!"

We bolted through the hallways. Outside there was a thick curl of smoke in the air. One of the firepits had tipped over and the flames were starting to spread across the grass. There was a group scattered around the fire. But, like, not necessarily doing anything.

A little ways away, I could see Tanner on his hands and knees, puking. Sarah was patting his back and looked like she was crying. I sprinted to catch up with Berry, who had cut across the green and slipped into a small shed at the edge of the property.

"Take this," she hollered, tossing me a shovel. It was about the same size as me.

Berry grabbed another shovel and then tore back through the grass toward the fire. A few boys were flapping at the flames with their jackets, an act that looked like it was mostly making the fire bigger. Gilly was nowhere to be seen.

Berry stuck her shovel in the dirt near the edge of the fire, then tossed a clump over the flames, which did seem to snuff them out. I did the same.

"Hey!" Tanner screamed, from his puke spot. "What the fuck are you doing to my FUCKING LAWN, you fucking fat COW?" With a strange grace, he wobbled toward us. "You think this is your fucking property?"

"HEY!" I held up my shovel, fully prepared to swing it like a baseball bat. "We're PUTTING OUT the fire. Even though YOU are an ASSHOLE. And you're too much of a pathetic sap to deal with your own SHIT."

"FUCK YOU, ANNE!" Tanner shoved his face into mine.

"NO," I boomed back, "FUCK YOU!"

"TANNER!" someone in the distance yelled. "Someone broke the back door!"

Tanner stumbled backward, disappearing into the crowd. "Fuck you, dykes."

In a haze of smoke, we shoveled clump after clump of dirt on the flames until all that was left was the smell of burnt and beer. The shouts of kids freaking out were suddenly drowned out by the sound of a siren.

Berry tossed her shovel on the ground. "They're here," she said, "let's go."

I handed my shovel to the kid behind me, who turned out to be Sarah. She stared at me, wide-eyed.

"Take it," I said.

Sarah blinked. Her face looked puffy. She took the shovel.

"At some point," I snapped, "you're going to look back at this and realize *you* were the asshole tonight. Whatever other bullshit you want to tell yourself."

"BYE!" Berry added, then burst into a jog.

I ran after her, sliding into her car while she revved the engine. We exited just as the firefighters hopped out of their truck. Little stones spat out from under our tires as we skidded past them and swerved through the open gate to the road.

"Fucking Tanner Spencer, fucking Sarah Pye," Berry muttered, her grip so tight on the wheel her knuckles were little white mountains. "Fucking Gilly Henderson."

"What did she think was going to happen?" I grumbled. "Like, did she really think Sarah was going to listen to me?"

Berry gripped the wheel.

"When you guys stopped being friends, did she say why? Like did you have a fight?"

"No. But Sarah Pye didn't like me, so it didn't take, like, a genius to figure it out. I mean, they made sure I knew without them saying anything."

Two lights appeared in the road ahead of us, which became a large silver truck that was going faster than we were, and slid past us so fast it was gone in a blink.

"Who's that?" I wondered aloud. Maybe it was Gilly.

"Mr. and Mrs. Spencer," Berry said. "Back from poker."

"Shit."

"Yeah."

The soft glow from Berry's headlights lit a dim path along the road. Mato hummed and squeaked as we sat in silence for the rest of the ride until we got to my house.

"Okay," Berry said, shifting into park. "Safe and sound."

"Thanks to you," I added. I cracked open the door. I could hear

Monty barking inside. "You saved the day," I said as I unbuckled my seat belt. "Like, really."

"Yeah." Berry looked down at the steering wheel. "Did you go to the party because you wanted to, like, make peace with Sarah, or because you like Gilly?"

"What?"

Berry's knuckles turned white as she gripped the wheel, "Can I just, like— Do you *like* Gilly? Like *like* her?"

"I don't—" My words stuck in my throat. "I mean, I had this moment where she seemed like someone I could like?"

"Even though she's super mean to you." Berry's voice sounded like cement.

"I mean, Sarah was mean," I corrected.

"Gilly *helped* Sarah be mean." Berry re-corrected.

"But she tried to speak up today. . . ."

"For like a *second*." Berry's voice cracked. "Like one second. And then Sarah said to shut up and Gilly did."

"I guess I felt like . . ." I could feel my palms sweating. "Like maybe there was more to her, than that?"

"Right. Sure. Okay." Berry nodded. "Okay, cool. Well. Good night."

I could feel something in the car, like a blanket of disappointment, as I peeled out of my seat and ducked out the door.

I stayed outside and waited for Berry's headlights to disappear into the night.

"ANNE!"

Lucy stood in the doorway, huffing like she was some sort of ticking time bomb.

"Get in here. Right. Now."

"What? People do parties on Tuesday here," I said, pulling off my sweater as I brushed past her into the house.

Inside, in the light of our living room lamps, it was clear that the color had drained from Lucy's face.

"Did you set Tanner Spencer's backyard on FIRE?"

TWENTY

The most I ever got in trouble was when I was in fourth grade. I had my friend Rebecca over after school one day and decided we should have an "adult tea party."

By which I meant a tea party for *adults*.

Obviously.

I can't remember what movie I or Rebecca had seen that inspired that particular combination of words. It could have been *Alice in Wonderland*. Rebecca had the idea that we should drink from fancy glasses, and it was *my* idea that we should have something the color of tea in those fancy glasses. And I knew just the thing! A bottle in the cabinet of the living room that had the cut-glass surface I prized and often ran my fingers over.

The liquid in the bottle was brown, like tea. Seemed like a solid connection to me. It also, tantalizingly, smelled like almonds.

And, okay, in my defense, I wasn't supposed to use the stove when my moms weren't home and so I thought having what turned out to be amaretto from the cabinet, instead of anything that involved boiling water, was a safe and suitable substitution.

Until a few glasses later when Rebecca barfed on the couch.

In that order.

I, upset, also barfed on the couch.

(Wow this story has way more mention of barfing than I was expecting. Anyway . . .)

At which point Millie opened the door to the sight of two innocent little girls sitting on the couch covered in barf and crying. I immediately confessed once I'd stopped barfing (not that I could hide what had happened because I was literally sitting in it).

Rebecca moved to Maine the next year. To this day I can't drink tea or smell almonds without feeling a little sick.

In *that* particular example, Lucy wasn't the new vice principal of my school. And no one's backyard was on fire. Also, in that example, I did the thing I was in trouble for.

On the night that I returned home from possibly the worst party ever, I could see as soon as I set eyes on her that Lucy was not up to hearing my side of the story. She stalked back and forth across the carpet, making this gesture that involved holding out and stretching her fingers, like she was trying to grab something very big that was hovering in front of her. Millie, meanwhile, sat in her robe, on the couch with a nervous-looking Monty in her lap.

When Lucy finally stopped pacing, I thought *she* might puke, she was so mad. "*Why* were you at Tanner Spencer's house?"

"I was invited to a party by one of his friends," I said. "It's not like I broke in."

Lucy folded her arms over her chest suggesting she might think that was exactly what I did.

"Tell us what happened," Millie said.

"Berry and I went to the party. It was at Tanner's house, which you know. They were all drinking. We were not. We hung out for a bit. I tried to talk to Sarah about the play. She did not want to hear anything I said. She like reverse-racism-ed me. Tanner asked us to go. Berry went to the bathroom. We heard people screaming. We came out and the grass was on fire. Berry got a shovel and *we helped them put the fire out*." I looked from Millie to Lucy. "That's *it*."

I couldn't tell if Lucy was listening. She'd started pacing again halfway through my riveting but succinct story.

"Lucy," Millie said quietly, over the sound of Monty whining.

"Tanner Spencer's father just called." Lucy spun around to look at me, her hands on her hips. "*He* said that you and Berry came to the party *uninvited* and yelled at Tanner and his friends and when they asked you to leave you pushed over one of the firepits."

"I did *what*?" My stomach landed with a splat on the floor.

Millie pressed her lips together.

"*Why* would I do that?!"

Lucy's phone pinged from the couch. She walked over to the coffee table and picked it up. "Well," she said, swiping her screen. "Michael Spencer just followed up with an email. *And* there's an email from Principal Lynde. And the school board."

I could hear all the electricity running through the house. Every buzz coming out of every lamp. I could hear the wind outside. The crickets. The tap of Lucy's fingers on her screen.

"According to Mr. Spencer's message," Lucy said, "Tanner, a girl named Sarah, a boy named John, and a girl named Gilly all saw you start the fire. Resulting in several hundred dollars' worth of damage to his property."

"*Gilly* said that?"

Was that her plan the whole time? To lure me out to Tanner's house? To make everything worse?

"Why?" Millie looked at me. "Who is Gilly?"

I seethed. "Okay, *all* the witnesses are Tanner's friends, Mom. They all *hate* me, so of course they're all going to *lie*."

Lucy was still looking at her phone. "Mr. Spencer said he is considering suing me or the school for damages."

"But I didn't do anything! Berry was there. Berry saw it."

"Well, they're accusing Berry as well," Lucy said, dropping her phone onto the couch. "So, you're both in trouble."

"I'm in trouble," I seethed. "Why am I trouble? I just told you, I didn't do anything."

"You didn't go over there knowing you were going to get in some sort of conflict with those kids?" Lucy asked, her eyes searching my face.

"No." I mean, I did. Ish. But then I believed the person whose idea it was to go over there. I believed it was at least possible that things wouldn't end up a mess.

"I told you to leave it alone. I *told* you." Lucy looked at the ground. "No one wins this fight, Anne. Not this way. Michael Spencer is not going to back down from this. You already have a recorded incident of assaulting Tanner at school."

"With PIZZA!"

"No yelling," Millie snapped.

"You don't even care about my side of the story," I fumed. "You just care about your job."

"I care about *your decisions*." Lucy's eyes got wide.

"Oh, like *you* don't make bad decisions? Like *your* decision to come to *Greenville*? To move us to a place where you knew people would basically hate us? Where there's basically only white people?"

"Anne." Millie held out a hand toward me.

"Anne, look. I . . . I know you're having trouble here," Lucy stammered. "This isn't like other places we've lived before. Okay? That's true. I'm having trouble. Millie is having trouble. We're all having to deal with conflict right now. But it's how we all deal with that conflict."

She held out her hand, ticking off my offenses. "Getting in fights. Yelling at students."

"Yelling?" I screeched. "You mean defending myself?"

Millie got between Lucy and me. "That's it. TIME! Everyone needs to take a breath. Right now."

My body was a bomb. "All I do is go to this stupid school and deal with their shit. And every day they figure out another way to make things worse. For ME. That's MY trouble. And now you're helping them."

"That's not what I'm doing." Lucy's voice hummed with fury. "I'm trying to find a way to make things better."

"We are," Millie added quietly, in what I'm sure was a quiet-voice attempt to get us to stop yelling.

It didn't work.

"Well, it's WORSE now. For me, at least. So, thanks." I turned. "Good night." As I walked away, I tossed a stick of dynamite over my shoulder. A quiet but definitive, "Fucking stupid."

"Fucking *stupid*?" Lucy's voice boiled. "You think being accountable for *your* actions is FUCKING STUPID? You think what Millie and I have to say is fucking stupid?"

"Yeah." I spun around. "I do."

"Well, then." Lucy crossed her arms over her chest. "Then you can pay for the Spencers' lawn. You can pay for the damages, not Berry. YOU! And until you do, no school play, no school activities. You go to class and you come right home."

"WHAT??"

Lucy shook her head. "Until we can manage this, until I know YOU can manage this, you are taking a step back. Because right now we are just—"

"I'm THE LEAD in the PLAY," I screamed. "This play is the ONLY THING I have in Greenville that's mine!"

Lucy pounded her fist in her palm. "This is all TOO much and it is affecting your judgment and your actions and your behavior in destructive ways."

"Lucy," Millie said quietly. "Let's just wait and talk about this tomorrow."

"THIS IS THE ONLY THING I HAVE in this WHOLE HOR-RIBLE PLACE!" My entire face was a scream. "YOU get to have your job and MILLIE gets her art and I get NOTHING!"

"ANNE!" Lucy's voice hit final warning.

My voice filled the room. "FUCK YOUR JOB. FUCK GREENVILLE. And FUCK! YOU!"

The word *you*, as in *you, my parents*, was the main bit. *Fuck* was not as much of a problem in my house. I mean, see above, it's a problem, but it's not a fireable offense. Because Millie believes, or believed, in the freedom of self-expression. But *fuck you* has never been okay.

"GO TO YOUR ROOM!" Lucy screamed.

So, I did.

I slammed the door so hard my corkboard fell off the wall. I put my headphones on, but I couldn't even bring myself to play any music. Because who would want to bring the happiest music in the world into this moment?

I was crying on my bed in Greenville, my clothes still smelling of smoke and dirt.

I texted Berry a hand-waving emoji, but she didn't answer.

ANNE
Hey. Tanner messaged my mom and said we started the fire.

What if Berry's parents were giving *her* shit because the Spencers were trying to get *her* to pay for a lawn she did nothing but save with her hard work after all Tanner's friends could think to do was pour their beers on it? Maybe Berry wasn't texting me because she *was* in trouble because I dragged her to a party because I told her it might be fun and it was the opposite of fun.

ANNE
I really hope they didn't call your parents too.
If they did I'm sorry. I am going to pay for the whole thing. OK?

There was a familiar whining at the door, which I cracked open so Monty could come inside. Downstairs I could hear a back-and-forth of angry whispers. Both Millie and Lucy came from families where their parents yelled at each other. So, with the exception of what had just gone down, both of them almost never raised their voices at each other, at least not when I'm in the house. It should be some sort of signal to them that whenever they do this harsh-whisper routine it drives Monty crazy and she ends up hiding under my bed.

I dragged Monty up *on* the bed with me because what good is a golden retriever if not to comfort you in a moment where everything is terrible?

My phone buzzed.

GILLY
I'm so sorry.

Monty whined.

ANNE
K

GILLY
Really I am!!!

ANNE
Well Tanner just messaged my mom and the rest of Greenville to say that me and Berry set his lawn on fire and you were a witness so maybe I don't want to talk to you right now

I waited for a response. Of course she knew about Tanner. Why wouldn't she? She was *his* friend.

ANNE
Goodnight.

A set of dots appeared next to Gilly's name.
Then they disappeared.
Then they appeared again.
And disappeared.

GILLY
I'm really REALLY sorry.

ANNE
Ok

I curled up on my side. I could hear Millie stomping around in the kitchen. Pots and dishes clattering. Time for a late-night stress snack.

GILLY
☾

I don't know if that meant go look at the moon, but I did. Even though I was mad at her. It was outside my window like a spotlight. Downstairs I heard Millie humming and burning toast, my second waft of smoke on another horrible day in Greenville.

TWENTY-ONE

Berry didn't text me back that night.

I called her twice before I left for school the next day (calling, the last and final straw in communication), but no answer.

I snuck out of the house early—Lucy wasn't there when I got up and Millie was on the phone—and got to school before the bell. I spotted Berry in the parking lot, doing tricks on her skateboard. The sky was gray and annoyed, with little clouds turning into even thicker clouds with every minute.

I ran over, darting around cars. "Hey."

Berry jumped off her board. She was wearing a green sweater with an angry set of eyes on the front. "Hey."

"Did you get my text about the money? The lawn? I'm going to pay for it."

"Yeah." Berry toed her board forward with her boot. "Yeah, my parents were pretty pissed when they got the email."

"I mean, we didn't do it," I said.

"Sure." Berry kicked her board forward. "But we shouldn't have gone to that party."

"I know." I sighed. "And I'm sorry they were shitty to you and I like dragged you into the worst idea ever. Like honestly I got basically screamed at by my parents about it yesterday. Like about 'my choices.' Even though Tanner is clearly a fucking liar."

I guess I expected Berry to be mad about the email, too. She just stared at me like I had a glowing orb on my forehead.

"They're making me quit the play," I added. "Because of the email. And a bunch of other things, I guess. The pizza fight. All that stuff."

Silence.

Horrible, uncomfortable, so thick you could cut it with a knife, silence.

"Okay, well . . ." I took a step backward. "Anyway . . . look, I'm sorry I brought you. And I'm sorry—"

Berry looked at me with stone eyes. "You really don't get it."

"Get what?"

Berry's cheeks turned their traditional bright pink. "You don't have to be sorry that I came to the party with you. I decided to go. I *wanted* to go with you. I *wanted* to make sure you would be okay."

"I know. I mean, thanks. I really appreciate it. I mean, I appreciate, like, everything you do to be a good friend. You're the best friend, Berry."

Berry's eyes flicked up to the sky just as the first drops of rain started falling. "You *don't* get it."

"WHAT?" Raindrops pittered and pattered down on my face.

And trickled down Berry's cheeks.

"Never mind." Berry reached down and picked up her board, the wheels spinning.

Suddenly I was chasing a speed-walking Berry threading through the parking lot. Like she was trying to lose me. "Berry!"

Berry didn't look back. "I need you to give me some space, okay? Please leave me alone."

The rain turned into a torrent as Berry sailed off. Endless sloppy raindrops. And me. Feeling more alone than even that first night in Greenville with the endless dark that would be my new home.

By the time I made it into the school I looked like a wet sponge, and not just because I was wearing yellow head to toe. Yellow, the color of caution, of which I apparently had none.

"Anne!"

I swiveled, my boots squeaking on the floor, to see Mr. Davidson shaking off his umbrella and taking in my yellow faux-fur parka, which was now about twenty pounds of fur and rainwater. "You're soaked. Fuzzy and soaked."

"Yeah." I flapped my arms. "Well. Yeah. Actually. Mr. Davidson. I have to talk to you."

"Let's get you dried off first," he offered, holding open the door to his classroom. "We have a few more minutes before first bell, and I think I have some paper towels in here somewhere."

Magically, he also had a thermos of tea and some cookies, which he spread out on his desk before handing me a wad of napkins. "Help yourself. You look like you need it."

"Uh, I'll skip the tea, thanks." I dabbed at my jacket. "Um. So I have to tell you—"

"You're quitting the play." Mr. Davidson sat down behind his desk. "I got an email from your mother this morning."

"Yes, well," I said, grabbing another sheet of paper towel. "My mom thinks, with everything happening, it's not a good idea. Plus, I basically am being framed for arson right now by a bunch of Forevers, and Berry hates me, which I can't really get into because I will totally lose my sh—stuff, if I do."

"The Forevers?" Mr. Davidson grabbed a cookie. "Who are the Forevers?"

"Like the people who act like they have been here since like the dawn of time," I explained, grabbing a cookie for myself.

"Ah." Mr. Davidson brushed the crumbs from his desk. "I see. Well, I'll be very sad to not have you in the play. I was looking forward to seeing your Pan."

"Will you *change* the play?" I asked, grabbing another cookie because they were really good. Kind of lemony. "Because of the letters. And the parents. Who hate it?"

"Ha-ha, no." Mr. Davidson flicked his hands. "No, I'm not changing the play because the *Pyes* feel ostracized by the existence of art that isn't a direct reflection of their experiences and tastes. This whole thing is a power play to get Sarah the lead, as I'm sure you've guessed. Despite their additional threat to withdraw funding for the costumes and sets, which is a traditional Pye donation to the school, our *Peter Pan will* go on. Trust me when I tell you this is not my first, nor will it be my last, tussle with Ettie Pye."

He winked. "I starred in *our* high school production of *Our Town* with her, did you know that?"

"No!" I wonder if that's where Sarah got her dress.

Or if her mom made her wear it.

He sat back, lifting up his sneakers and placing them on the desk. "You know," he said, "I've been here for as long as any so-called Forever. My family are very pillars-of-the-community types. And for as long as I've been here, there has been a general resistance in this place to anything new."

"Someone else who's also a pillar told me Greenville has a stick up its . . . um . . . behind," I admitted.

Davidson perked up. "HA-HA! Yes. That would be my great-aunt Beverly! Yes, that is her common Greenville Gripe. The stick. Yes."

"Wait. She's *your* great-aunt?" I did some fast math. "So Principal Lynde is your . . ."

"Cousin." Davidson nodded. "Yes. She is also the owner of a stick, but I will deny saying that if you repeat it."

Small towns.

Mr. Davidson took a long sip of tea. "You know, when I was young,

Aunt Bev used to take me to see plays in other cities. We took a trip to New York once and I saw *Guys and Dolls*."

"Really? I love 'Sit Down, You're Rockin' the Boat.'" I grinned. "But I've only seen the movie."

"Marlon Brando!" Mr. Davidson clutched his chest dramatically. "Heartthrob."

"Exactly." I smiled.

"Gosh, that's a great one." Mr. Davidson shook his head. "One day we'll have to put aside some time to compare our love of musicals. OH! And we should invite Beverly. You know she was quite taken with you the day you all came to take her portrait."

The school bell rang. Mr. Davidson gathered up his tea and cookies. Then he looked at me, pointedly. "Don't quit."

"My mom—" I started.

"I'll talk to your mom." He tossed the lot of wet napkins in the bin just as the door opened and students flooded in.

"Okay."

"Come to rehearsal today."

"Okay." I could feel tears stinging the corners of my eyes. "Thank you," I said. "Really. Like. Thank you."

Mr. Davidson waved me off with a gentle flick. "See you after school."

Mr. Davidson, clearly, was one of the few people in Greenville who a person could call a kindred spirit. By which I mean that he was clearly a fellow lover of marvelous things.

I truly hoped he also loved disco.

I skittered out of the classroom and into the hallway, which was flooded with students, a mix of Forevers and locals and probably a bunch of kids in between, jostling and shoving each other down the hall, trying to make it to the other side of the day.

I stepped forward and was swept into the flow, not really sure of anything beyond the one person I needed to find.

Berry.

Who didn't want to talk to me. And by the time I got to homeroom, was nowhere to be found.

TWENTY-TWO

Between looking for Berry and getting full-on glares from Tanner, Sarah, and Gilly for the rest of the day, it was kind of a mess. It was like every second between talking to Mr. Davidson and going to rehearsal was like another pin being pushed into my brain.

Like here's how upset I was:

I ordered pizza for lunch. *Greenville disgusting pizza*. And then I *ate it* by myself, sitting on the still-wet steps writing and deleting texts to Berry.

I mean, look, I take a person's request for personal space very seriously. If someone says they need you to back off, you absolutely need to back off. But there was also the look Berry gave me right before she skated off into the rain. Like I was the biggest numb brain ever. Like, okay, not unlike the look I was sure I was giving Lucy the night before.

So I didn't send the many texts I wrote to Berry.

Meanwhile, I couldn't miss the look Gilly gave me from her seat at the lunch table with Sarah and Tanner and John. Like some fugitive message of concern lobbed at me from inside the fort or something.

I wasn't up for it. Like. Everything was falling apart; I couldn't afford to do one more thing that would take the ground out from under me. Maybe Lucy was right. Maybe all my choices were making everything worse. For everyone.

But then, of course, by that standard, after school I could have just gone home and *not* gone to rehearsal.

But Mr. Davidson seemed so sure. And a sliver of me just didn't want to give up. So I went.

Rehearsals were after school in the chemistry lab, of all places. I guess because the band was in the music room. On the way there I ran into future magical fairy, Minnie, with new and improved wings on her back. And even more eyeliner. It was like her face was morphing into a fairy face more and more every day.

"You look awesome," I cheered.

"Coat hangers!" She pointed at her back.

"They worked great."

"Anne!" Mr. Davidson popped his head out of the doorway of the chemistry lab. "Hey, Minnie! Come on in."

Inside, Gilly and Tanner and Sarah and John were sitting at the chem table at the front of the room. Gilly was kind of folded in on herself. She looked up at me with huge eyes when we walked in. She looked . . . surprised.

"Hi," I said. "Uhhhhh."

Minnie looked around the room. "Awkward," she whispered.

"No." Tanner stood up from his stool, shaking his head. "What the fuck is she doing here?"

"Tanner!" Mr. Davidson clapped his hands together. "I will not have that language in this room."

"You're not supposed to be here," Sarah added from her perch, with a level of assurance that seemed . . . weird.

Like, was the small town rumor mill that strong that everyone already knew the results from my fight with Lucy the night before? We still didn't have curtains up. Was that it?

I scanned Sarah and Tanner's faces, avoiding looking at Gilly.

Or did they just think it was obvious that accusing me of an actual crime would be a solid way of taking Peter Pan away from me?

"Miss Shirley is a player in our troupe." Mr. Davidson closed the door with a decisive click and turned back to the classroom. "And as a member of this cast, she is here for—"

"She also *destroyed* my backyard," Tanner cut in. "There was, uh, major damage? So maybe a destructive person like that shouldn't be allowed to be the lead in a school play?"

I mean, a brief study of the history of actors would say otherwise, but I digress.

Suddenly I could picture Tanner and his dad looking at whatever char spot on their back lawn was left after we put out the fire. I could see Tanner's dad typing the word *damage* into his email. Something about that word was like a kinetic bomb in my brain.

Damage?

To *his lawn?*???

I wanted to jump on Tanner's head and scream.

How about my *lawn, you* jerk? *How about the lawn you and your terrible friends spray-painted and I never even told anyone! Because* I'm *not a dick! And* you are!

But before I could think of jumping or screaming, I felt Mr. Davidson's hand on my arm.

"My original understanding of your initially stated quarrel, Sarah, reinforced by you and your mother's letter and letter campaign," he explained, smoothly, "was that you were concerned that the *content* of the play was not to your standards and was in conflict with the heritage and values of the school. I have addressed these concerns with your mother and with all levels of the school administration at a meeting an hour ago, at which point I noted that *Peter Pan* was one of the first productions at this school, *and* the original production featured a female lead. So this play and its cast are entirely in keeping with our values. And so, we will be performing *Peter Pan*. And Anne will be our lead."

Did that mean he'd talked to my mom? Also, cool about the school's history with *Peter Pan*!

I stared at the side of Mr. Davidson's face. His jaw flexed.

"Okay, yeah, well, it's also clear that she's got some vendetta against us, so maybe it's not okay for her to be in the play," Sarah sniped. "Maybe it's about *that* now."

"That would be a matter to take up outside of this production," Mr. Davidson rebutted. "For the moment, we will continue with rehearsals."

A hot stillness settled over the room. Possibly because I was still bubbling.

"What if *we're* not okay with that?" Sarah said, looking at Tanner.

There was a scuffling on the other side of the door. Like someone was listening? Then, like out of nowhere, Minnie let out a long groan. "Oh, whatEVER, Sarah. Give it a fucking break."

"Language, Minnie," said Mr. Davidson.

Someone else snickered.

"Oh, you think this is funny?" Tanner was dialing his phone. "I'm calling my father."

Taylor, the kid with the drums, sat up. "Can we just rehearse without you calling your *dad*, dude? Like, come on."

"Mr. Spencer." Mr. Davidson's voice was tight. "Please put your phone away for the duration of this rehearsal."

"She fucking tried to set my house on fire." Tanner pointed at me with his phone, which was still ringing. "That's fraud."

Sarah crossed her hands over her chest and bored a glare into my chest. No one said anything about how technically, okay, *if* I had set Tanner's lawn on fire, which I didn't, it would have been arson and not fraud.

Also, come on, that's funny.

Tanner held his phone up to his ear. "Dad?"

"Stop." Gilly pulled herself to her feet. Or foot. Since she was still in her boot. She looked like a small tree springing up from the ground. A tiny tree, but still a tree.

Tanner looked up, seething. "I'm on the phone."

Gilly held up her phone. "Okay, well, tell your *dad* that I have texts from *Sarah* that say some *other* kid knocked over the firepit that night, not Anne or Berry."

"GILLY!" Sarah spun around to stare at her.

Gilly's voice wavered, "T-tell him you told Vice Principal Shirley that I was there, but I wasn't because I went home before the fire even started. And my *dad* picked me up, so he can verify that. Tell him I said I'll show the text to Vice Principal Shirley, Tanner, if you don't stop this . . . now."

Tanner froze, his phone an inch from his cheek. I could hear his dad shouting through the speaker.

Tanner hung up.

Sarah tossed her pages down onto the floor with a slap. "Fuck you, Gilly."

Mr. Davidson swayed slightly. "Oh my" escaped his lips.

Gilly took a deep breath. "No. Fuck you, Sarah."

"OKAY!" Mr. Davidson held up his hands and stepped into the line of rage. "That's enough f-bombs for today. Sarah and Tanner and Gilly, that's at least one too many each, so you can go to the office and pick up a detention slip. Everyone else." He sighed and looked at his watch. "That's a wrap for today. We'll take this up tomorrow. So have your lines memorized."

The Forever crew filed out of the room, each taking a long look at me as they left. Gilly was still struggling with her crutches, which clearly Tanner and Sarah weren't going to help her with anymore.

"Hey." I stepped forward, pulling back a stool so she could get out. "Thanks."

"I mean." She pulled a crutch into position. "It was kind of the least I could do."

"Well, thank you anyway." I slid out of her way. "I'm sorry you kind of— I mean I'm sorry you lost— I mean I'm sorry your friends—"

"Are assholes," Gilly finished for me, hopping forward. "This whole town is full of assholes."

"I used to think the same thing," I said, "but to be honest Greenville is kind of proving me wrong. Like more and more every day. And I'm also kind of an asshole sometimes." I pointed at myself with my thumbs. "Like I'm cool but I'm ALSO a person who starts pizza fights, so . . ."

"Yeah." Gilly stared at the door. "Yeah. I'm pretty sure they're not going to talk to me again."

"You never know." I shrugged.

"Yeah, when they decide they're not talking to someone, they kind of stick to it," Gilly told me.

"Well, *I'm* talking to you," I offered. "You know, if you're into that."

An idea flashed over her face. "Hey."

"Hey."

"Do you want to come with me to the Fall Dance next weekend? Since I'll probably be going by myself." Her eyes got wide. "Not that that's why I'm asking you."

My face got hot. "Why are you asking me, then? Because I'm talking to you?"

Gilly shook her head. "No! I *want* to go with you. To the dance. Because . . ." A small smile curled the corners of her lips, "You're pretty cool, like I said. What do you say?"

She reached out and touched my hand. Which almost caused her to fall over.

You know when that thing you've been kind of secretly dreaming of happens and then suddenly that secret dream is revealed and you feel, like, exposed and giddy and scared all at once?

"Okay."

Gilly's phone buzzed. "Oh, that's my dad, I bet," she said. "I gotta go. But it's a date, right?"

"It's a date."

Gilly hopped away and I sat down in a seat in the empty room that was once the site of my standoff.

I looked at my phone.

There were three texts from Berry.

BERRY
Hey. I hope everything goes okay today.

BERRY
You deserve to be a star.

BERRY
Just FYI.

Without thinking, I tapped the little Berry icon on my phone, which was a picture of one of the sculptures from her secret garden, and called her.

People do that, you know: just call.

Suddenly there was a ringing in the hallway very close to the door. I bolted out of the room to find Berry frantically silencing her phone.

"HEY!"

"HEY!" Literally every part of her face was red. With her green hair, she looked like a radish. But, like, in a cool way.

"I didn't know you were here."

"Oh." Berry shoved her phone in her pocket. "I was just checking on you. To make sure you were okay."

"Since how long?"

"I mean, I heard Davidson tell Sarah off." Berry smiled. "And I heard Gilly stick up for you. That's pretty nice. And. I mean, yeah."

"So you heard the whole thing basically."

The smile slipped from Berry's lips, replaced with the same look from this morning.

"I'm glad Gilly stood up for you," she said. "And I'm glad you're okay."

And with that Berry hopped on her board, risking Principal Lynde's wrath, and zipped down the hallway.

Really not wanting to risk *any* wrath, I walked to the front steps and I strapped on my skates. Diana Ross's "Upside Down" blasted on my headphones as I rounded out of the parking lot and headed home, chasing the last slivers of light.

TWENTY-THREE

That night, when I got home from our second somewhat-failed-but-ultimately-very-successful play rehearsal, Lucy's car was in the driveway, but not Millie's, and Monty didn't do her "Anne is home" bark when I opened the door.

"Hello?"

"In here."

Lucy was waiting for me in the living room, in a very worn pair of yoga leggings and her second-favorite school mascot sweatshirt, celebrating the Homerville Bears with a picture of a bear that I swear is a panda (not a bear), but no one asks me about these things. She looked . . . tired. Her hair was down and not sprayed up into a helmet. Which was interesting.

"Where's Millie?" I asked.

"Millie thought we should talk," Lucy said. "Alone."

"Okay." I dumped my bag. "You mean about the play? Mr. Davidson told me you thought it was okay. Right?"

"Yes." Lucy shook her head. "I mean, no."

I froze. "I'm confused."

"No, I just wanted to say—" Lucy stepped forward. "I just wanted to say I'm so sorry, Anne. I'm so sorry I didn't believe you. I knew you didn't do anything to the Spencer yard, but I didn't tell you that. I should have and I'm very very sorry. It's just with everything happening, I got so caught up with being worried about the you who is my daughter at Greenville and all that's going on that I forgot about . . . you."

Looking at her, in her own skin, a rare occasion, I realized that while I spent a week in a white T-shirt trying to fit in, Lucy had spent every day since she'd arrived in Greenville in a crisp green prison suit, trying to get Greenville to treat her like anyone else doing her job.

"So, I'm very sorry."

"Thank you," I blurted out. "And I'm sorry I told you, you know, 'fuck you.'"

"Thank you." Lucy let out a long slow breath. "I knew this was going to be hard, I knew Greenville was going to be hard."

"Medium hard," I joked halfheartedly. "Standard hard."

"Really hard," Lucy added. "I know you handle yourself so well with all this stuff—mostly. We've been so many places and you adapt, you're much better at this than me when I was your age. I think some-times I forget that it's a big thing to ask a teenager to handle herself well when it seems like everyone's against you—like everyone wants you to break. I forget that as much as I know what it's like to be on the outside, I don't know what it's like for you to be on the outside. I don't know what it's like to be the only person who looks like you in a whole town. I mean, I know but I don't know. And I should have talked to you about it more, and I'm sorry."

A lump swelled in my throat. "I mean . . . they wanted to see us both fail, right? Maybe for reasons that were different but kind of simi-lar? I don't know."

"Is that how it feels?" Lucy let out another long breath and put another elastic in her hair, which was clearly already tied up with at least two elastics.

"Yeah," I said. "It feels pretty horrible."

"I don't know how to make this better," Lucy admitted. "I really don't, Anne. It's my *job* and I don't. And every night I go to bed and I try to think of how to make it better, and every night I can't think of anything. So I just lie there and worry."

"I mean you did most of it already," I said. "No matter what some of Greenville says, and a lot of what it says sucks, I know you and Millie love me for who I am. You tell me that all the time. Like a mil-lion times. You taught me how to disco and let me run with that. I am one hundred percent me and I know you and Millie are cool with that.

I think there's lots of kids who don't get that from their families. You know, here in Greenville even." I smiled. "So, good job."

"Hey." Lucy wiped her eyes with her sleeve. "I'm supposed to be giving you the speech." Her voice was croaky.

"You gave me all the speeches," I said. "So, so, so, so many really great and let's say well-thought-out speeches. And you apologized for not believing me when I told you I didn't set Tanner's house on fire. So we're good. And please don't stop what you're doing. I won't let you fail, Mom. I mean, we're not failing. You're not. So go to sleep."

"Thanks, kid."

"And I"—I took a deep breath—"I should have told you, you know, what was happening. So I'll do that now."

"Yes." Lucy looked deep into my soul. "You have to tell us, Anne, we won't break if you tell us something feels broken. Okay?"

"Okay."

The front door opened with a dramatic slam as Monty bounded in the room the way golden retrievers do, like there's a party going that they almost missed.

"Okay, that's good." Lucy bit her lip. "We love you so much, kiddo."

"Damn right we love you, kid. We love you with all our bones and muscles," Millie crowed.

And then Monty jumped on me, and I crashed to the floor and bonked my head on the side table.

Small detour to big family hug, but we got there.

Crying is good for you, did I tell you that? It's like the body's filtration system. So it's probably good we spent the rest of the evening watching a live-action *Cinderella* and crying.

Who doesn't—if not love—then at least appreciate, a mean step-mother?

(Relax! Not me! Anymore! Geez.)

That night, Mr. Spencer sent a very short email saying he would no longer be seeking damages. He didn't say why, but I could guess. And we just sort of let that go because I do think there's a right and wrong way to win certain battles. Plus I had two moms who loved me *and* a friend who looked out for me *and* a date. What did I care about a dick like Mr. Spencer?

The next morning, Lucy and Millie confirmed both that I would be able to be the lead in *Peter Pan* (yes!) and be able to go to the dance with Gilly (yes!).

TWENTY-FOUR

Leading up to the play, on top of rehearsing for *Peter Pan*, which is a script that is just way more complicated than you think it is, most of my time was spent drowning in fabric, because in addition to playing the starring role, I was also the only person in the cast who could sew. Except for Sarah's mother, that is, who informed Mr. Davidson in what I heard was a pretty snippy email, that she was making Sarah's Wendy costume. But no one else's.

Fortunately for us, we at least had the funding for the costumes, care of our new patron, the enigmatic and exuberant Beverly Lynde, who wrote a choice letter about the Pyes that I won't share because it was very funny, but *very* rude. There was also a check enclosed.

I made all six pirates', six Lost Kids', and Hook's costumes. Because Gilly needed to stay off her feet, she was a sitting Lost Kid, with big bell-bottoms to cover her cast.

With the scraps, I made extra pirate gear for Monty and Bjorn. They looked adorable. Bjorn hated his and ate the bottom half, and I had to throw it away basically.

For my costume I was pretty much set, as any fashionista would be. I already had the tights, I just needed to stone them and take in my tunic so it looked more Panlike. Minnie and I actually stoned our tights together. Minnie was upping her makeup and accessories game each day, which was catching on with the cheerleading and debate teams, so maybe there's hope for the rest of Greenville yet.

Oh right. Yeah, Tanner and Sarah and John all stayed in the play. Like, the day after our standoff they showed up for rehearsals with their lines memorized and everything. I think Sarah and Tanner especially really wanted to be there. Sarah was like *putting in the work* as Wendy every rehearsal and asking for notes and everything.

So after Tanner tried to set me and Berry up for arson, we set to work rehearsing our sword-fighting scene, which was a little nerve-racking considering. And afterward Tanner came up to me with this, like, weirdly apologetic vibe and asked me if I could find him buttons for his cufflinks (we ended up using some from Lucy's vice-principal drag).

Maybe Greenville just all had this pent-up creativity and they just needed to let it out? Like the game changer was when we got Tanner his hat. Suddenly every time I turned around, there he was in the hallway working on these one-handed flourishes with his feathered hat and *no soccer jersey*! Like, I didn't even know Tanner had regular shirts. He does!

With the leftover Bev money, Mr. Davidson ordered a proper flying apparatus. It was a complicated harness with industrial straps that was somehow supposed to fit under my tunic. The first time they strapped me in and three kids from the soccer team hoisted me up over the stage, Lucy nearly passed out.

"It's not as dangerous as roller-skating," I reasoned, dangling over her head while my stomach muscles strained to keep me from looking like a dead spider.

"Don't tell me that," Lucy grumbled as I spun and finally was lowered to the ground.

Gilly also didn't think it looked safe.

"I'm just flying in and flying out," I reasoned. "Plus the guys they'll have the night of the show will be professional . . . hoisters."

A couple of days before the dance, Millie asked me what was going on with Berry.

I didn't say it, but I was looking for Berry, like a lot, in school. Every time I turned a corner, she was flying out of whatever room I was in. In every class she came in last and left first, spending most of her time with her face buried in a book. She also wasn't replying to my texts. Even the really funny ones.

Whenever I talked to Millie about it, she got this weird look on her face. Like this little wrinkle in her forehead.

"Should I call her?"

"Do you want to?" Millie asked.

"Yeah. I mean, I miss her." Every time something happened, I'd think about talking to Berry about it. Like when I was flying, I wanted to look down and see Berry waving at me with her fuzzy green hair.

I wanted to know she was okay.

I wanted to talk to her, but I didn't know what I needed to say.

The night of the dance, I took out my tuxedo again and laid it out on the bed. Lucy peeked in just as I was putting together my shoes and accessories.

"The velvet tuxedo," she said appreciatively. "It's very you."

"It is, isn't it?"

Lucy wiped her eyes with her sleeve. She was wearing her sweatshirt with the logo that was a woodpecker (as a school mascot!). I had suggested, and Lucy was thinking about it, that she start a "school mascot" day at school so she could wear her favorite sweatshirts to school.

"You know I was thinking about how you said it's good I'm staying Anne in Greenville," I said, pulling out a sparkly bow tie and then putting it back. Too much. "I think I can be Anne *of* Greenville too."

"Yes, you can." Lucy pulled out something from behind her back. A huge corsage with *giant orange roses*. "Because they sell these here."

"ORANGE ROSES!" I squealed. "AHHHHHHHHH! THANK YOU!"

Monty whined from the doorway. Either because she felt left out or because she had to pee.

"I'll walk her," Lucy said, releasing me from the hug. "You get dressed."

"Thanks, Mom."

"And have fun!" she called from the stairs.

Technically a velvet tuxedo wants for a top hat, but I figured my first dance, I would just do big hair instead. So several cans of hairspray later, once I had molded my hair into a shape I was thinking of as "campfire big," I floated down the stairs. I would say I looked like a Creamsicle. Like a velvet Creamsicle with a cloud of sherbet hair on top.

"TA-DA!" I assumed a jaunty pose at the bottom of the stairs.

Millie said she thought I looked like a fancy cheese stick. Which I accepted.

"All right, then, Fred Astaire," Millie snorted, grabbing her robe to cover her pajamas. "Come on, Monty. Try not to get too much fur on Captain Orange as we drive her to the dance."

"*Empress* Orange," I corrected, taking a few long steps to make sure the pants wouldn't split. You never know with vintage trousers. And really the last thing I needed was a crotch incident.

By the time we got to the school, the parking lot was full. Kids were spilling out of cars, posing for selfies, hugging, dancing toward the front door, which someone had decorated with fall leaves and a wonky but effective cut-out pumpkin.

"Have fun!" Millie called out as I stood on the curb, peeling a layer of Monty fur off my legs.

"I will," I called back.

I strode up to the front steps, adjusting my coat. I passed the kid Marcus who was playing a Lost Boy and a girl named Jennifer who was in my math class.

But no Gilly.

I didn't want to sit and ruin my pants, so I stood off to the side of the steps, trying to look casual and not worried. Casual but cool.

"Anne."

Berry stepped up onto the curb.

"Holy COW!"

Her hair was up and sprayed into a pouf of green. Instead of her usual coveralls she was wearing a black-and-green-checkered blouse and liquid-black leggings with boots that buckled up to the knee with acid-green clasps. Her lips were painted bright green to match the glitter around her eyes. She looked like what a cool alien would look like going to prom, in the nineties.

Not that I was there, in the nineties.

She looked really, really cool.

Berry was clearly overcome by how cool *I* looked. "Wow! Nice tux!"

"I mean! *You* look amazing." I gawked. "Where did you get that shirt? Did you get that from Greenville?"

"It was my dad's." Berry shrugged. "He used to be cool. What can I say?"

"Your dad is clearly the best," I marveled.

"You haven't experienced the fashion marvel that is Harry Blythe," Berry added. "You should see what he wears on his birthdays. It is . . . a whole thing."

"I'll take your word for it." I rubbed my chin in exaggerated evaluation. "I mean, maybe I'm coming over to your house to raid your dad's closet."

"I'm sure he'd be thrilled." Berry put her hands on her hips as she assessed. "But *this*, this really takes the cake. I'm sorry I underestimated the tux earlier. It is very cool."

"Hey." Without warning, a ripple of nervous ran through my body. "I've like really missed you."

"Oh." Berry looked at her boots. "Yeah. Well. I just, yeah."

"Can we, like, I would love to hang out with you again?"

And then everything was slow motion as Berry looked up at me. With her big eyes and her freckled cheeks.

And I got it.

"Berry." The name escaped from my lips.

How could I have missed it? This person who just showed up and was so amazing from the first moment? This secret-garden painter, asphalt rider, my friend, my superhero, had been my true true this whole time.

"Anyway. I know you're waiting for your date." Berry pointed at the door. "I should go in. Make an appearance."

There was a series of sharp honks. I looked up to see Gilly's hand waving out the window of a big black truck.

"Hey! Anne!" she called.

There was a slight metallic rattling of buckles as Berry disappeared. "Bye."

And then it was like there was just this big empty space. A Berry-shaped space.

"Hey!" Gilly hobbled forward as her dad honked and roared off. "You're here! Am I late?"

"No." I couldn't breathe. "Uh. I mean, no worries."

Gilly's hair was all pinned up with little flowery clips, and she was wearing a yellow dress with little yellow flowers on it, with a matching yellow sweater. Her cheeks were flush from the short walk from the truck, and she leaned on a crutch to wipe the sweat off her forehead. "Geez, these crutches make everything take forever."

"You look great," I said, trying to shake whatever it was that was making everything feel like molasses.

How could I not have noticed?

"Hey!" Tanner was wearing a navy suit matching Sarah's navy dress. They waved as they walked toward us.

"Hey," Gilly said, cautious.

"You guys look great," Sarah said quietly. "Are you going in?"

"Yeah," Gilly said, "in a second."

"Okay, well." Tanner nodded. "We'll see you in there."

Gilly seemed to wait till they were out of earshot to release a relieved sigh.

"So, you guys are all good," I asked in a low voice. I wondered if they'd talked since the chem lab fight. Maybe not. I mean we'd all spent a week in rehearsals, so I knew Gilly was at least able to be in the same room as Tanner and Sarah, but I hadn't seen them talk.

"Yeah." Gilly touched her chin to her shoulder. "I mean, Sarah's been texting me, more and more, I suppose. She was angry, but . . . I think we're still friends? I don't know, I probably should have stood up for myself a long time ago." She looked up at me. "I'm sorry I asked you to do it."

"What do you mean?"

"At the party? I thought. If *you* talked to them. Like, then everything would be fine, you know? And we could *all* hang out? It would be fixed."

"Yeah, well," I said, "it probably would have been better if *you* had talked to them. Since they're your friends."

"Maybe." Gilly smiled up at me. "But it all worked out! We don't have to talk about it anymore."

A chill crept up my coat sleeve. She didn't really get it. I mean, she asked *me* to fix something *she* needed to fix. After all that happened? And now it was just . . . fine, in her eyes?

"Um. Okay," I offered. "What do you want to talk about?"

Gilly looked over my tuxedo, her eyes pausing on my multiple accessories. "That's quite the, uh, outfit."

I took this to mean she wanted to talk about my outfit. I flexed the lapels. "Thanks. I like yours too!"

"Thanks." Gilly's head bobbed slightly. Then she looked like she wanted to change the conversation again. A silence stretched out between us like gum.

Finally I cut the awkward with, "We could go into the dance now, if you're like, ready?"

"Yeah, sounds good." Gilly's hands gripped her crutches. "Let's go."

The gym was decorated mostly with the orange-and-green-fabric leaves you get at craft places, all of which faintly smelled like vanilla, which combined with the smell of teen sweat to create a curious Greenville funk. The funk did not match the music, which was, I would say, modern dance electronica.

"Sorry, I can't really dance," Gilly yelled over the bass as we made our way into the gym.

"It's okay," I yelled back. "This music kind of sucks anyway."

"What?" She hadn't heard me.

"Nothing!"

Gilly did that little nod again.

I scanned the room for Berry. I mean how hard can it be to find someone lime green in a sea of pastels and navy formal wear?

Tanner walked over with a chair and put it next to Gilly so she could sit. I took Gilly's crutches and leaned them against the back of the chair.

Gilly rested her hands in her lap. "I guess it's probably not as exciting as other dances you've been to."

"It's pretty much the same!" I nodded along with the music.

Gilly shouted something I couldn't hear over the bass, so I leaned closer. "What?"

"Nothing," she shouted back. "I love this song!"

As the bass built on the dance floor, more and more kids streamed into the crowd, jumping in unison like they were trying to smash a hole in the floor together.

Somehow, I was standing with the same group of kids that, like, a week earlier had tried to erase me from Greenville High existence, and it felt like I was still standing on the edge of a cliff.

Because I still wasn't where I needed to be.

My eyes darted over the crowd. That's when the music on the dance floor faded, and the first beats of tinny metal funk came over the loudspeakers. Tanner shot Sarah a confused look. I searched the auditorium for an explanation.

"Did you put this on?" I asked Gilly.

"Put what on?" Gilly shrugged.

" 'Funkytown.' "

"Wait." Gilly looked up at me. "Is this, like, *your* song?"

"It's a song I like," I shouted. "Like, a lot."

Gilly nodded blankly. "Oh. Right."

I turned and spotted Berry strutting along the edge of the dance floor, a flash of green hop-stepping along the sidelines.

Berry.

"Gilly!" I squatted down by her chair. "Um. I have to say something!"

"What?" A confused look flashed over Gilly's face.

"I want to thank you for inviting me to the dance. And I think you're really cool and possibly after this we can be friends," I hollered, "but there's someone I need to go dance with. Now."

Gilly looked at the ground then up at me. "Berry," she said.

"What?"

"It's BERRY!" Gilly yelled over the music, a small smile on her lips. "It's OKAY. GO!"

Officially it is possible everyone knew but me.

I bolted across the dance floor, through a soft sea of not fabulous suits and spaghetti strap dresses, to the far end of the floor, where I saw her, dancing.

Let's say, when she really cuts loose, Berry is an amazing dancer. I'd seen only flashes of her brilliance earlier at the mini putt. Tonight she was using every bit of her body from her fingers to her toes. She hopped when the music called for it.

"BERRY!" I screamed.

Many, many people stopped their tepid movements to this amazing song and stared.

In mid-jump, Berry spun around to face me.

I knew what I had to do.

I took a long run, dropped to my knees, sliding across the dance floor, friction building on my velvet pant legs as I skidded to a halt about a foot short of where I wanted to be.

And then Berry stepped forward and met me so the pose would be perfect.

"I'm SO SORRY!" I screamed up at her, over the music.

"Why are you sorry?" Berry screamed back as she grabbed my hand and pulled me to my feet.

"BECAUSE!"

Berry searched my face. For signs of intelligence, possibly. "BECAUSE WHY?"

All the little details, like the flecks of green in her eyes. Or the way her lips pouted when she relaxed her face, or when she was looking at me when I was sweating profusely in velvet. The three freckles that formed a perfect triangle on the top of her right cheek. The tiny heart on her nose. The way she wiggled a little when she had a great idea. The many shades of pink her cheeks turned when she was upset or happy or nervous, like a human mood ring.

"BECAUSE IT'S YOU!"

"ME WHAT?"

"It's YOU that I LIKE," I bellowed. "But it's MORE than that. You're weird and I'm weird and when we're together it feels AMAZING instead of strange. Because you're awesome and I just want to hang out with you all the time!"

"You want to hang out with me?" Berry's face swam in front of mine, surrounded by glowing dance lights. "Your friend?"

"NO." I shook my head. "I want to BE, like, WITH you!"

"Are you SURE?" Berry eyes searched my face.

My throat was starting to vibrate from screaming on the dance floor. "YEAH, OKAY. I know I'm late. But I'm here now and I will MAKE IT UP TO YOU!"

Berry did a little spin. I grabbed her hand and spun her back into me. "Okay," she said.

"So now what?"

Some slow song came on. Not disco. Something else. "Aw," some kid yelled, "I love this fucking song."

I took a small step forward. "I was thinking I should kiss you if that's okay."

Berry considered. "You're very sweaty."

"Deal breaker?"

Berry shook her head and held out her hand. I reached out and my fingers laced with hers. I thought maybe I could feel her heart beating, but it might just have been my heart finally beating loud enough for the both of us.

"Okay, here I go."

"Okay, stop talking now."

It was a pretty sweaty kiss. But it was our first kiss. Which would make Greenville and Greenville High, as the site of that kiss, a very important place, maybe my favorite place, after that.

Berry's lips were soft and they tasted like green lipstick. Which weirdly tasted like cherries.

Berry pulled her face away and smirked. "There's green all over your chin."

I kissed her again. I didn't care.

When your heart's exploding, a little lipstick on the chin is pretty much no big deal.

TWENTY-FIVE

Where does this story end?

Not that it has an actual end, of course, because I'm still here and my story's still going.

But this story, this one of many stories of me and Greenville, should probably have some sort of end.

I mean, one ending could be of me flying.

Because what's more magical than flying?

Up in the air, in my sparkly green Peter Pan outfit (yes, I stoned the whole thing), a set of very large citizens operating a crane connected to a metal wire connected to a metal harness you could kind of see under the outfit in a way I was worried looked like a diaper, but Berry said it didn't.

I flew over the heads of all of Greenville, or at least the heads of Tanner and his fellow pirates.

Tanner didn't even freak out when I almost put his eye out (foam) sword fighting. Of course, I apologized backstage afterward—it *was* a mistake—I think I was just super in character and also I'm not a great sword fighter. Tanner was, happily, more excited that he was killing it as Hook, which he was.

Speaking of, Sarah, who I thought was a great Wendy, even stood next to me and held my hand up when we took our bow at the end of the play, all while Greenville High's gathered parents, or those who cared about something other than soccer, put their hands together for our stellar performance.

Small victories, is what Lucy calls it.

After the play, our big opening and closing night (high school), Mr. Davidson threw a huge party for the whole cast and crew and their parents at Beverly Lynde's house. Which was amazing, mostly because Bev's house is maybe the most amazing house I've ever seen in all of time, let alone Greenville, and I got to show it to Berry, and *she* loved it.

Plus, Beverly wore all green velvet for the occasion, including, I kid you not, a hoop skirt that made it almost impossible for her to walk through her own doorways.

You cannot beat Bev Lynde for fashion.

As if to match his aunt's pizzazz, Davidson drove his mint-condition Coupe de Ville that he wipes every day with an old T-shirt, but never drives, to the party (so he could show it off, obviously).

Still buzzing from our standing ovation possibly, Mr. Davidson said next year we're going to up the ante, theater-wise.

"Let's really blow their socks off," he told me as he cut me a piece of Peter Pan cake and plopped it on a paper plate with the same theme. "It's time."

What could that mean?? *Guys and Dolls*?! *Grease*? DOLLS AND DOLLS??? Talk about having an agenda.

Millie and Mr. Davidson ended up meeting at the party, and now she and Mr. Davidson are, like, best friends, by the way. She's even using him for her next series, Small Town.

Tanner's dad didn't come to the after-party, which was kind of sad, but Gilly's did. And he brought her daisies and told everyone how proud of her he was. Which was embarrassing, but I think in a good way, from the look on Gilly's face. He also gave me a daisy and a pretty solid linebacker clap on the back.

I can't tell if Gilly actually wants to be friends, or what it meant that she invited me to the dance. But for now, like the rest of the Forevers, she looks happy.

And I'll take that any day.

Sarah's mother also came to the party, looking like an older Sarah with big earrings and big hair. She shook my hand and told me I gave a magnificent performance. Then, like two minutes later, Berry told me her mom saw a social media post where Sarah's mom said my performance was campy and overdramatic and she accused me of putting on airs! The campy and overdramatic bit is a tautology of sorts, which, she can look up what that means. I might have overplayed it a little but, hey, I just really enjoyed putting my hands on my hips in an angular fashion and talking in a loud, high-pitched cheerleader tone for all my lines.

Peter Pan *is* campy and overdramatic. He's a kid who wants to be a kid forever. He fights pirates. He runs a club of "Lost Boys."

"He's not an accountant!" I fumed to Millie.

"Everyone is entitled to their opinions," Millie said, licking the green icing off her fork. "That's art, baby!"

Berry later reported that Sarah's mom's post got no likes and one person who replied, "Well, I thought she was great."

And that got a bunch of likes.

So maybe all of Greenville is ready to move on.

Most importantly, Lucy and Millie both thought my performance was amazing. Even if Lucy had to close her eyes when I was soaring overhead. Millie said I looked happiest when I was soaring.

OH! You know who *else* was a fan? Principal Lynde. I kid you not, she sidled up to me by the chips and dip at the party and told me she thought I was "incredibly brave" for getting in the flying apparatus.

"I like a student with a bit of steel in their veins," she said, with a nod.

"Really?"

"Quite a lucky thing for this school," she added. "To have two new bold talents under our roof. I look forward to see what you'll bring next!"

Who knew all I needed to do to get Principal Lynde's respect was put on a harness and fly over the gym in a Peter Pan pose?

(Davidson admitted later that he might have played up the dangerous elements of the flying apparatus. Which says a lot about Principal Lynde. But still. I'll take it!)

Aside from *my* parents, Berry's parents were possibly the most exuberant parents at the play and the after-party. Berry's dad was wearing yet another shirt, gold with huge cuffs, that I plan to steal at some point.

Instead of flowers, Berry brought me a bright orange top hat.

Because Berry Blythe, who is officially my girlfriend, by the way, is the most amazing.

We left the party early, hopping in Mato and peeling off into the sunset. As we crested the hill, I put on Berry's current favorite song, "Hang On to the Night" by Tegan and Sara, a Canadian pop duo who also happen to be twins. "Hang On to the Night" is from their 2016 album, *Love You to Death*. Which is a great album, actually.

I like this song mostly because I like the way Berry looks when she sings along to the lyrics. You think I like disco; you should see what Berry looks like when she sings, which she does more and more these days. Like when Berry sings a song, she's *into* it.

She sings it like she's telling you a truth you don't necessarily see right away. A truth about you and her, her and me. Her voice gets louder and louder and I roll down the windows as she gently turns the wheel to follow the curves of Greenville's many impossible roads. Which are now my roads.

Just like Berry is mine and I am hers.

We are not Forevers, but we are here.

Home.

And that's a great place to end a story, I think. Our wheels are turning and we are flying. We're going somewhere. We're on our way.

ACKNOWLEDGMENTS

Thank you to my love, Heather Gold, who has been the source of many Anne-like adventures. You are bright, bold, amazing, and you are the disco in my life.

Many, many, *many* thanks to Melissa de la Cruz for bringing me onto this project and gifting me this incredible opportunity.

Thank you to my editor, Kieran Scott Viola, who shares my joy for all things Anne and made this writing process such a joyful romp, as all writing processes should be.

Thank you to the whole team at Hyperion who worked on this book and helped Anne come to life!

Thank you to my agent, Charlotte Sheedy, for everything.

This book is a tribute to the joy the story of *Anne of Green Gables* has brought to me and countless other readers over the decades. I am very grateful this book exists, and thank you to Lucy Maud Montgomery for writing it.

Thank you to Grace Ellis, Kim Trusty, Lukas Blakk, Cory Silverberg, and the countless other writers and artists who have been nice enough to let me reach out to them for support and advice.

Thank you to my queer communities for helping make me into the artist I try to be today.

I have tried to give you as much information on all of Anne's favorite music and theater productions as possible without making this book seem like a wiki. Thank you to all the artists (including Sylvester, ABBA, and Lipps, Inc.) who made the music that fills my soul. I highly recommend, if you haven't already, listening to all these tracks. They are life changing.

Thank you to Canada, my home forever no matter what.

The GORGEOUS cover of this book was designed by Marci Senders. The figures were illustrated by Shirley Zhou. Type and background were illustrated by Jyotirmayee.

If you are an LGBTQIA+ person in need of support, the Trevor Project is the world's largest suicide prevention and crisis intervention organization for lesbian, gay, bisexual, transgender, queer, and questioning (LGBTQ) young people. For support, text START to 678-678, or phone 1-866-488-7386, or go to www.thetrevorproject.org.